THE BLIND
SWITCH

THE BLIND SWITCH

LYN FARRELL

W❂RLDWIDE

TORONTO • NEW YORK • LONDON
AMSTERDAM • PARIS • SYDNEY • HAMBURG
STOCKHOLM • ATHENS • TOKYO • MILAN
MADRID • WARSAW • BUDAPEST • AUCKLAND

The Blind Switch *is dedicated to my daughter and former writing partner, Lisa Fitzsimmons.*

Lisa and I wrote the seven-book series "Mae December Mysteries" together under the penname Lia Farrell. During our days writing as a team, Lisa tried her best to keep my tendencies to write ever more Byzantine plots under control. I miss her input, insights and fine writing.

WORLDWIDE™

Recycling programs
for this product may
not exist in your area.

ISBN-13: 978-1-335-73666-6

The Blind Switch

First published in 2021 by Camel Press, an imprint of Epicenter Press, Inc. This edition published in 2022.

For questions and comments about the quality of this book, please contact us at CustomerService@Harlequin.com.

Harlequin Enterprises ULC
22 Adelaide St. West, 41st Floor
Toronto, Ontario M5H 4E3, Canada
www.ReaderService.com

Printed in U.S.A.

BLIND SWITCH:

A horse being caught in a pocket behind or between horses which prevents a free course from being pursued.

ACKNOWLEDGMENTS

I wish to particularly thank and acknowledge the contributions of two people to this book: Dr. Bob Stuart, Chief Medical Officer, Advocate Aurora Health Care, Wisconsin, and Officer Robert Pfannes, Chief, City of Ann Arbor Police Department, Ann Arbor, Michigan. Both men are now retired.

Dr. Stuart provided the medical expertise about the care of the murder victim in the book. He and I talked for several hours and he read and reviewed draft chapters. Any errors in medical terminology or procedure are mine and not his.

Officer Pfannes and I also spent multiple hours on the phone discussing police procedure. After talking with him, I came to the realization that police work is as noble a calling as medicine, teaching or the ministry. He was particularly helpful with understanding the jurisdictional issues in the book and the mindset the police have in investigating crimes. Any errors in police procedure are mine.

I also wish to acknowledge Jennifer McCord, Associate Publisher and Executive Editor, and Phillip Garrett, President, Epicenter-Coffeetown-Camel Press. I have worked with Jennifer since 2012 and with Phil for a year. Both of them have been extremely supportive as I moved away from writing with my daughter, Lisa, to writing on my own. I miss working with her. She is a talented writer and a superb editor.

The MSU Creative Writers group and my critique group, Three Woman Writers, provided valuable feedback.

Finally, I want to say thank you to my friend Daniel Mazzuchi, M.D., who explained apprenticeships for trainers in the racing world and took me to the track many years ago. Those were the days my friend.

PROLOGUE

Saturday, October 5

IT WAS ALMOST midnight on Saturday night when Danny pulled into the parking lot in front of the apartment building where he lived with his girlfriend, Tracey. He got out of the car and locked it, wincing at the pain in his right wrist. He hadn't called her to say he would be late and knew she would be furious. He swallowed hard, suffused with guilt for all the lies he had told her.

"Daniel Kidd Parrish, where the hell have you been? Why didn't you call me?" Tracey's black eyes were flashing. She was standing in the living room, speaking through clenched teeth. Turning away, she threw her hands in the air with an "I give up" gesture. Even with a scowl on her face she was gorgeous, slender and lissome. Her long, dark hair fell down below her shoulders.

He gestured to his right wrist, which was in a splint, wrapped in white gauze. "At the Urgent Care," he said. "Sprained wrist. Sorry I didn't call, couldn't get any reception inside the building."

"Oh, Danny," she ran to him. "I'm sorry for yelling at you. It's just that I was worried sick. How did this happen? Are you in a lot of pain?" Her eyes were filled with compassion. He pulled her close with his left arm.

"Working at the track isn't like working in a hair

salon, you know, Trace. I have a dangerous job. Damn horse stepped on it."

"Really?" she hesitated, looking confused. Then her brows drew together in a frown. She narrowed her eyes in suspicion. "Danny, are you telling me the truth? That doesn't sound right. You've never been injured by a horse before."

He felt a quiver in his stomach. He hated lying to her and had been doing so for months. This wasn't the first injury related to his stupidity. "I don't know what was going on with Boyd's Boy. He was antsy all day. He kept rolling his eyes and jerking on his lead whenever anybody came close."

"I doubt a yanked rein would've sprained your wrist. Did he step on you?" Tracey pursed her lips and pulled away from him, rubbing the back of her neck. "I don't think I'm getting the whole story."

"Just leave it, Trace. I did something dumb, that's all. Could you get me a beer?" Danny asked. He glanced at the mirror on the wall and quickly adjusted his expression, not wanting her to see the fear on his face.

"Fine," she said with a tight smile, "but that big black stallion loves you. You've been able to handle him since he was a colt. I want the whole story, Danny. You are lying. I can always tell. It's time to tell me the truth."

After drinking the beer, Danny took a deep breath and forced himself to tell her. It wasn't easy. They had wanted to buy a house together. Renting was throwing their money away. Both of them had been saving a little from each paycheck. But at the rate they were going, they would be collecting Social Security before they could afford their own home. He was impatient to get her what she wanted. He had been gambling. And losing, big time.

"Gambling? Oh Danny, you've been an idiot! Have you been betting at the window at least? You haven't been going through a bookie, have you?" At his nod, her face pinched. "You may as well tell me. How much do you owe?"

"Fifteen thousand," he lowered his head, staring in shame at the floor. He couldn't look at her. He started to leave the room but the sound of her crying made him stop. "Please don't be mad at me, Trace. I was only doing it for us. I found a little house for sale. It's near the track and needs some work, but it's affordable. I thought we could fix it up together." He swallowed, looking at her now, pleading. "Dockery, the man I place my bets with, sent some muscle to the track today. They sprained my wrist and I have a couple of busted ribs." Danny clenched his jaw, touching a sore area on his face. He told himself to be a man and not to break down.

"My Uncle Joe had a gambling problem," Tracey said in a weary voice. "We never knew what happened when he disappeared. Two weeks later, his body washed up in the river. The thugs could put you in the hospital next time, or worse." She shook her head. Her chin was quivering and tears formed in her dark eyes. She brushed them away angrily.

His shoulders slumped in defeat. "I have a week. That's what they said. A week to come up with all of it. What are we doing to do?" He looked up at her. "If I can't get the money together by then, we're going to have to leave the area. Maybe I should leave first and then you can join me, once they stop looking for me."

"Let me think," Tracey began to pace the small room.

"I can get a small advance on my paycheck, probably a couple of hundred dollars. You need to talk to your boss in Rosedale. Maybe you could get a loan from him." She came to a stop, looking thoughtful. "Don't you have a rich relative? Didn't you tell me once you had an aunt, or a stepmother or something? Someone with some money?" She looked at him intently.

"My birth mother is well-to-do, she married a successful lawyer after she had me," he said. "Her name is Cara Summerfield. She gave me the money for my training, but I'm not asking for her help now. Not when it's my stupidity that's landed me here."

"This is your *life* we're talking about, Danny," Tracey said in a charged whisper. "You're going to have to ask her for help or I will!"

Danny shook his head and walked down the hall to the bedroom, holding an arm around his ribs.

ONE

WAYNE NICHOLS, RECENTLY RETIRED Homicide Detective, was looking at himself in the full-length mirror on the door to Lucy's closet. He had left the Sheriff's Office in January, although he had done some part-time work for them since. It had been hard to completely cut his ties to the office. Today, however, he was interviewing for a new position. He was dressed in a new charcoal suit, a white shirt and a diagonally striped red and gray tie. Turning around he saw his long-time girlfriend Lucy Ingram, an ER physician, looking at him with a perplexed frown on her face.

"Is that what you're wearing for your interview at Rosedale Investigations?" she asked.

"Why? What's wrong with it?" Wayne never had to think about what to wear when he worked for the Sheriff's Office; it was either a uniform for formal ceremonies or a suit and tie for investigative work. Dressing in a suit for police work was known in the crime business as *plainclothes* and had been worn in place of a uniform for over a century. It was a way to denote the rank of Detective or above. Officers of lower rank were required to wear uniforms.

Since he and Lucy had been living together, many of Wayne's old suits had mysteriously vanished to be replaced by newer and far more expensive models. Lucy raised her eyebrows and Wayne was moved by how beautiful she was, dressed in a white silk robe with red roses twining down the sleeves.

"Scuttlebutt in town is that Rosedale Investigations is a very informal business. I really want this to work for you," she said.

"Would you like to pick out my clothes then?" he asked, amused by the importance she placed on his appearance.

Lucy emerged from the walk-in closet shortly thereafter carrying a pair of chinos and a striped shirt. Wayne had never seen either garment before, and while he had little to no interest in his wardrobe, his visual memory was impeccable; his girlfriend had been buying clothes for him again.

Thus, apparently appropriately-attired for the upcoming job interview, Wayne joined Lucy at the breakfast table. He had woken up thinking about the issues he might face in this new venture—should he be offered a job with the agency. It was a private investigator firm owned and run by a man named Patrick Devlin Pascoe, originally a detective with the Nashville post. The firm had been in business for five years and they were looking to hire a senior investigator. Ben Bradley, his friend and Sheriff of Rosedale, asked if Wayne would be interested. Although he had been retired from the Sheriff's Office in Rosedale for only a few months, Wayne was already bored and feeling at loose ends. Lucy worked long hours in the ER and her stressful job didn't leave much free time to spend with him.

His biggest concern was that his interrogation style, honed over years of dealing with low-life criminals, wasn't going to work for the type of person who sought the services of Rosedale Investigations. He assumed most of the people who came through their doors would be the well-heeled business community of Rosedale. It occurred to him that Lucy's interviewing style might work better with this population. When he entered the kitchen, she was cooking French toast and served him a single piece on whole wheat bread with coffee and fruit. There was no butter on the table. No syrup either, just a little jar of strawberry jam. In addition to improving Wayne's wardrobe, Lucy was working on his diet.

He took a sip of coffee. "I'm trying not to get ahead of myself here but I need to be prepared for their questions. I assume they'll ask how I get information from people. My style might be a bit antagonistic for their clientele. When a person comes into your ER with a complaint, how do you get to the underlying issue, especially if you suspect the patient finds their problems hard to talk about, or is lying?"

"Unless the patient has some run-of-the-mill disease like diabetes, is obviously overdosed, or a trauma case, they hardly ever tell me the whole story right off the bat," she said. "For instance, if a patient got injured in an embarrassing way or it's a sexual issue, they often withhold information. And it's *always* hard to get them to open up about which illegal drugs they are taking, even when I reassure them everything they tell me is confidential."

Wayne frowned. Lucy's unwillingness to report illegal drug use or in fact any crime except child abuse was a sore point between them. "Setting aside your covering-up of criminal acts for the moment, how do you get to the heart of the matter without coming across as putting your patients on the spot?"

"By listening empathically and avoiding yes or no questions. Open-ended questions that require the patient to tell you a bit more about themselves work best." She smiled at him. "You're a good listener, and you're patient. Just don't forget to smile, Wayne. You know you look kind of grumpy unless you're smiling." She looked at him then, sweetly exasperated. He stood up from the table and kissed her good-bye. Opening the back door to leave, he heard her low voice say, "Come home safe."

He turned around to see her apprehensive face. "You have been saying that quite often lately. I'm out of the Sheriff's Office now. You don't need to worry about me getting injured." He smiled and started to tell her how lucky he felt to have her in his life. "You are everything…"

At that moment Lucy's pager rang and she pulled it out of her pocket, waving Wayne away so she could listen carefully to the message.

As he got into the truck, Wayne wondered if Lucy had some sort of premonition that something was going to go wrong. It was odd that she would fret now, when he had left his job in violent crime behind. *The only thing that could hurt me now would be stubbing my toe on the leg of my desk*, he thought, shaking his head at his lovely girlfriend's concerns.

WHEN HIS GOOD friend and former boss, Sheriff Ben Bradley, learned his office was taking a massive budget cut, he had reluctantly raised the question of Wayne leaving the office.

"I hate asking you this, pal," Ben said. "But would

you be interested in taking early retirement? You have enough years in to qualify for a pension and I've been sensing lately that you might be ready for a change."

Ben's request coincided with Wayne's own feelings that it was time to start a new chapter in his life. He had spent his career dealing with the motives for murder—obsessional love gone wrong, greed, and revenge—except for a tiny handful of cases with great outcomes. He smiled remembering the day he had found a missing toddler who had crawled under the front porch to take a nap. The little boy had emerged with sand in his hair, completely nonplussed by his frantic mother's emotional reaction. He had also rescued a pregnant woman from a flood-swollen river. He hoped doing private detective work would mean more of that type of case. It might give him a sense that he was making a difference. Seeking justice for the dead didn't often generate heartfelt appreciation from those left behind.

When Wayne agreed it was time to officially leave the Sheriff's Office, Ben said, "If you're going to retire, I'll need to take your gun and your badge."

It had been one of the hardest days of his life. Handing over his weapon and badge felt like he was being stripped of his identity. It took enormous courage to put them in the hands of the Sheriff. Since then, whenever Wayne patted his inside jacket pocket for a badge that wasn't there, he felt rootless. *What was he if he wasn't a Detective anymore?*

SETTING ASIDE HIS memory of that painful day, Wayne drove to the address of Rosedale Investigations, parked his truck and walked into the agency which was located in a remodeled home just off the main square. A sign on the front door said, "Come in." When he opened the door, a tinkling bell heralded his arrival.

He'd seen Billie Jo Bradley's picture on the agency's web page. When she walked into the entryway, however, Wayne realized her photos hadn't done her justice. She was much more attractive in person. She had a heart-shaped face, straight dark eyebrows and sparkling brown eyes. While her face was truly lovely, her outfit was definitely not. She was wearing an alarmingly short black miniskirt, green and red striped tights and a pink sweater that barely covered her slim midriff. It looked to Wayne like a costume for skateboarding.

"Detective Nichols?" she asked. Wayne nodded and put out his hand to shake hers. She had a small, soft hand. "I'm Billie Jo Bradley. Come on in. You can hang your jacket up on those hooks there." She turned away from him and called down the hall, "PD, Wayne Nichols is here."

Patrick Devlin Pascoe, a retired Homicide Detective from the Nashville post, was in his mid-70's, solidly built, with dark eyes and gray hair cut in a military buzz. Several years earlier he had helped Sheriff Ben Bradley with a case and Wayne remembered Ben saying Pascoe was a "good cop." High praise indeed. Wayne had checked both PD and Billie Jo out thoroughly before his interview, running them through the available police databases. He found no criminal background for either one, although Billie Jo did have several speeding tickets.

"Good to meet you," Pascoe said and he shook Wayne's hand in a bone-crushing grip.

"Thanks for seeing me, Detective," Wayne said.

"Call me PD," the older man replied gruffly. "I'm not

a detective any more. That's a young man's game." As they walked down the hall into the conference room, Billie Jo scooted ahead of them. She was wearing red high-topped sneakers, Wayne noticed. They were hard to miss.

"Welcome to our elegant conference room," Billie Jo said with a grin, gesturing to a banged-up card table and chairs. "I've ordered a new table. The old one belonged to our prior investigators. They took it with them when they left. Coffee?" she asked, gesturing to an antique dresser on the side of the room.

"Thank you, yes. Black, no sugar," Wayne said.

She poured the coffee for both men and hovered, clearly wanting to stay.

"You can go now, Billie Jo," Det. Pascoe said firmly. The young woman frowned slightly but departed. PD turned to Wayne saying, "Let's get right down to it. I've been running this place for about five years now. It's been a successful venture. We had two senior Investigators who were married to each other. They decided to retire a month ago, leaving me short-handed."

Wayne nodded.

"When I quit the Nashville post, I was going to wash my hands of the crime business, but I don't know anything else. Don't have a family you see," he shrugged.

"Sort of my situation too," Wayne said. "I've been a homicide detective for nearly twenty years, the last seven here in Rosedale. Prior to that, I worked in Detroit, investigating murders there."

"What was your solve rate?"

"My solve rate in Detroit was fifty percent, which is high in this line of work as you know. In Rosedale, we've solved all of the murders, not that there have been that many. I've been compared to a bloodhound. Once I catch a case, I never stop until I nail the perp. Of course, I realize I wouldn't be chasing criminals here, and would need to modify my interrogation…that is my *interviewing* style."

"What made you become a cop originally?" PD asked.

"It was the sense of camaraderie that exists in the force. It's been like a family for me. I grew up in foster care and missed out on that. I loved the physical nature of it, the long hours, the mental challenge and the sense of doing something important." Wayne knew it was more than that. He had really become a murder detective to give the victims of crime what he had never been able to give his foster mother: a timely justice.

"Do you think you would miss the adrenaline rush we get from chasing bad guys? There isn't much excitement in this kind of work."

"When I was young, I needed it," Wayne admitted. "Over the years, though, I find while I still enjoy solving a case, giving people bad news has become harder and harder, the worst being times when I've had to deal with the murders of young victims. I'm looking forward to dealing with *life* and setting death aside."

PD nodded. He seemed pleased with Wayne's answer.

"What do you see as your flaws as a homicide detective, other than the difficulty of giving people bad news?"

"I think we all hate doing the death knock," Wayne said, taking a deep breath and remembering the all times he had to tell people about the loss of a loved one. "In terms of other issues, I have a hard time sharing my feelings, something my girlfriend complains about, and I take all my cases to heart. I can't sleep, hardly even eating when dealing with a case. Even now when working a murder, I work nearly twenty-four seven until we catch a break."

"You sound like me," PD smiled. "Your Sheriff, Ben Bradley, came to see me once about a case. The deceased was a young man named Tom Ferris. There was a connection between Ferris and one of my unsolved ones, a kid whose death was ruled a suicide. I knew it was murder. Bradley closed that case for me. He's a good guy."

"Without question," Wayne said. "I notice your receptionist, Billie Jo's last name is Bradley. Is she related to Ben?"

"Something like a fifth cousin, she tells me. Do you have any old cases that haunt you?" PD's eyes were intent on Wayne's.

Wayne nodded, feeling an old remorse rise in his chest like an oncoming train—remembering little Ruthie. Pascoe's eyes narrowed. He had obviously picked up on Wayne's discomfort.

"Is there some reason you want to know?" Wayne asked, stalling.

"I have a feeling we are quite a bit alike, but I can't work with someone whose approach I can't respect," PD said.

Wayne sighed inwardly, knowing he wanted the job and that sharing Ruthie's case was the price he had to pay.

"There was a case in Detroit, my first as lead detective, which almost made me resign from the force. It was a couple who had tried for years to have a child. They finally had a little girl, Ruthie, and nobody could have been more adored. She was five when she went missing. She had been playing in their fenced backyard. Ten minutes later, when her mother went outside to get her, she was gone." Wayne forced his breathing to slow, trying to regain control, dampening the pain he always felt when he failed.

"A whole team was assigned to the case. We set up a whiteboard with photos. One day I totally lost it when I saw all the pictures of Ruthie had been taken down. They had been replaced with pictures of what she had been wearing—her little red jacket and rain boots. I left the police post furious, got Ruthie's picture blown up to poster size and put it in the center of the board. I made every one of them look at it morning and night. We brought in sniffer dogs and tracked her to the edge of a small pond. She had apparently climbed the fence, or was grabbed and taken from outside the yard. The scent vanished at the edge of the pond. We got hundreds of tips. I investigated every single one personally. The only clue was a little stuffed giraffe that was her favorite toy. It was found behind the garage with her blood on it. Although the case is still open, as are all unsolved murders, we stopped active investigation at Christmas that year."

"That's a tough one." Pascoe's expression was understanding.

"Every year since, I get out her file and go through the entire thing again to see what we might have missed. The National Association of Missing and Exploited Children 'ages' her photo each year. I keep it on my computer so I will recognize the child, if I ever spot her. I'm still in touch with detectives on the force in Michigan. If anything is ever discovered, even her remains, they've agreed I can tell the parents."

"I assume the parents blamed you," Pascoe said.

"No, in some ways that was the worst thing of all," Wayne said, pausing to regain control. "They couldn't have been nicer. They never blamed me, or anyone else on the team. They still send me Christmas cards." Wayne felt tears rising and blinked them furiously away. "I've got some questions for you now, PD," he said.

"Shoot," he replied.

"What kind of work do you do here? In the past, PI's did a lot of surveillance to document infidelity, but most of the time now I believe divorce is a 'no fault' situation."

"I still do a lot of that kind of work. Tennessee is both a 'fault' and a 'no fault' divorce state. Normally I'm called when there is a pre-nuptial agreement that specifies that the wife gets no financial settlement if she commits adultery. Most of the time she denies playing around, and I get called on to find the truth."

"Interesting. What other kinds of cases do you get called in on?"

"I often get missing person's cases. It's become a sort of a specialty of the firm. In fact, Billie Jo got a call this morning from a woman who's looking for her son who was adopted at birth. That will be an interesting one. All our work is completely confidential except when there's violence involved. Then I call the cops."

"What is Billie Jo's role in the organization?" Wayne asked.

"It's a bit complicated," he paused. "I became friends with Billie Jo's grandfather, Aaron, when we were both soldiers in 'Nam. He married, but lost his wife when she ran off with another man. She left their young daughter behind with him. When the daughter, Melanie, was in her twenties she got pregnant. She never revealed who the father was. By then Aaron was struggling with emphysema, so he asked me to keep an eye on her and the baby. Melanie did a good job until she got ovarian cancer," PD shook his head sadly. "Aaron was already dead by then. After she passed away, I decided to become more closely involved. Billie Jo was waiting table, going to college at night and needed a place to stay. I had just bought this place and said if she would supervise a renovation, she could live here once it was done. She's bright and ambitious, keeps asking to be involved in interviews, etc. She's become a whiz with the computers. Wants to get her Investigator's credentials. She's eager but way too young."

There was a brisk knock on the door and at Pascoe's shout to "come in," Billie Jo re-entered the room. Wayne wondered if the girl had been listening outside the door.

"The job is yours if you want it, Wayne," Pascoe said, glancing at his assistant who sat down at the table. "We'll put you on the payroll by next week if that works. Billie Jo here will send you the particulars of salary, benefits, etc. on email."

"Did you tell him about the model we use?" Billie Jo asked PD.

"No. You go ahead," he said.

"We use a different working model than in most organizations. There is no 'lead' person on any of our cases. PD and I, and now you, will all work as a team. We divide up the tasks and stay connected until the issue is resolved. Everyone has equal standing."

"Yeah, it's something she's talked me into. Found it

difficult at first, but now I like the idea," Pascoe said, looking slightly embarrassed at acquiescing to the girl's quirky ideas.

"I'm taking an English class in night school and my professor has us analyzing the old detective stories. She tells us to watch for people in the story, beyond the detective, who help solve the case. She pointed out that a team approach, especially having women on the team, works well. Women can often intuitively sense what happened."

Wayne and PD exchanged a look. Wayne found Billie Jo's ideas intriguing but a bit off-kilter. He shifted in his seat, uncomfortable with relinquishing the control of being the lead Detective. He cleared his throat.

"As you are well aware, Billie Jo, law enforcement is a strict bureaucracy, like the military. Tell me a bit more about your model. It's new to me," he said, looking at the twosome.

"Let me tell him, PD," Billie Jo said brightly. "One thing I've learned in my classes is that human beings crave stories—stories that make sense of their lives. When something happens that disrupts a person's story, they want the narrative reconstructed. That's what we do. We pull the threads of the story back together. It's like mending a hole in a spider web."

Wayne nodded, although he wasn't sure he fully understood, but decided not to pursue the point. "As soon as I get the information on employment specifics from you, I'll be in touch. Although as a cautionary note, I'm not interested in being an employee. If I take the job, I'd like to be a partner in the firm."

"Then all of us have some thinking to do," PD said and they shook hands good-bye.

Still pondering Billie Jo's rather cryptic remarks, Wayne walked out to his truck and called Miss Dory Clarkson, his best friend. She had also recently retired from the Sheriff's Office and since she was the finest natural investigator he had ever met. He hoped talking with her might shed some light on spider webs, the solving of mysteries and the nature of narrative.

TWO

Miss Dory Clarkson, an aging but still-glamorous African American woman, was getting a manicure when she received Wayne's call. She pushed the button to accept the call on her cell phone with her left hand. The manicurist was applying bright magenta polish to the fingernails of Dory's right hand.

"What's up, big guy?"

"I just finished a job interview with Rosedale Investigations and wondered if you might be available for lunch? My treat."

Dory had recently taken so-called *early* retirement from the Sheriff's Office. Although in her case early was a bit of a misnomer. She was secretly well past the usual retirement age, but as she had never provided her birthdate to the office, the fiction was preserved. Plus, skin of color didn't wrinkle much. She still felt and looked like she was in her fifties. No one would ever guess her age, certainly not her boyfriend, Al, who needed to be kept in deep darkness about the entire subject. *Especially since she was a good decade his senior.*

"I am at your service," she said. "What time were you thinking?"

"Now?" Wayne asked hopefully.

Dory looked down at her navy jeans and old sneakers. It would never do to be out in public in such a state. She was lucky Michelle worked out of her home in the

Flower Pot District, just down the street. She was able
to cut through back yards and enter through Michelle's
back door whenever she needed her hair or nails done.

"No dice, honey. I could, however, meet you in an
hour at Emil's."

She heard an irritated sound; Wayne hated to be kept
waiting. The grunt was followed by a brusque, "Fine.
See you then."

Michelle finished her excellent work, adding a tiny
gold star to each of Dory's nails. Dory paid her bill, tipping the woman generously and slipped out the back
door. Arriving back at her house, she walked into her
bedroom and opened her closet door. She had recently
added two rooms to her small home. Friends thought she
should have added a whole master bedroom suite, but
Dory decided she's rather have a bathroom and dressing
room. Her glamorous master bath had a claw foot tub
and marble wainscoting. The second room was given
over to a dressing area and an ample closet.

Walking into the closet, Dory looked at herself in the
mirrored wall and decided she would wear a figure-hug-
ging magenta sheath she had just purchased. It would
match her fingernails. She was hardly sylph-like (the
word voluptuous sprang to mind) but she still looked
damn good. Once sufficiently glamorous, adorned with
four-inch stilettoes and gold jewelry, she set off to meet
her dear friend, Detective Wayne Nichols.

WHEN DORY BREEZED into Emil's, a recently-added upscale Italian restaurant in Rosedale, she spotted Wayne
sitting in the back corner. He was nicely dressed, no
doubt the work of his girlfriend Lucy, but from the look
in his eyes, she guessed he had just downed his sec-

ond scotch. She slid into the booth, smiled and said, "What's going on? You look like someone just ran over your dog."

"It's not that bad, but you're right. I'm not a happy man. I ordered a glass of wine for you."

Dory nodded and the waiter brought her a glass of red wine and some hot bread sticks.

"As I told you on the phone, I just had my interview with Rosedale PI Investigations. It's run by this old murder detective, PD Pascoe. He offered me a job, although we're still working out the details."

"So why the second scotch and the harried look?" Dory asked.

"I suddenly realized that my whole thirty-plus years in law enforcement have come to a halt. The day I turned in my gun and badge to the Sheriff, I felt I'd surrendered my soul, but it wasn't until after the interview today that I knew my former career had ended."

"I do have nice shoulders, should you need one to cry on," Dory said with a smile. "You know, Wayne, I'm feeling pretty much the same way. I started working part-time for the Sheriff's Office when I was only seventeen. And now that I'm…well let's just say I'm not a teen-ager anymore."

"You must really be rattled, my friend. You almost told me your age, a secret that's been more closely guarded than the gold in Fort Knox," Wayne grinned.

"Did they give you a job offer?" Dory asked.

"They did and I've decided I'm going to take it. Wayne Nichols, Private Investigator," he shook his head. "It doesn't seem real. Used to be law enforcement looked down on those guys. We thought of them as cop 'wannabes.' But PI's do a lot of important work these days—background searches, surveillance and missing persons. Top PI's often work directly with law enforcement, serving subpoenas, testifying in court and working cold cases."

"Doesn't sound bad at all, Wayne. Sounds like being a cop without having to go to the morgue, get out in filthy weather or chase bad guys," Dory smiled. "As a matter of fact, having been retired now for a month, I will admit to feeling a smidge restless. I'm the one that should be looking for work. You were offered a nice gig with Evangeline Bon Temps' husband, Jason, doing corporate security the week after you left the Sheriff's Office. I thought you were going to take it."

"I was, but after thinking about it some more I realized being a security guard didn't sound very challenging," Wayne said, downing another large swallow. "In thinking about our joint unemployed status, it occurred to me that you might want to work for Rosedale Investigations, too. I have a feeling they'd be open to adding more people."

Dory sipped her wine and nodded. "You're right that I might be interested. This doing nothing but shopping and eating out is not exactly good for my razor-sharp mind or perfect figure. Lately when I wake up in the morning, I think about what I'm doing that day and realize there's nothing pressing. Most of the time I feel downright bored. What did you think of Pascoe and his sidekick, Billie Jo? The scuttlebutt around town is that they are good at their jobs."

"Interesting duo. Detective Pascoe is sort of an older version of me. The girl, Billie Jo, is a smart cookie and good with the computer but she dresses weirdly. Despite her youth, she seems to have PD wrapped around her little finger."

"Word on the street is that she's ingratiated herself into being a quasi-Investigator without any credentials."

"I'd say that's about right. She said something that I wanted to get your take on. Apparently, they don't have a lead investigator on any of their cases. She and Pascoe have a very tight working partnership but use what she called a spider web approach to solving their cases. Everyone contributes equally. What does that mean to you?"

"To me it sounds freer, like you wouldn't have to worry about stepping on someone's toes by coming up with a new idea. Very appealing."

"Hmmm. She said one other thing too. She said that people need narrative, stories that made sense of their lives. When they experience a divorce, a death or something else disruptive, it breaks the story line. What do you think about that?" Wayne looked at Dory inquisitively.

Dory looked thoughtful for a moment before saying, "Sometimes I think we all see ourselves as the main character in a story or a movie. When something happens we can't get our heads around, we feel like there's a scene missing in the film. And if someone can help make sense of what has happened, we experience a sense of relief."

"Lucy says a lot of her patients get that 'ah ha' moment when she tells them their diagnoses. The spider web idea is new to me but I don't seem to have a choice if I want this job. One other thing I wanted to mention. I told the Rosedale PI duo I don't want to be an employee. Provided we can come to an agreement on the finances, I'm offering to become a partner in the firm."

"I have to say this has been a very enlightening sort of 'ah ha' lunch, Wayne. I'll follow up with the twosome and see if they have another opening. If so, I'll apply for a job there. If we both get hired, we could actually be partners. What do you think?"

"I think you're one of the smartest people I know," Wayne sat back with a smile. "And I'd love to have someone I could count on fixing that broken spider web with me."

THREE

CARA KIDD SUMMERFIELD set her coffee cup down on the shining granite surface of her kitchen island and gazed out her front window. October mornings were usually clear and warm in Tennessee, but it had been raining since midnight. Lightning from the storm woke her early, so close it lit up their bedroom windows. The glare revealed the chiseled profile of her handsome husband. *He slept with the total immersion with which he did everything*, she thought, fondly.

Grant hadn't even moved when the thunder boomed, and didn't stir when she got out of bed. She padded down the hall with its shining dark wood floors, past bedrooms that should have housed their sleeping children. Catching sight of herself in the hall mirror, she saw dark eyes and shoulder length wavy hair. *I still look young enough*, she thought, but despite years of hormones and multiple *in vitro* fertilization procedures, there had been no babies. *Except for my first—my perfect baby boy*, she thought taking a deep breath, trying to dispel her grief.

The doctors could find no medical reasons she and Grant couldn't get pregnant, but she knew the truth. She had conceived and carried a baby to term after all. While it wasn't her fault, she still blamed herself—believing it was because she had given in to her father's pressure to give baby Danny up for adoption—that God or Mother Nature was still punishing her. *If only I could go back in time to that awful day*, she thought. *I would keep him close forever.* For a moment she could feel her baby's solid warmth against her chest and tears pricked her eyes. When she heard Grant getting out of bed and opening the door to their en-suite bathroom, she quickly wiped her tears away. *He can never know*, she thought. *Grant's pride in his masculinity couldn't take knowing it was his fault they didn't have a family.*

It was only after Grant left for work, and Cara managed to temporarily set aside her regret about Danny's adoption, that she was able to sit down at her desk to respond to emails and update her increasingly busy calendar. The kitchen window was open and she heard the mail truck turn into their subdivision. Moments later she saw Charlie, her postman, walking toward the house. He didn't have an umbrella and was dodging raindrops. She walked quickly to the entry and opened the elaborate door just as he rang the doorbell.

"Hello, Mrs. Summerfield. Got a package for you and a couple of letters." Charlie had a weather-beaten face and pair of faded blue eyes. His hair was iron gray and curly. This morning it was tinseled with raindrops. She liked him.

"Thanks for bringing it up, Charlie," Cara said, smiling. She took the mail from his hands. "I have an extra umbrella I could lend you."

"No thanks. I've got my hands full, literally. Don't have an extra hand to hold an umbrella." He grinned and turned back toward the mail truck. Then, noticing a small white envelope he had accidently dropped on her lawn, he picked it up. "Sorry," he said and handed it to her.

"Not a problem," she told him and waved goodbye. She walked back to the kitchen and set the circulars and bills aside to open the package. It was one of the books her husband had ordered for his office with its mostly empty floor-to-ceiling walnut bookshelves. This one was a recent biography of George Washington. Grant read compulsively, but not because he enjoyed it. He was a "people person" and would chat happily with anyone. Reading bored him. He was always setting books aside, after reading only a page or two, to make a phone call or check his email. Still, he was going to be interviewed soon for the local paper. As an up-and-coming politician, he needed to be prepared. They always asked what the candidates were reading.

She set the book down and turned to the small envelope Charlie had retrieved from the rain-soaked lawn. It was invitation sized, probably something else she would have to attend. But it was addressed to Cara Kidd, her maiden name. A funny premonitory quiver slid across her shoulders. She set it down and took another sip of coffee. It had gone cold. Her hands trembled. She had a nearly overpowering desire to rip the little envelope in half and toss it into the wastebasket but forcing herself, she opened it.

Dear Miss Kidd, I'm writing you on behalf of your son. Danny's in trouble…

SHE HAD ONLY seen Danny once since he was born, just one late-night meeting ten years ago. He had apparently browbeaten his adoptive parents, the Parrish's, for months before they gave him her name. He sent her a private message on a website for children trying to lo-

cate their birth parents, asking if she would meet him.
She had been profoundly shaken, but could not resist the
chance to see her son again. Cara bit her lip, thinking
of the gangling adolescent with a thatch of near-black
hair that fell across his fine dark eyes.

Cara had met her husband, Grant, at the age of twenty-
one, four years after the agonizing choice to give baby
Danny up for adoption. She never told Grant about the
baby and an illegitimate stepson wasn't something he
could handle. Not with his political career skyrocketing.
And she doubted he would be very understanding about
two decades of being lied to either. She drew in a shaky
breath, trying to set aside the agonizing pain she always
felt, recalling the day the social worker took her baby
away. *It had been raining then, too,* she remembered.

She swallowed and turned her attention back to the
letter.

*Danny's in debt—to some frightening guys from
the racetrack. After they sprained his wrist and
broke his ribs, he confessed that he owes them
fifteen thousand dollars. They've given him only
a week to come up with it. He's left for work now
and would be incensed if he knew I was writing
you. He hopes to talk his boss into a personal
loan. It's a long shot. Could you please help him?
I'm afraid he will disappear or leave me if he can't
get the money. Hopefully, Tracey*

Tracey had included a photo of the two of them,
standing in front of an aging apartment building. They
were holding hands, both of them smiling. Cara's breath
caught in her chest, they looked so sweet and young.

STASHING THE LETTER in her purse, Cara opened her kitchen desk drawer and pulled out her savings account passbook. It was only the second time Danny had ever asked for money. The first time it was for an equestrian apprenticeship program. Even at sixteen, he knew he wanted to be a horse trainer. She still felt the thrill of seeing him after so long, coupled with a wave of fear that Grant would discover her lies. But her husband happened to be out of town and although she went back and forth a thousand times in her mind, in the end she met her son at a coffee shop.

She hadn't planned to give him any money, but when she heard how passionate he was about becoming a racehorse trainer, she felt herself melting. She agreed to pay for the apprenticeship, but asked why he hadn't asked his adoptive parents for help. He told her they were totally against gambling and feared he would get into that life working at the track. His adoptive mother's dad had been a professional gambler. When the father died, all their assets were confiscated. Danny's mother had grown up in dire poverty and was still enmeshed in bitterness. When Danny told them he wanted to be a horse trainer there had been a God-awful fight. He had stormed out, saying he was never coming back. Cara wondered, in the ten years since she laid eyes on her son, if they ever reconciled.

This time it wasn't Danny but his girlfriend, Tracey, who asked for help and, given the situation, Cara didn't hesitate. She would send him the money he needed to pay off his debt and a few thousand extra. She only needed an address to send a certified check to. But picking up the envelope she felt her heart start to race; the rain had obliterated most of the return address. She looked carefully at the postmark, but even that was hard to read. She had a magnification app on her phone, something her optometrist said would help her forty-two-year-old eyes. Holding the light above the envelope, she could decipher only three letters. The rest of the return address was illegible. She felt like a bird trapped in a closed room, fluttering frantically against a glass window. *You failed him as a newborn, and your decision to pay for his racehorse training apprenticeship led to this,* her conscience said.

She forced herself to calm down, to think. As a part of the local community service her husband asked her to contribute, Cara volunteered to landscape and maintain the Post Office gardens. In the three years she had been keeping up the garden, Cara had met the Postmistress, Marianne, and they had become friends. Maybe her friend could read the address with some scanning equipment. Cara grabbed her purse, keys and raincoat. Twenty minutes later she was standing in Marianne's office with the envelope in her hand.

"Thanks so much for seeing me," she said. "I received an invitation today. The rain wiped out the return address and I want to reply to it. It's just another one of these political fund-raisers, but I'd like to attend. Can you help?"

"Surely," Marianne said. She tall and thin, in her mid-forties. Her children were away at college and she often helped Cara with the garden. She held out her hand for the envelope. When she switched on her desk lamp, Cara's heart fell.

"I've already tried looking at it under a light," she said softly.

"Hmmm. I see what you mean. If you can wait a

minute, I will look at this under UV. We have a full-spectrum camera in the back." Marianne left her office and walked through the double doors to the mail-sorting room.

By the time she returned, Cara was chewing on her fingernails. She pulled part of one nail off with her teeth, knowing her manicurist would be outraged. "Did you find anything?" she asked.

"We could tell that it came from a small town located near Nashville. The zip code was incomplete, but the first four digits were 3721. We also deciphered a little of the street address. It was smudged, but we're pretty sure it is from Donelson, Tennessee which has a 37214 zip code. Your letter carrier, Charlie, helped me with this. He remembered dropping the letter and felt it was his fault. He said to tell you how sorry he was. It struck us both as odd though. If it's a local fund-raiser event, why would you get an invitation from there?" Marianne looked at her curiously.

"Maybe they delegate fund-raising invitations to an out-of-town mailing service?" It was the best Cara could come up with on the spot, and even to her it sounded lame. She felt guilty lying to a friend, but she'd been doing it for so long about Danny, it had become automatic. A therapist she had seen some years before said she was leading a double life. "You can't live a lie forever," the counselor said gently and urged her to tell Grant about Danny. But memories of her pregnancy and baby son remained walled off, in tightly locked compartments—except for the nights Danny came to her in dreams.

Realizing her friend had been waiting for her response, Cara said, "Thank you, Marianne. I'm not going to worry about it any longer. After all, if they want me to attend some event, they'll probably follow up. I'll be coming by here tomorrow morning around 7 a.m. to work on the flowerbeds if you want to join me?" Cara smiled encouragingly.

"Not a chance, Kiddo. It's my day off and I'm going to be lazy," Marianne grinned. "I have a new man in my life. Decided it was time to invite him to stay over."

"Good for you," Cara said, smiled and took her leave. Sitting in her car in the Post Office parking lot, she tried to think logically about her next steps. The first thing was to call information. Maybe there was a Daniel Parrish, or a Daniel Kidd, with a listed phone near Donelson, Tennessee. She dialed information but the operator found nothing, which meant he didn't have a land line and accessing a street address was now out of the question. She typed "Daniel Kidd" into her phone finding 172 profiles for that name on LinkedIn. The name Daniel Parrish was similarly common. It would take days to go through all of them, but googling "horse racing" on her phone revealed a large racetrack called Nashville Downs only two hours from Rosedale.

She briefly considered driving there and asking around the track for Danny. *I could see him again*, she thought and felt a thrill run through her whole body before realizing she had no idea what she would tell Grant about her absence. He had a big political fundraiser coming up and was counting on her being beside him. No, she needed someone else to locate Danny and it had to be soon. As a condition of paying off his gambling debt, she would insist that Danny attend Gamblers Anonymous meeting. Gambling was a serious problem and she wasn't going to enable that behavior. The extra money could go toward whatever he and Tracey needed, but it wouldn't be for gambling.

Leaving the Post Office, she drove to Citizens Community Bank. A few years after they married, Grant asked her to quit her pre-school teaching job. He hadn't wanted her to work outside the home, preferring her to be available to travel with him and support his career. She made so little money that it wasn't a sacrifice, and in those years she thought it wouldn't be long before she was pregnant...again. She had always banked her paychecks and any extra money Grant gave her in a personal savings account. When her father died, she had inherited some money from him and added that to the account. *All along I thought the day might come when Danny would need my help*, she thought. Standing in front of the bank teller, she requested two certified checks, one for fifteen thousand dollars and one for three thousand.

"Who should I make these out to?" the young teller asked.

"Make the large one out to Daniel Kidd Parrish," she said. "Leave the name on the second one blank for now if that's okay." The teller looked at her expectantly. "A gift for my...cousin," she added.

"Pretty nice gift, I'd say," the teller said. "Any time you want another cousin, just let me know. I'm available for adoption." He grinned. "Do you want a slip with your balance?"

"No need," Cara said, feeling a small lurch in her stomach knowing her balance had been cut almost in half with this withdrawal. She felt the pressure of time bearing down on her. She had to get Danny the money before those horrible thugs got their hands on her son.

Thinking about him possibly injured severely, she swallowed hard—trapping a sob in her throat.

Returning to the car, she felt in her purse for a tissue and pulled one out. As she did so, her library card fell onto the car seat. At a recent fund-raiser for the local library, she'd overheard a woman say she had hired a private detective to trail her husband. She suspected he was having an affair. It was impossible to go to the police and report the threat against Danny. Maybe a private investigator could find him.

Coward, the critical voice inside her head said. *You don't even have the guts to find him now when he needs you. And you didn't insist on keeping him after he was born.*

But, I was only seventeen, she pleaded in her own defense.

You were a coward, Cara.

After a few moments getting herself together, she typed "PI firms, Rosedale, TN" into her phone. A listing for Rosedale Investigations gave its location and phone number. She pressed the call button and when a young woman answered, made an appointment for the following day.

FOUR

Tuesday

BILLIE JO BRADLEY heard the sound of the tinkling bell as the door to Rosedale Investigations opened. She quickly closed the document she was reading on her computer and walked to the front entry to welcome their newest client. An attractive dark-haired woman hesitated at the threshold.

"Mrs. Summerfield?" Billie asked, and when the woman nodded said, "Please come in."

After introducing herself and ushering her new client into the conference room, Billie Jo offered her water or coffee. When Mrs. Summerfield declined, she got out her computer tablet and sat down across from the woman at the rickety card table.

"How can we help you, Mrs. Summerfield?"

"Please, call me Cara. Excuse me, but I thought I was meeting with Detective Pascoe. You look way too young and pretty to be interviewing clients. Is he here?" The woman gave Billie Jo a sweet smile that transformed her face.

"He'll be back soon, but we can get started now. I'm a partner with the firm," she said. *It was a total lie, but sounded impressive.* "Can I have your full name and address…"

"It's Cara Kidd Summerfield," the client said and went on to give the rest of her contact information.

"Do you work outside the home, Mrs. Summerfield? I need a work number if you have one."

"Not now," she answered after a brief pause. "My husband's in politics, so I attend a lot of events with him and on his behalf."

Billie Jo sat up a little straighter. "Are you married to Grant Summerfield?" *I hope this case isn't going to involve him cheating. He seems like one of the good guys.*

"I am," Cara's voice was very quiet now. "Grant and I don't have children together and he doesn't know that..." her voice trailed off. Billie waited patiently as the woman hesitated and cleared her throat. "I have a son. His name is Daniel Kidd Parrish. He was born when I was seventeen, four years before Grant and I married, and was adopted as an infant by a Mr. and Mrs. Richard Parrish. My son has been beaten up—because he owes money to a bookie—and I need your help to find him. Before you do anything, however, I need your assurances that this is completely confidential."

"Absolutely anything you tell me is confidential, Mrs. Summerfield. Do you have any ideas where we might start?"

Just then Billie Jo heard the back door to the house open, and the sound of kitchen cupboard doors opening and closing. PD must have stopped at the grocery store. He was always buying food for her, saying she was too thin. She stood up. "Excuse me for a minute please, Mrs. Summerfield."

Billie Jo walked to the kitchen at the back of the house seeing PD take a six-pack of beer out of the grocery sack and put it in the refrigerator.

"Thought you weren't drinking," she said, giving him a look. "Our new client is here. Her name is Cara Summerfield. Come join us."

"*Our* new client?" PD asked, looking at her slant-wise. "I thought we had agreed that you don't *do* initial interviews. You aren't a partner yet, Kiddo."

Billie Jo turned around and PD followed her back to the conference room. "Mrs. Summerfield, this is Detective Pascoe," she said, her voice sounding a bit sulky.

PD and Cara shook hands. He took the chair next to Billie Jo across from their new client and said, "Sorry I was late. What can we do for you, Mrs. Summerfield?"

"Your young partner has been getting my contact information," she said.

At the word "partner" PD cast Billie Jo a vexed look. "Now that I'm here, you can tell me the issue."

Cara took a deep breath and began, "I became pregnant with my high school boyfriend, Rafe, when I was seventeen. When I told my parents, they sent me to live with my aunt for the duration of the pregnancy." Cara rubbed her hands together and twirled her diamond-studded wedding ring around her thin finger. Billie Jo and PD waited quietly for her story to emerge.

"Even though I wanted to keep him, Dad convinced me that it was better for me and the baby if I gave him up for adoption. My mother was already battling breast cancer and she agreed." Tears were rolling down her cheeks by then, unchecked. Billie Jo handed her a box of tissues. Cara wiped her face and continued to speak. "I only held him once before they took him away. The nurses said he went to a foster family for the waiting period, and I had six weeks to be sure, but I didn't change my mind. My parents brought me back home where I finished high school and went on to college. I married my husband, Grant, four years later. I never saw my baby again until he tracked me down when he was sixteen. That was ten years ago."

"Does your husband know about Danny?" PD asked.

"No," she said quietly. "I never told him or Danny's biological father, Rafe Marston, either. His parents moved out of state before I found out I was pregnant." She pulled an envelope from her purse. "This came in the mail yesterday from Danny's girlfriend, Tracey. My son owes fifteen thousand dollars in gambling debts and is being pressured to pay up. She asked me to send them the money, but I can't read the return address." Cara handed the envelope to Billie Jo, who read the letter while PD studied the envelope.

"Tracey sent a picture as well." Cara handed the photo to PD with a shaky hand. "My friend at the Post Office thinks that it's a Donelson, Tennessee zip code, but I couldn't find an address or phone number. I'm willing to send them the money, but I don't know where to send it. According to his girlfriend, Danny only has a week to come up with the money."

"We have numerous databases in the office. I can practically guarantee that we can find your son," Billie Jo said brightly.

PD frowned. He had advised Billie Jo many times not to promise things to clients that could prove impossible.

Cara asked Det. Pascoe a few questions about their rates and gave them the three thousand dollar cashier's check she had just gotten from the bank, quickly writing the name of "Rosedale Investigations" as the recipient. Billie Jo took the check.

"I've got an event to attend this evening and should get going." Cara stood up and pushed her dark hair back from her face. "Is there anything else you need from me?"

"We need to be able to get in touch with you as the case develops. What's the best way to do that?" Billie Jo waited with her fingers poised over her tablet's keyboard.

"Here's my card." She fished it out of her purse and put it on the table between Billie Jo and PD. "It's best to email me. I don't want my husband to know I contacted you. I'll check my email frequently, but if it's urgent and I don't respond within a couple of hours, you can call or text me." She took a deep breath and lowered her shoulders with a visible effort. "Thank you both. I'll let myself out."

The duo met each other's eyes as Cara left the room and the front door closed behind her. PD looked furious.

"If I hear that you have introduced yourself as a *partner* to a client again, I'm going to be seriously angry," he said. "And we've talked before about you promising more than we might be able to deliver. You've *got* to stop doing that." He narrowed his eyes and Billie Jo flushed. "Start checking through the databases for a Daniel Kidd Parrish. He's twenty-six, lives in the Nashville area and could work at Nashville Downs racetrack," PD said. "Can you find him with that and the photo Mrs. Summerfield gave us?"

"I think so. We have facial recognition software now. I just bought it." At PD's frown she colored, "Don't look at me that way, PD. We needed it."

"How much did it cost?" PD asked.

"It wasn't that bad," she gave him a guilty smile.

"How bad?"

Avoiding the question, Billie Jo said, "Let me do a little online research. It's possible that I can track down Danny's adoptive parents and get an address. Or his cell phone number may be in that new database." Billie Jo smiled at Det. Pascoe, trying to distract him from asking about the cost of the facial recognition software again. It had been steep.

"I presume there will be bill coming for the software?" PD said looking at her intently. "When it arrives, you are to give it to me immediately and you are grounded with respect to making any more purchases." Billie Jo nodded, looking embarrassed. Minutes later, the doorbell tinkled.

FIVE

PD PASCOE STOOD up and pulled his cell phone from his pocket to check the time. "I think that's my interview," he said to Billie Jo, who was giving him a quizzical look. "She's a little early." Moving towards the front door, he said, "Ms. Clarkson? Come on in. We're back here."

A beautifully dressed African American woman who looked to be in her mid-fifties entered the room. "I'm Dory Clarkson," she said, smiling at PD with an outstretched hand. "You must be Detective Pascoe."

"Good to meet you, Dory. We're not formal around here, so please call me PD." They exchanged a handshake.

Turning to Billie Jo, Dory said, "My friend Wayne Nichols told me all about you, Billie Jo. I gather you are the brains of the outfit."

PD rolled his eyes as Billie Jo nodded and preened a little.

From the tops of their heads right down to their footwear, Dory and Billie Jo were a study in contrasts. Dory had light brown skin, wore a fitted coral sheath, a silver necklace and high heeled shoes. Billie Jo was wearing pink flip-flops with the rest of her biker-chick outfit. Her T-shirt was off-white and hung loosely from her shoulders showing a black bra strap, something PD had told her repeatedly was unprofessional.

Billie Jo looked like a kid standing next to Dory, but from their non-verbal behavior PD sensed the two of them would like each other. His previous female investigator hadn't liked Billie Jo, although her husband quite definitely had. He was always hitting on the girl, the wife was continually furious and PD felt he was walking on eggshells trying to mediate the issues between them. If they hired Dory, and she and Billie Jo got along, it would be a relief.

"You're Wayne Nichols' friend?" Billie Jo asked. Dory nodded. "We're hoping to bring him on board soon. I didn't realize PD had scheduled an interview today, I usually do the scheduling around here," she gave PD a quick slanted glance saying, "I'm happy to meet you."

Dory gave an infectious laugh, glanced at PD and winked. "Is this a good time? I just live around the corner in the Flowerpot District, so I could come back later. And yes, Wayne is a dear friend. We've worked together for years."

Billie Jo tilted her head smiling. "Now's a perfect time for us to talk. Can I get you a glass of iced tea? It's Red Zinger."

Dory included both of them in her grin. "I'd love some."

"C'mon with me to the kitchen," Billie Jo said and practically skipped out of the room.

"That's fine, I don't want anything. Not that you asked," PD said, under his breath. He followed the sound of their voices back to the kitchen, amused at the contrasts between the two women and their obvious clicking.

AN HOUR LATER Dory left, having nailed down a job offer. She also wanted to be a partner. Her final words as she sailed out the front door had been a promise to return on the following morning to get started. As the front door to the firm closed, PD turned to Billie Jo. "Well go ahead, girl, do your computer magic and track down Mrs. Summerfield's son. I'm going to make some calls."

It didn't take Billie Jo long to access a little-known cell phone directory online. There were several Daniel Parrish's, but only one of the numbers had a Nashville area code. She wrote it on a slip of paper and brought it into Det. Pascoe's office.

PD picked up his cell phone and entered the number for Daniel Parrish. After three rings he heard a woman's voice saying a very quiet, "Hello."

"Could I please speak to Daniel?"

"Who is this?" She demanded. Her voice sounded young and frightened.

"I'm a private investigator who has been hired to find Mr. Daniel Parrish," he said. "Is this Tracey?"

"You just leave him alone!" She shouted, and the line went dead.

He stared at the phone in his hand and pressed "redial" but this time no one answered. He would try again later, but if Daniel was as frightened as his girlfriend had sounded, he might be in the wind already.

PD called out to Billie Jo who had returned to her desk. "I called Danny's cell phone number and a woman answered. She hung up on me when I said I was trying to find him. Nobody answered when I called back."

"She probably thought you worked for the bookie," Billie Jo said. "I'll text Cara and let her know, but I'm guessing somebody needs to go to Nashville Downs and look for Danny in person if she won't answer that phone."

"Neither of us can go. We have the jewelry theft to investigate and I am looking into the embezzlement at the insurance agency," PD said.

"Luckily, Dory and Wayne start tomorrow. Maybe they would like to go on a little road-trip."

"Right. Can you make Wayne and Dory's employment agreements? I'll call our two new partners and tell them where they are headed."

AND HOUR LATER, PD heard the sounds of Billie Jo gathering her papers and locking the front door. He glanced at his watch. It was four o'clock in the afternoon.

"See you tomorrow," Billie Jo said. "I'm going up to my private quarters to change. You can call if you really need me."

When PD decided to remodel the old house, Billie Jo had been evicted from her low income rental. It took careful probing before she confessed to living in her car. Although unsure in the beginning, PD ultimately decided she could live in the upstairs floor of the house. During the renovation, Billie Jo had worked closely with the contractor. On the main floor, they created a waiting area with a couch and chairs, a handicapped accessible bathroom, an office for PD, a reception station for Billie Jo, a conference room and a kitchen. Upstairs, Billie Jo had a living room with a Juliet balcony, a bathroom, and a bedroom with a walk-in closet.

"It's not quitting time yet," PD shouted after his assistant.

"It is for me," she called back, cheekily, "I have a date."

Of course you do, PD thought and sighed, wondering for the hundredth time whether hiring such a young person had been a good idea.

SIX

Wednesday

DORY CLARKSON WAS standing in front of her closet, naked—surveying its contents with a gimlet eye. She and Wayne Nichols, who was due to arrive shortly, were driving to Nashville, Tennessee on their first assignment for Rosedale Investigations. When they talked the night before, they decided to split up as soon as they got to the Nashville Downs racetrack. Wayne would start checking local medical facilities and Dory would go to the track. She sighed wondering what one wore on a non-race day to the track. *A big hat?*

There was a section of Dory's closet totally devoted to hats, some as big as hula-hoops, decorated with artificial flowers in brilliant colors Mother Nature never created, but she was pretty sure you didn't wear a hat on a day when there were no races. Jodhpurs? Paddock boots? Dory was curvy, there was no getting away from it. Her traditionally built African American body was not enhanced by snugly fitted, bottom-hugging pants.

"Still, needs must," she told herself firmly and pulled out an old pair of Ralph Lauren stretch jersey pants with leather patches on the inside of the thighs, short black boots and a clingy low-cut top. After all, she might be *forced* to lean forward to elicit an important clue from a gentleman. She smiled at the easy simplicity of manipulating men.

Wayne beeped the horn of his truck in her driveway an hour later. It was still only 8:00 o'clock in the morning. He was smartly dressed in a dark suit, pale blue shirt and tie. He had a new haircut too, neither of which was enough to curb Dory's exasperation.

"Wayne Nichols, have I not told you repeatedly not to honk your horn in the Flowerpot District? Especially this early," she said irritably, loading her gear into the back seat. Male manipulation clearly didn't work very well on her partner. But thinking of the word partner, she grinned. They were finally partners. Equal *'we have each other's backs'* partners. Life was indeed sweet, despite horns honked in driveways way too early in the morning.

"What did you bring?" Wayne asked

"Nothing but the staples: coffee, blueberry muffins, bananas, Clementines and water. Did you look up the directions? I checked the distance last night. It's only a couple of hours."

"We should be there right around ten," Wayne said. "Did you get all your paperwork done for Rosedale Investigations?"

"Sure did. I'm a partner, same as you. When I started all this, I didn't know how much money would be involved—didn't realize I'd have to *pay* for the privilege of working there." Dory raised her eyebrows. "I've worked all my life for Rose County, so I wasn't thinking that in order to be a partner in a private firm, you have to buy in. How did you come up with your share?" Dory asked, grabbing the rearview mirror of Wayne's truck to check her eye make-up. Her eyeliner and mascara were perfect.

Removing her hands firmly from his mirror, Wayne replied, "I still had the money from the sale of my old condo in the bank. Not that you earn any money in savings these days, but it was enough. What about you?"

"Had to pull out a big chunk of my retirement to buy-in," Dory said. "Hope this PI business ends up being sufficiently lucrative that whenever I decide to quit, I'll have made money on my investment. I sure don't want to end up in the county nursing home."

"Don't think that would ever happen to you, my friend," Wayne said. "And if it ever did, I would stage a break out."

The two of them smiled companionably at each other.

An hour later, Dory was bored. It was an early fall day and the billboards along the freeway were interesting for a while. When that paled, she focused on the flowers growing on the sides of the highway. Her tablet had a plant identification app and even speeding past, she found some of their names. She identified goldenrod, purple asters, Black-eyed Susan's and cattails standing erect in the water-filled ditches. However, Wayne's damn pick-up rattled even on the freeway and it needed suspension work as well. Next time they would take her car. She looked up the Nashville Downs racetrack on her tablet and read some of the text to Wayne.

"The track was built in 1990 and was originally called the Dueling Grounds Race Course. It was built on a farm located at a slight bend of what is otherwise a perfectly straight Tennessee-Kentucky border. The property was the site of numerous duels in the 1800s. Dueling was legally abolished in both Tennessee and Kentucky in 1827. The track conducted steeplechase races in its first years, but removed the fences and switched to flat racing in

1992. The first meet featured the Dueling Grounds International, whose seven hundred and fifty-thousand dollar purse remains the richest in racing."

"What's your plan once we get there?" Wayne asked.

"I thought I'd check the Personnel office first, to see if Daniel Parrish is employed there, and if they have a home address for him."

"Doubt they will just hand over the information, despite the get-up you're wearing. Especially since in my experience the personnel office is normally staffed with young females. I have observed that males are more susceptible to your considerable charms," Wayne said and chuckled.

"Don't you worry about me, Pardner," Dory drawled. "I brought a letter Sheriff Bradley wrote for me some time ago saying that I was employed at his office as an Investigator. What's your plan by the way? And when do you want to connect later?"

"I was going to start with the local Urgent-Care facilities, assuming Danny probably sought medical help from his brush with the bookie's debt collectors, but last night Lucy said I should skip that and check the local hospitals. There are three of them, plus Vanderbilt which has a Level 1 trauma center. Probably save myself some time by checking there first."

"And you think they'll just tell you stuff about a patient? Ha!"

"That's another thing I thought about. I'm not in law enforcement now, but am still available for major crimes with the Sheriff's Office. I'm going to check in with the Nashville Police post to see if I can get their okay to obtain information from the hospital. Luckily, the track is located within their jurisdiction," Wayne said.

"Didn't think you even knew how to work the web, my friend," Dory said giving him a little cat grin.

"Lucy did it for me," Wayne said shortly. Lucy was already bugging him about learning to search the web on his own; he didn't need Dory to nag him about it too. "I've already applied for my license as a private eye. Still have to take the two-hour exam, but then I'll have my license. And Billie Jo supplied me with a letter of employment from Rosedale Investigations which is licensed as an agency. I figure with my work history as a detective and the letter, I should be good."

"I looked up the requirements too. The fees weren't too bad. You have to pay to apply, for the fingerprinting and the license, once you get it. They usually look for former cops, people with undergraduate degrees in criminal justice or lawyers. Luckily, I have all those years with the Sheriff's Department," Dory said. "How about I take your letter of endorsement from Rosedale Investigations with me? Having both letters might help me with the girls from personnel."

Dory and Wayne stopped for a coffee break at a sandwich shop on the outskirts of Nashville. The place was close enough to the track that Dory surveyed the clientele with a shrewd eye. They were mostly young guys, clean-cut and in a hurry. Young professionals on the rise, she thought. Not likely to be involved in collecting unpaid gambling debts. She pulled the photo of Danny from her purse and looked carefully at the crowd. Daniel Parrish wasn't there. Having finished their coffees, they drove the remainder of the way to the racetrack.

As advertised, Nashville Downs was beautifully landscaped. In fact, the photos on the website didn't do it justice. Turning into the track and following the signs, they came to a large brick building with wings on either side. Arriving at the main entrance, Dory hopped out of the truck, grabbed her purse and waved good-bye. Wayne turned back on Old Clubhouse Lane, headed for the local police post.

Walking into the large building, Dory found herself just outside an auditorium for yearling sales. To her right was the Auctioneers podium. A young man was leading a chestnut filly into the arena. The horse's feet hit the ground with the distinctive clip clop. Dory moved into the stadium and made her way to the seats. It was a slow business as the horses were led in, walked around the arena and the bidding began. She looked carefully at everyone. The men—and it was an exclusively male province—all looked intent and serious. After ten minutes, Dory left. She hadn't seen Danny Parrish. When a young woman walked by, she asked where the Personnel office was.

"Down the hall," the woman said and gestured to her right.

"By chance do you know this young man?" Dory asked, pulling Danny's photo from her purse. "His name is Daniel. Does he work here?"

"Yeah, Danny. I've seen him around, but not in three or four days," the young woman said and Dory felt a rising satisfaction. She had hit the right racetrack first thing. Then a trace of worry rose in her chest. He hadn't been seen in several days. That could mean Wayne was right to visit the medical facilities.

She located the personnel office and asked the receptionist, a sweet looking girl, for a Daniel Parrish. "I know he works here. I'm trying to get his contact information."

"We don't give out that kind of information," the girl said, starchily. Dory decided to play the mom card.

"His mother is looking for him. She hired me to find him. You know how mothers are. She's is worried that something bad has happened to her son. Is there a supervisor or boss I could ask?" Dory smiled. She checked the name-plate on the woman's desk saying, "I hate to put you on the spot, Denise, but I'm sure if your mother was worried, you would want to help."

"If you continue to ask me to violate policy, I'll have to call Security," the girl said coolly and her bright blue eyes hardened. She didn't look all that sweet any more.

"I'm a Private Investigator and there is concern that a crime may have taken place," Dory said, assuming a confident stance, shoulders back.

"Your Investigator ID?" Denise asked, holding out her hand.

Drat. "I have a letter here from Sheriff of Rose County in Tennessee," Dory said, pulling it out from her purse.

The girl glanced at the letter before saying, "This letter is for a Detective Wayne Nichols."

Damn! I pulled out the wrong letter. As Dory rummaged in her purse for the correct piece of paper, she heard Denise click on the intercom.

"Security," the girl said into a microphone. "There's a woman here impersonating a Private Investigator. Come to the Personnel Office, ASAP."

SEVEN

AFTER LETTING DORY out of the car, Wayne drove to the Nashville City Police post and walked inside. He felt at home as soon as he entered the building. The Duty Sargent's face wore the universally suspicious expression of a long-time cop. Scantily-clad prostitutes were waiting for their pimps. A furtive little guy, who might be a jockey, was leaning against the wall. Wayne's cell phone chirped and he saw a text from Dory. It read "Danny works at Nashville Downs. Struck pay dirt right out of the gate." He grinned at the news and Dory using the local vernacular.

"Excuse me, Sargent," Wayne said, moving to stand in front of the tall desk. The height of the desk was deliberately intended to make people feel intimidated when speaking to the officers who occupied the tower. The Sargent had bristle-short hair, lines on his face that drew his mouth down at the corners, and a flattened nose. He looked like a brawny ex-prize fighter whose face had been a casualty many times. His nametag read Sullivan.

"I'm Detective Wayne Nichols from Rosedale."

The Duty Sargent looked at him carefully. "What do you want?" he asked with a distrustful note in his voice.

"I would like to talk with a Detective whose patch is the Nashville Downs racetrack. I'm looking for a missing person."

Noting a little scuffle among the prostitutes, the Sargent bellowed into the microphone. "Any of you ladies want to spend another night in the can, keep that up." The girls settled as an obvious pimp came through the door and left with three of them. "Hang on, Detective," he said turning his attention to Wayne again. He clicked the switch on the intercom saying, "D'Angelo to the front desk."

"Thank you, Sully," Wayne said, and the Sargent nodded. Five minutes later, a young man with dark curly hair walked into the waiting room. The Detective was sharply dressed in a nicely-tailored suit and tie. His shoes were shined and his outfit looked classy. Lucy had been teaching him how to identify expensive tailoring and this was definitely it. Wayne rose and extended his hand.

"My name's Wayne Nichols. I'm a Detective with the Sheriff's Office in Rosedale."

"Detective Tony D'Angelo," the young guy said with a little note of pride, and Wayne guessed the rank of Detective was recent. They shook hands.

"Is there some place we could talk privately," Wayne asked and at the gesture from D'Angelo followed him down the hall and into an office.

"Have a seat," the young detective said. "What can I do for the forces of law and order in Rosedale?"

"First, I need to say that I recently retired from the Sheriff's Office, although I'm available if there is a major crime. I'm starting work for a Private Eye firm in town."

"Okay," the young man said, frowning and looking slightly irked at the lack of full disclosure at the outset, "Why are you here?"

"I'm looking for a young guy named Daniel Parrish, or he may go by the name Daniel Kidd. He works at Nashville Downs as a trainer. He's gone missing after a set-to with some local muscle working for a bookie. They assaulted him over an unpaid gambling debt."

"Sounds like a crime and it's not in *your* jurisdiction," Detective D'Angelo said. His hazel eyes that had already rested suspiciously on Wayne narrowed to pinpoints.

"I'm not interested in the crime. That's your business and it might not even have been reported. I just want to talk to the kid. He has family in Rosedale who are worried. His mother wants to make sure he's among the living."

"Ah, mothers," D'Angelo said and his face softened. He clearly knew about mothers.

Wayne took a breath, feeling his old guilt rise. He had never known his own mother who abandoned him as a toddler; and his foster mother, Jocelyn, was now dead and gone. He had waited too long to find her and when he did, she was serving time in prison for killing her husband. Nobody had bothered to unearth the decades of abuse she had suffered before she snapped. Her inept counsel hadn't even offered a plea of self-defense. Wayne still winced when he thought about his decision to run away from her home at seventeen, abandoning Jocelyn to her husband's abuse.

The day he had achieved her release from jail and had delivered her to family in Michigan's Upper Peninsula, he felt whole and clean. Leaving the UP, he and Lucy drove across the Mackinaw Bridge in a snow as fine as a mist. The sun was shining and Wayne felt the skies open. The shame released him then, like an eagle loosening its talons, but in the last few years, his feelings of guilt has returned to haunt him. *You finally got your foster mother out, but it took you decades to get around to it,* the punishing voice in his mind said. *And she was dying by then.*

"Are you asking us to look into the beat down?" D'Angelo said picking up his pen and forcing Wayne's mind to return to the present.

"No, just wanted you to know that I'm in town on your patch. Your police Chief, Paula Crawley, has collaborated with our Sheriff on cases before. Hopefully, it won't be a problem for you if I check local hospitals for Daniel Parrish. My partner, Investigator Dory Clarkson, is looking for him at the Nashville Downs racetrack."

"Beyond staying out of your way, what else do you want?"

"Would you be willing to check to see if a Daniel Parrish is in your system?"

"I'll check the criminal database," D'Angelo said and quickly entered the code into his computer. A few minutes later he said, "Nothing for a Daniel Kidd, or a Daniel Parrish, or anyone else with either of those last names. Sorry, the guy isn't in the system."

"Thank you very much, Detective. Any chance he's a subject of an existing case?"

"Hang on," D'Angelo said and walked from the room. When he returned he had an older Detective with him. The man was tall and thin with gray hair and a long nose. "This is Detective John Stoneman, my Supervisor. He's got an active case, a John Doe, who was pretty badly beaten. No id on him. He's at Vanderbilt. Could be your guy."

"I'm Detective Nichols," Wayne said, introducing himself, and shaking hands with Stoneman.

"You told D'Angelo that our Chief has worked with your Sheriff before. I will want to check with her before going much further, but if the John Doe is Daniel Parrish and you can ID him, it would give us somewhere to start," Stoneman said.

Having thanked both Detectives and saying he would inform them if he could identify the hospitalized patient, Wayne left the post and walked out to his truck. He was on the way to Vanderbilt when his phone made the incoming text sound. It was the most recent text from Dory.

"Come back to the track NOW. Screwed up. They called Security."

"Don't RUN, I'm OMW," Wayne texted back. He swung his truck around, missing the siren he had in Rosedale and headed back to Nashville Downs. He hoped Dory would stay put until he arrived. Nothing fixed guilt in the mind of a Security guard or a cop more than a runner. And those tight pants and high-heeled boots his partner was wearing didn't make for good sprinting gear. Glancing in his rear view mirror, Wayne was at all not surprised to see a cop car following him.

An hour later, with Dory still in custody of the track security personnel, Wayne had no choice but to call Detectives D'Angelo and Stoneman and ask for help. Although clearly irritated, they arrived and talked Security into releasing Wayne's still-fuming partner. Walking outside afterwards, Wayne thanked the Detectives gratefully. Dory was still making injudicious remarks under her breath about the use of "racial profiling," until Wayne poked her in the ribs and hissed, "You need to apologize."

Dory's expression softened and she said, "Detective Stoneman, I have to say that both you and Mr. Handsome here from 'Nashville's Finest' have been a big help. I do appreciate you springing me from the joint." She grinned at D'Angelo. He brushed off her compliments with an embarrassed smile but it was obvious he was pleased. Detective Stoneman's facial expression remained grim.

"I trust you won't need any more assistance today," Stoneman said, looking up from his cell phone that had chirped with an incoming text. "You two are to stay *below* law enforcement's radar. Am I clear?"

"Crystal," Wayne said.

ONCE BACK IN Wayne's truck, Dory punched the address for Vanderbilt hospital into his GPS. It took twenty minutes to get to the hospital and park in the area reserved for police. Luckily, Wayne's windshield still had a police sticker with no expiration date. They walked up to the Information desk and asked if a patient named "Daniel Parrish" or "Daniel Kidd" was in the house.

An older black receptionist (whose nametag read Ms. Woods) made a note of Danny's name. After checking her computer she said, "No patient by that name."

"He could be in the ICU," Wayne said.

Ms. Woods glanced at her computer again, "Sorry, as I just *said*, no one here by that name."

"Maybe he's not listed by name. Could be he's listed as a John Doe. It's a police case. We could really use your help."

"And maybe the patient was already discharged," Ms. Woods said crisply.

Wayne knew he was being deliberately stalled. He drummed his fingers on the desk. "I doubt it, since according to the Nashville police, he is at this hospital," he said irritably. People who used their jobs to inflate their own sense of superiority made his blood boil.

"Not on my list. Possibly transferred to Nashville General." The woman was clearly not cooperating. Wayne felt his level of frustration rise. His collar felt tight. He shot a glance at Dory who stepped forward.

"Ms. Woods, we don't want to put you in a bad position here. I can tell that my partner, who is used to dealing with low-life criminals, as opposed to model citizens like yourself, is coming on *way* too strong." Dory cast Wayne a mock irritated look. "Have you been asked to keep the information confidential on the John Doe patient? I'm Dory, by the way."

"I can only look up a patient by name, Miss Dory, and for any patient the subject of a police case, I'm supposed to call the on-duty social worker and if necessary, the cops. If you'd care to wait, I'll call her. We have a line of other people behind you that I'm *supposed* to be waiting on," Mrs. Woods's mouth tightened primly.

"Yeah, how about you do that and ditch these folks who are holding up the line," a man behind Dory said clearly.

"Can we just go up to the ICU and take a look?" Dory asked hopefully.

"Not without a pass key for the elevator," Mrs. Woods said, firmly. "I'll call the social worker." She pushed a button on her console as Dory and Wayne retreated to the seating area.

Every few minutes Wayne looked up, checking the clock, watching visitors and hospital personnel entering the lobby, emerging from the cafeteria and passing through the automatic doors. Twenty minutes later, with no sign of a social worker, Dory glanced toward the exit and swallowed. She poked Wayne in the ribs. He stood up respectfully, his stomach clenching. Detectives Stoneman and D'Angelo had entered the lobby and they were clearly furious.

"What the hell's going on here?" Detective Stoneman said. "I got a call saying somebody was harassing a volunteer at the Vanderbilt Information desk. Thought we were done with you two."

EIGHT

WAYNE SHOOK HIS head apologetically saying, "Detectives, I am so sorry. My partner, Investigator Clarkson and I were just trying to confirm the identity of the John Doe patient. We planned to let you know if it's the person we are trying to locate. Apparently the volunteer on the Information desk has been told to call the cops if anyone asked about the kid. We can't get into the ICU without a social worker okay and a special elevator key."

The Detectives exchanged glances, obviously trying to decide whether allowing Wayne and Dory to stay in the hospital was sufficiently important to their own investigation to let things proceed. At that moment, a young woman arrived, spoke with Ms. Woods, walked over to the two local Detectives and handed them an elevator card. Stoneman gestured to his partner and they stepped away. They were out of earshot but Dory could see Det. Stoneman shaking his head. Something had to be done. And it didn't take the experience of a Private Investigator to tell that the two Nashville Detectives were about to forcibly evict them from the hospital.

"I've got an idea," Dory whispered to Wayne and walked over to the Detectives. "I wonder if a steak dinner and drinks would help repay you for interrupting your day. Our agency would cover the cost. Your choice of restaurant. But if you'd rather not dine with us, the offer still stands. You can take a rain check for any time in the future," she smiled winsomely and touched the arm of the young Det. D'Angelo who looked at his supervisor.

"Fine," Det. Stoneman said brusquely. "But this is the last time we're helping you out. We have other cases we need to be working. We'll take you up to ICU." As Wayne walked over, he added, "Your partner said she'd cover dinner and drinks. I need your word that you will leave the area immediately afterwards. Got it?"

Wayne gave Dory a surprised look, complete with raised eyebrows, but nodded. All four of them proceeded toward a private elevator. Detective Stoneman inserted the key card and the elevator doors opened. Nobody spoke on the way up to the tenth floor. When the doors opened, they were greeted with quiet, classical music and lush potted greenery. It looked more like a lobby in an exclusive boutique hotel than an intensive care unit.

The Nashville Detectives appeared known to the nursing staff because after a brief conversation, they were allowed into the unit. The lights were slightly dimmed and the noise reduced by sound-dampening flooring. When Det. Stoneman pulled the door open to the patient's room it was clear his existence was teetering on the edge. His life was being maintained by a matrix of tubes—a tube to deliver pain meds ran into the vein in the patient's arm. There was a catheter in his bladder and an endotracheal tube in the patient's throat. Danny, if indeed it was Danny, was having trouble breathing.

Dory watched the young man breathe, glancing at the blood pressure cuff on the patient's arm. The cuff would inflate and deflate and a digital readout appeared on the monitor above his bed. The display showed multiple other numbers too, most of which Dory didn't understand. The only indication of the patient's individuality was his shiny black hair.

As she stood beside the hospital bed a wave of sorrow struck Dory. Her woman's heart felt for this young man, for all he had suffered. Then another pain hit her, thinking of his mama, who never forgot her baby boy. At only seventeen, it must have been awful for Cara, pressured by her father into making such a life-altering decision. Dory felt tears rise in her eyes, thinking of all life had already inflicted to those two, the mother and son and wondered who had suffered more. She stepped away, unable to bear the pain of looking at the young man any longer.

"Is he going to make it, do you think?" she whispered to his nurse.

"Are you family?" the woman asked.

"No, but I'm here on behalf of his mother. She hired us to find him."

"Then I'd say she needs to get down here soon. That is, if she wants to see him." The nurse looked at her intently.

When Dory walked back into the young man's room, she saw Wayne pulling out the photo of Danny and Tracey. He bent down to look carefully at the patient's face, comparing it to the photo.

"Do you think it's Danny?" Dory whispered.

"Hard to say," Wayne answered and handed the photo to Det. Stoneman who also looked at his features—distorted by tubes, blackened eyes and a mouth stretched wide by the breathing tube. Stoneman shrugged. A few

minutes later they left the unit and returned to the waiting area by the elevators.

"There was no i.d. on the body when he was brought
in, I take it?" Wayne asked.

"No wallet on him. Poor guy was dumped outside
the hospital behind the ER. He was barely breathing
when an ER nurse found him and brought him inside."
Det. D'Angelo said.

Wayne heard his cell phone beep. It was a text from
Billie Jo. She had found a street address for Daniel
Parrish.

TWO HOURS LATER, Wayne and Dory had mostly repaired
their fractured relationship with the Nashville Detectives by employing the soothing effects of food and
alcohol. Dory joked and flirted with D'Angelo during
dinner, feeling all the while like they were running
out of time to reunite Danny with his mother while he
was still among the living. They were on the point of
departing when Wayne turned to Det. Stoneman and
said, "If the John Doe in the ICU is our guy, he has a
girlfriend named Tracey Dimond. She could identify
him for you. We could run out there tonight and see her.
Might save you a trip."

"Didn't think you had an address," Det. Stoneman
said, narrowing his eyes.

"It was on the envelope of the letter she sent his
mother," Wayne lied. "Okay with you?"

"No. We will be visiting Miss Dimond tomorrow
morning. You two are now returning to Rosedale," Det.
Stoneman said firmly.

"If you do get a positive identification, or if the patient's condition changes radically, could you give me

a buzz? Here's my card," Dory whispered quickly to Detective D'Angelo who nodded.

"Thank you again for all your assistance." Wayne said and shook hands. They left the restaurant and walked out to Wayne's truck.

"I assume we are going out to Danny's address," Dory said, watching Wayne's face carefully. She would have killed him if he said no.

"Of course we are," Wayne said. "And then we are going to rapidly skip town. We can call Miss Billie Jo on the way back. It's after hours, but since she lives on site, she'll probably get the phone. We can give her an update."

THE ADDRESS BILLIE JO found was for a small apartment building east of town that was pretty run-down. One of the apartments had a broken window and the trash had not been picked up recently. There was a large overflowing dumpster at the end of the building. They parked the truck and walked up to the door marked 1C. A slender young woman with a markedly distressed expression threw open the door before they knocked.

"Is this the residence of Daniel Kidd Parrish?" Wayne asked. "I'm Wayne Nichols and this is Dory Clarkson. We're from Rosedale Investigations."

"Have you found him?" she asked, sounding desperate. The girl was slim as an arrow, wore jeans and a cotton knit sweater. Her hair had been done in braided cornrows and her face bore the traces of tears. "Where is he? Is he okay? I've been just frantic."

"May we come in?" Dory asked. "Are you Tracey?"

The young woman nodded and opened the door further. "Please sit down," she said gesturing to an old couch. The furniture was minimal, but the place was spotlessly clean.

"I'm sorry to tell you this, but we believe Daniel Parrish is in critical care at Vanderbilt hospital. We were unable to formally identify him from the photo that you sent to Mrs. Summerfield, but we're pretty sure it's him."

"I've called every hospital in town. Nobody said he was a patient."

"That's because they didn't have any id on him," Dory said.

"I'm going there right now," she said and reached for her purse and keys.

"Hang on a second, Ms. Dimond," Wayne said. "We were just there and even with our credentials we had to get the local Detectives investigating the case to get in."

"Detectives? The case?" Tracey asked and sagged down on the couch.

"Yes. He's in pretty bad shape," Wayne said.

Tracey seemed like she was having a hard time catching her breath and Dory walked over to the galley kitchen and got a glass of water for the girl who drank a few swallows, coughed and took another sip.

"Detectives Stoneman and D'Angelo are coming to see you tomorrow morning," Wayne said. "They will take you to the hospital for a formal identification. In the meantime, I can assure you Danny's getting excellent care."

Tracey nodded, still looking stunned.

"Do you have someone who could come and stay with you tonight?" Dory asked.

"No, no family left." The girl gestured at their small apartment and Dory's heart ached for her.

"What about a girlfriend then?"

"I could see if I can stay with one of the other beauticians. Her name is Courtney."

"That would be a good idea. Rosedale Investigations hired us to find Danny, at the request of Mrs. Summerfield, Danny's birth mother."

Tracey looked somewhat relieved at this information. A bit of color came back into her face. "She got my letter then," she said softly.

"Do you mind giving me your cell phone number?" Wayne asked.

"Not at all," Tracey said and read it to Wayne, who entered it into his phone.

"Here's my card. We'd appreciate your calling us tomorrow once you've seen Danny," Dory said. "And please don't mention to the Nashville Detectives that we stopped by."

"I won't," Tracey said. She stood up and reached for her purse and keys again. "I'm going over to my friend's house now."

"Good idea," Wayne said and they said their goodbyes.

Once on the road, Dory dialed Billie Jo's number at the office. The phone rang four times before they heard the girl's sleepy voice. Dory flipped it to speaker.

"Billie Jo, it's Dory. We're pretty sure we've found Danny. He's in the ICU at the Vanderbilt hospital. It was difficult to do an absolutely solid identification because he's hooked up to so much medical machinery. We just left his girlfriend's place. The Nashville Detectives are picking her up tomorrow morning. They promised to call once she's formally identified him."

"Good work, Dory. Are you on way back here?"

"We are. Once tiny little thing," Dory said. "Hope it's not a problem. We had to buy a couple of local detectives some dinner. A little alcohol helped pour oil on troubled waters."

Billie Jo laughed. "Bit of a problem, were they? No worries. PD says it happens all the time when you invade their territory. Just hope it really was Daniel Parrish you found," she said in a slightly worried tone.

"Me too," Dory said, "Bye."

AS WAYNE AND DORY drove back to Rosedale in a deepening twilight, Dory broke the silence saying, "I am so worried about that poor young boy in the hospital. I asked the nurse about his prognosis and she hinted he might not have very long."

Wayne didn't respond right away. Having worked with Wayne for years, Dory knew the signs; her partner was thinking. Because he cogitated so long on questions, Dory had secretly dubbed him the "Long Thinker."

Five minutes later, Wayne took a deep breath and then said, "My mind is running along a related track, Dory. I'm having a hard time not being a Detective, I guess. I know all we had to do was find him, but I want to nail the bastards who beat the kid up. We don't have the name of the bookie who ordered the hit either. He's probably already known to the cops. I hope Stoneman and D'Angelo can get the thugs for attempted murder."

"There's something bothering me, Wayne," Dory said. "I wondered why Tracey didn't ask about the money. I heard her say Mrs. Summerfield must have received her letter. You'd think she would have asked about the money, worried the bookie and his thugs might come after her for the debt." She took a shaky breath. "Poor kid."

"They won't come after her. They'll know she doesn't have any money. And it's bad business beating up a girl."

They drove a while in silence. It was getting dark. Dory turned the radio on for a while, but found nothing she wanted to listen to. She flipped it off. "If Mrs. Summerfield wants to lay eyes on her boy again, I think she needs to get on the road, whether she tells her husband about her son or not," Dory said.

"Unless she fesses up, I wonder how she's going to explain being out of town to her husband. Tracey can do an informal identification, of course, but she wasn't wearing a wedding ring and the cops prefer a family member," Wayne said. "I also wonder how much money Mrs. Summerfield has access to without the husband starting to be suspicious. Fifteen thousand dollars is a big chunk."

"What do you think our next step should be?"

"I believe it has slipped your mind that we are not working alone on this case. My guess is by the time we get into the office tomorrow morning Miss Billie Jo will have our next steps all thought out."

"Ah yes, repairing the spider web," Dory said. "Well, if I have anything to say about this, I think we need to head back here as soon as possible. And on our next trip, we need to have Mrs. Summerfield with us. The spider web of Cara Summerfield's life has just been torn to shreds."

NINE

Thursday

THE FOLLOWING MORNING, both Dory and Wayne arrived at Rosedale Investigations by eight o'clock. Billie Jo was yawning when she let them into the house. She was barefoot, wore what looked like hastily-donned pink leggings and a mostly-unbuttoned pajama top.

"I haven't had any coffee yet," she said sleepily. "Come on in, you guys. Sorry, but I need to take a shower and then I'll join you in the conference room. PD is expected soon." She headed upstairs.

Half an hour later, all the members of the Rosedale Investigations team, with Billie Jo now fully clothed, although in an eye-popping outfit, had assembled in the conference room.

"I got this new conference table yesterday when you two were on your field trip," Billie Jo said. "The old one was shot." The new table was oak and large enough to accommodate twelve people, although it was still surrounded by four old card table chairs. They were probably next on Billie Jo's list.

"I gather from your call the kid you saw is in bad shape," PD said. He was dressed formally in a suit and tie. Wayne wondered if he was meeting with some big wigs in town or perhaps a former client.

"While we couldn't make a positive id, I think it's

critical that Mrs. Summerfield gets down there ASAP," Dory said.

"I plan to call her as soon as our meeting is over," Billie Jo said. "What do you think, Wayne?"

"It seems to me that as far as the agency goes, we have met our obligation. We agreed to find Danny, and although we are awaiting official notification, I believe we have found him. As a former cop, I wanted to nail the bastard who ordered his beating, but I don't see any way to do that. Even if I were still a Detective, we have no jurisdiction in the Greater Nashville area. Just hope the Detectives we met, Stoneman and D'Angelo, will get on it," Wayne said.

"I have some information to add to the picture," Billie Jo said. "I found Danny's biological father yesterday. His name is Rafe Marston. Mrs. Summerfield, *nee* Kidd, listed him on Danny's birth certificate as the father. He and Cara Summerfield were high school sweethearts according to the school yearbook I dug up. When she gave the baby up for adoption, she never informed the father she was pregnant," Billie Jo said.

"I trust you didn't actually *contact* Mr. Marston," BD said, coolly. "Mrs. Summerfield did not give us permission to get in touch with him."

"No, I didn't. Just located him in case…" Billie Jo's voice trailed off.

"In case what?" PD asked, pointedly.

"In case Danny Kidd Parrish doesn't survive," Wayne said in a voice that sounded like a death knell. All four people seated at the table were silenced for a few moments.

"I assume it's still up to Mrs. Summerfield as to

whether she tells the father about his son... Or her husband," Billie Jo said.

"Of course it's up to her, but I think it would be both ethically and morally wrong of her not to tell the boy's father," Dory said. "Especially now."

"And there are his adoptive parents to consider too," PD said.

"We seem to be in pretty deep waters here. Let's just take this one step at a time. The first thing to do is to find out if Mrs. Summerfield wants to see her son. If she does, I'd like to go back to the hospital with her," Dory said.

"I'm calling her now," Billie Jo said and reached for her cell phone, putting it on speaker.

Wayne turned to PD asking if Billie Jo should be the one to make the call.

"She has to learn and making mistakes is how you learn," PD said, topping up everyone's coffee as the phone rang.

"Hello," Cara Summerfield's quiet voice came over the phone.

"We found Danny, Mrs. Summerfield. Sadly, he's been beaten-up pretty badly and is at Vanderbilt hospital in Nashville. What do you want to do next?"

Both Wayne and PD looked at the girl in exasperation.

Wayne whispered, "We don't even know for *sure* if it's her kid." Billie Jo waved their concerns away with an airy hand.

Cara Summerfield's voice came clearly over the speaker. "Of course, I want to see him. Just let me think a moment. I need to look at my calendar." She paused and then said, "Actually, it's going to work. My husband is leaving for an out-of-town meeting. He's only going to be gone for the day, but I can be at your office by 10 a.m. And thank you, Billie Jo," she said and rang off.

"I think that's as far as we can get on the Summerfield case today," PD said. "I have both your Partnership Agreements here, which you need to sign." He passed out the stapled contracts. "I also wanted to bring you up-to-date on several other cases the firm is working on. We're checking out an embezzlement that took place at a local insurance firm and a case of some stolen jewelry the owners didn't choose to report to the police."

"Why was that?" Wayne asked.

"It's a wealthy family and they would prefer to deal with the matter privately. They know the police have a poor record of locating stolen jewels. They are usually fenced and melted down before they can be recovered."

Wayne nodded. He knew it was true.

"Dory and Billie Jo, would you like to work the jewelry theft? It's gold jewelry, dating from the 1920's." PD pulled out two case files and flipped one open to show a photograph of the missing necklace.

"I certainly would," Dory said, smiling.

"Me too," Billie Jo said.

"You'll need to start by interviewing the residents at the family home. It's an important family, the Cantwells. Here's the address," PD said, handing out pieces of paper to both women. "Wayne, would you like to start on the embezzlement case?"

"Sure thing," he said.

"I've been tracing the money through the computer," Billie Jo said. "I don't have it nailed down, but it looks like an inside case."

At that moment, Dory's phone rang. "Sorry, this will

just take a minute," she said and stepped out of the conference room. When she came back in her face looked frozen with shock.

"Who was it Dory," Wayne asked.

"That was Detective D'Angelo. By the time they got to the hospital this morning with Tracey to identify him, Daniel Kidd Parrish was dead."

"It appears you will have to talk with Mrs. Summerfield again," Wayne said. "You did jump the gun on this one, Billie Jo," he said in a serious voice.

"PD, would you tell her?" Billie Jo pleaded. "Or you, Wayne? Dory?"

"On the phone? No way in hell," Dory said frowning and both men shook their heads.

Billie Jo's mouth was tight and she swallowed. Her hand trembled as she picked up the office phone.

"Jesus, Girl. Do *NOT* dial that number!" PD said, shaking his head irritably. "What are you thinking? You don't give *anyone* this kind of news over the phone and this is the boy's *mother*! You, and I do mean you, Billie Jo, are going to have to tell her in person."

TEN

BILLIE JO BRADLEY and Dory Clarkson rang the doorbell at 1778 Blacksmith Trail half an hour later. Dressed in a black business suit and heels, Dory looked over at her young colleague and frowned. Billie Jo was wearing jeans and a midriff-skimming T-shirt. The house was in the new Steeplechase Subdivision. The homes were all elegant and perfectly landscaped, surrounded by emerald green lawns and flowerbeds filled with lush white hydrangeas. Each home sat on a two acre parcel and all their exteriors were clad in brick or stone. It was a neighborhood for the discriminating and the well-to-do.

PD had been insistent that the news of Danny's death had to be given in person. Such a visit was standard practice but both women were dreading delivering the "death knock". When they rang the doorbell, Cara opened the front door. Recognizing Billie Jo, she whispered, "I told you yesterday I'd be at your office this morning at nine. Luckily, Grant just left for work."

"We needed to see you in person," Billie Jo said. "This is my colleague, Dory Clarkson. She's is a new partner with Rosedale Investigations."

"Come in," Cara said, after looking quickly at the neighboring houses on either side. No one was outside and there were no twitching curtains.

"Is there someplace we could talk?" Billie Jo asked.

"Of course," Cara said and led them down the dark

floored hallway. Shafts of light came through from sky-lights and lit the floor in bright squares. She led them into a spacious sitting room and gestured for them to be seated. Dory and Billie Jo chose chairs and Cara took the cushy blue sofa.

"May I ask why you are here? You told me yesterday that Danny's in the hospital," Cara bit her lips. It looked like she was trying not to cry. Billie Jo and Dory exchanged discouraged glances and Cara noticed.

"What is it? Why are you really here?" Cara put her hand up to her mouth and cried out, "Oh, God, what's happened to him?"

"Mrs. Summerfield, I regret to inform you that Danny Kidd Parrish died early today in the hospital in Nashville. We are so awfully sorry for your loss." Dory's words were formal, but her chin quivered.

"Me too," Billie Jo said in a whisper.

Cara slumped on the love seat, seeming to shrink away from them as her voice rose in an anguished wail. After some time she got control of herself and looked at the two women with tear-filled eyes. Dory stood up, walked over to Cara and sat beside her, holding her hand. Dory was unable to stop her own eyes watering as Cara began to wail again in a terrible paroxysm of grief.

Billie Jo didn't know what to do, but finally remembered the tissues in her purse. She grabbed some and handed them to Dory. Ten minutes later, both Dory and Cara managed to stop crying.

"I just feel so cold," Cara said, "I'm shaking." She looked down at her hands that were visibly trembling.

"You're going into shock," Dory said. "Billie Jo, get Mrs. Summerfield a blanket and make her a cup of hot tea with sugar." Billie Jo scuttled from the room. "Mrs.

Summerfield, I'm sorry to tell you this at this awful time, but since Danny was beaten, the police are looking into what happened. And now that he has passed away…" Dory stopped speaking and swallowed, "It's likely the Nashville police will initiate a formal investigation."

Cara was breathing shakily. She blew her nose and wiped her shocked eyes.

"We're pretty sure the cops will be coming here," Billie Jo said. She had returned with a blanket and a cup of hot sweet tea.

"No. They can't," Cara said, shaking her head.

"When we went to Nashville to locate Danny, we had to tell the local police we were in the area. They will want to talk to you in person. It's just part of regular investigative work."

"You know my husband doesn't know about Danny. What can I do?" Cara said looking up at Dory pitifully.

"There is only one thing you could do to forestall this. You could go to them. If you present yourself at the police post in Nashville and talk to Detectives Stoneman and D'Angelo, it will meet their needs and prevent them from coming here."

"You said yesterday you could get away for the day," Billie Jo said. "Do you want to see Danny? If so, we are ready to go when you are."

"In case you were up to it, I already put a thermos of coffee, donuts and fruit in the car," Dory added, kindly.

HALF AN HOUR LATER, the three women were en route to Nashville. Billie Jo was driving. Dory sat beside Cara in the back seat.

"Do you want to talk?" Dory asked, her voice sweet with compassion.

"I'm responsible for my son's death," Cara said. He voice was choked.

"No you weren't, Cara. You can't blame yourself. It most likely the 'muscle' for the bookie that beat him up."

"I wish I had never listened to my father. I should never have given Danny up for adoption. It's just *against nature* to separate a mother from her baby."

"You gave him a fine home, Cara. From what we were able to learn, Mr. & Mrs. Parrish were good parents to Danny. They weren't able to have or adopt another child, and all their love would have been poured into your son," Dory said. "Did you ever see him after his birth?"

"Somehow he managed to get my name from the Parrish's when he was sixteen and came to see me." She stopped talking, visibly striving for control.

"Mr. and Mrs. Parrish would probably be willing to meet with you and tell you more about your son, if that's what you would like."

"They will hate me," Cara said, bitterly.

"Why do you say that, Cara? You gave them a wonderful boy. I'm sure they are grateful."

"I paid for Danny to become a racehorse trainer. That was what allowed him to work at a track and probably the reason he got into gambling. When I asked him why he hadn't gotten money from his adoptive parents for the apprenticeship, he told me Mrs. Parrish's father was a professional gambler. When he died, all their assets, including the family home, were seized. Apparently, Mrs. Parrish and her mother struggled to survive for years after the father's death." Cara started to sniffle again. "Mrs. Parrish was opposed to Danny's career choice and she was right. It was gambling that killed my boy. And my money gave him that life." She started to cry again.

WHEN THEY STOPPED at a rest area a bit later, Cara had fallen asleep. Dory slipped into the front seat.

"If Danny was beaten to death, isn't that murder?" Billie Jo asked quietly.

"More likely manslaughter or attempted murder," Dory said. "Thugs who beat up people with gambling debts never intend to kill the victim. They wouldn't collect the debt that way. I'm sure the Nashville Detectives are looking into it. I keep having to remind myself that investigating a murder is not my job anymore."

The two were quiet for a while as the car sped down the freeway. The yellow-green vegetation of late summer flashed by—giant thistles with purple flowered tops, teasels that had turned brown already, bright yellow goldenrod and Queen Anne's lace. Dory heard the sound of her cell phone buzzing with an incoming text. She glanced at it, seeing her partner, Wayne's name pop up.

She showed the text to Billie Jo. It read *"Danny's cell phone was turned in to Sheriff's Office in Rosedale this morning."*

Dory immediately dialed back. "Who turned it in?" She whispered. "Cara is sleeping, so I'm keeping my voice down."

"It was dropped off at the front door of the Sheriff's Office. The office CCTV camera was on, but only caught a young person in a hoodie and jeans. The phone's already been tested for fingerprints, but nobody in the system left it," Wayne said.

"Can you get into Danny's cell phone?" Dory asked. The permeation of the market with iPhones had made it much harder for law enforcement. Those phones were practically unbreakable unless you knew the code. "Try using Tracey or Cara."

"Already did. No dice, but I called Tracey and she knew his code. It was Boyd's Boy. That's the name of the horse he trained."

"Who had he called on the last day?"

"He called the stallion's owner, Austin Cantwell. He's a bigwig in the area. Owns a number of racehorses as a partner in a syndicate. He's counting on Boyd's Boy to make money for him this year."

"Do we know for sure Danny was in Rosedale earlier in the day? It's quite a ways from Vanderbilt hospital," Dory said.

"Yes. They triangulated cell towers and Danny was definitely in Rosedale on the day before he died."

"So somebody drove him all the way from Rosedale to the hospital in Nashville," Dory murmured.

"The Sheriff's deputies are looking for his car in Rosedale and the Nashville cops are looking for it there. I'm thinking of running out to talk to Danny's employer, Austin Cantwell."

"Hold it a minute there, big guy," Dory said. "You can't do that, Wayne. Not without Sheriff Bradley's approval. We aren't in law enforcement any more, remember? We were hired to find Danny and we have. Talk to PD and have coffee with Sheriff Bradley if you wish, but you are not the lead Detective investigating a murder anymore."

"Damn it, Woman," Wayne said, but after a moment added, "You're right. I can probably get what I want from the Sheriff. Just having trouble adjusting. I want to nail the bastard that ordered the kid beaten to death. What are you doing right now?"

"Taking Cara Summerfield to see Danny in the Nashville City Morgue."

"He's not in the City Morgue, Dory. The body still is at the hospital. The pathologist won't release him."

"What's his name, their pathologist?"

"*Her* name is Shirley Llewellyn-Jones. She's from London and was educated there. I talked to her. She has that great upper crust British accent. Apparently, Dr. Jones has the same bloodhound tendencies of our own Dr. Estes in Rosedale. She says she has a 'nose for murder' and is doing the gamut of testing."

"Does she have a cause of death?"

"Not yet. He was definitely beaten though, and it was pre-mortem. He had three broken ribs, a sprained wrist, a black eye and bruises on his back in the area of the kidneys. However, Dr. Jones doubts it would have been enough to cause death in an otherwise healthy young male. I'll call and tell her you're on your way, shall I? She'll want to do what she can to make Danny look presentable for his mother."

"Thank you, partner," Dory said, meaning it.

ELEVEN

BILLIE JO, Dory and Cara pulled up in front of Vanderbilt hospital half an hour later. The facility had been built of red brick. Sections with multiple stories jutted out on either side of the main entrance. The structure looked like it had been created out of giant Lego blocks. A second floor glass walkway connected the major wing of the hospital to another building atop a gleaming glass crescent. A series of outside staircases led down to a grassy park interspersed with trees and flowerbeds.

"Mrs. Summerfield, would you like to take a walk in the garden while we find Danny?" Billy asked. "It often takes a while to find someone in a complex this large."

Cara nodded. She got out of the car and walked down the stairs to the hospital garden. Her head was down. She looked as if she had aged twenty years since she learned Danny died.

"Let's find the pathologist," Dory said and the two women entered the hospital. It was a circuitous route to the morgue which, like most such chambers, was in the basement. They knocked on the stainless steel door with its sign labeled VUMC Morgue, B503. There was no response to their knocking, but the door was unlocked and they walked in. Three walls of the room were made from row upon row of rectangular steel drawers containing the bodies of the dead. The highest level drawers were about twelve feet in the air, taller than anyone could reach. In the center of the room there were four white tables, each with a neck rest for a body.

"How do they open those top ones?" Billie Jo asked looking upward. "They are way above my head."

"I presume they open electronically and probably can be lowered down for viewing," Dory responded just as Dr. Llewellyn-Jones entered the Morgue. She wore a long white lab coat, dark-rimmed bifocals and looked irritated.

"Dr. Jones, I'm Dory Clarkson and this is my colleague, Billie Jo Bradley," Dory said and walked forward with her hand outstretched. She withdrew her hand quickly when she noticed Dr. Jones was wearing blue rubber gloves. They looked sticky. "I hope my partner, Detective Nichols reached you. He said he would let you know we were coming."

"Yes, he did. He said you wanted to see a John Doe who was brought down here from the ICU. Since then, the police gave me his name—it's Daniel Kidd Parrish. Neither of you look to be his mother, though." She looked at both women critically.

"We left her to walk the grounds in front of the hospital while we came on ahead. I hope it was okay that we entered your space without permission."

Dr. Jones lifted an eloquent eyebrow and frowned. "I would appreciate you waiting for me, should you ever need to visit again. Viewing a body is a confidential matter." Then using a remote she pulled from her pocket, the pathologist pointed at a second level box. It slid open and swung down to the level of a table. Dory and Billie Jo walked over to see the boy they had hoped to find alive for his devastated mother. Despite the pathologist's best efforts, he looked gray and waxy.

Dr. Llewellyn-Jones bent down and gently brushed the boy's hair away from his forehead.

Dory swallowed and looked away. "My partner said you haven't established a cause of death."

"Not yet. I am still waiting for the results from the lab. However, I can tell you that it is highly unlikely he died from the beating he received shortly before his death. When I spoke to Detective Nichols, he mentioned the young man was in debt to a bookie. Bookies do employ muscle to extract money, but in all the years I have worked here, I have only seen one such death. If the person dies, the thugs are sacked, I understand."

"Do you have a working hypothesis?" Dory asked.

"I am not in the habit of *sharing* my hypotheses," Dr. Jones said in a cool tone. She waited for a moment before saying, "However, since you have come with his mother, I shall deviate from my usual policy. There are two possible causes for Danny's death. Either he died from a weakness already present in his body, like a heart defect, or kidney problem, and the stress from the beating brought it on. Or, he was forced to ingest or was injected with a drug that killed him. I am inclined to the latter," she said.

"I presume the local Detectives, Stoneman and D'Angelo, have already called. They probably asked you to let them know the cause of death."

"Indeed they have. I told them the same thing I've told you. I haven't a lot of time this morning, so I suggest you get the boy's mother and bring her down to see her son. I will move his body into the viewing room."

THEY FOUND CARA SUMMERFIELD sitting on a bench in the gardens. She was learning against the backrest and her eyes were closed. The sun lit her lavender cardigan twinset and gray slacks. Tears had dried on her face, leaving streaks in her otherwise perfect make-up. She opened her eyes as Billie Jo and Dory walked up.

"Are you ready, Mrs. Summerfield?" Billie Jo asked.

Cara took in a deep breath and nodded. She stood up and silently followed the two women up the outdoor staircase, into the hospital, rode the elevator down to the basement and walked along a silent corridor until they reached the door marked "Morgue." Cara winced when she saw the word.

Dory knocked on the door and they heard the voice of Dr. Llewellyn-Jones saying,

"Come in."

Dory took Cara's arm and ushered her through the doorway. "Cara Summerfield, I'd like to introduce you to Dr. Llewellyn-Jones. She is the hospital pathologist."

"I'm very sorry for your loss," Dr. Jones said formally and shook Cara's hand. She had removed her blue rubber gloves, Dory noticed. "When you are ready," she said and gestured to the far wall where they could see an interior window offering a view to an adjacent room. When Cara nodded, the pathologist pushed a button that pulled aside the curtains covering the viewing window.

Cara walked over and looked through the thick glass. Daniel Kidd Parrish lay on a table in the room, draped with a white sheet except for his face. The lighting was softer than it was in the Morgue and Dory was pleased to see that he looked more lifelike.

"I've been told to ask you to confirm his identity, Mrs. Summerfield. Is this your son, Daniel Kidd Parrish?" the pathologist asked.

"It is," Cara said in a near-whisper. She turned her face away. "Could I be alone with him?" she asked.

"Of course. Come with me and I will take you inside the room," the pathologist said. Cara and Dr. Llewellyn Jones exited the Morgue. Moments later they entered the adjacent viewing room and stood beside Danny's body. The pathologist then left Cara alone in the room after closing the window covering to provide her with complete privacy.

Fifteen minutes later, Cara rejoined Dory and Billie Jo. She no longer seemed shaken, very sad, but silent and composed.

"Are you ready to leave now?" Billie Jo asked and Cara nodded.

"Thank you, Dr. Llewellyn-Jones. Could you let me know the cause of death once it's established?" Dory asked.

Dr. Jones shook her head. "No, but I will inform the Nashville Detectives. They will decide whether or not to inform you. That's Vanderbilt's policy."

"We'll check with them," Dory said and the three women headed for the door.

Glancing over her shoulder Billie Jo saw the pathologist open the drapes to the viewing window, look at Danny once more and make the sign of the cross. The woman clearly cared about the people who required her ghostly ministrations in this place; the house of the murdered dead.

RETURNING TO THE parking lot, Billie Jo started the car and entered the address of the Nashville Police Post into her GPS.

"Are we going to the visit the police now," Cara asked in a very small voice.

"I think that would be best," Dory said. "Unless you are ready to tell your husband about Danny. In which case, they will come to see you. I think you should consider it, Cara. That way you would have Grant's support during what will be a difficult conversation."

"No. It's too late now. There is no point in disrupting Grant's life since he will never be able to know Danny. I just wish I had known my son better. I missed out on so much." Cara leaned back against the seats and started to weep silently.

"Let's go," Dory said and rapidly texted Wayne asking him to inform the two Nashville Detectives that they were en route.

Half an hour later, the trio parked their car at the police post and walked inside. Approaching the Duty Sargent, Dory said, "We'd like to speak to Detectives D'Angelo and Stoneman, please. It's in regard to a case they are working."

"Your names," the Duty Sargent said.

"Investigator Dory Clarkson, my colleague Billie Jo Bradley and Mrs. Cara Summerfield, Danny Parrish's mother."

The bored expression on the Duty Sargent's face softened slightly as he picked up the microphone and said, "Detectives Stoneman and D'Angelo to the Lobby ASAP." A few minutes later, the two Detectives appeared.

D'Angelo was sharply dressed in a navy blue suit, pale blue shirt and red paisley tie. Detective Stoneman wore an old rumpled brown suit. He had dark circles under his eyes and looked tired.

"Good afternoon, Dory," Detective D'Angelo said. "I got a call from Detective Nichols, so we were expecting you."

"I'm Billie Jo," the younger woman said, holding out her hand to shake with both Detectives in turn. "And this is Danny Parrish's mother, Cara Summerfield."

"It's a pleasure to meet you, Mrs. Summerfield," D'Angelo said kindly. "Please come this way and we can talk." The good-looking Detective led the way down the hall to a small interview room.

TWELVE

ONCE IN AN interview cubicle, Detective D'Angelo introduced the women to his Supervisor, Detective Stoneman.

"Good morning," Det. Stoneman said brusquely. "I assume you are the boy's mother?" he asked, glancing at Cara.

Cara nodded.

"Why are you here this morning?" Detective Stoneman asked.

Dory nodded encouragingly to Cara who began by saying, "I have just come from saying good-bye to my son," she paused briefly and cleared her throat. "His name is Daniel Kidd Parrish. Dory said you would want to talk to me because his was not a...natural death." She stumbled a little over the last words and pulled a tissue from her purse.

"Just thought we would save you driving to Rosedale, since we were already in the city," Dory said cheerfully.

"Thank you. We do have some questions for you, Mrs. Summerfield. Go ahead D'Angelo."

D'Angelo expressed his condolences for Mrs. Summerfield's loss, saying how sorry he was. Cara nodded at him, eyes brimming. "We regretted asking you to do the official identification of Danny. We tried to contact his adoptive parents, but they are on a cruise in the Caribbean. To your knowledge, was your son in regular touch with Mr. & Mrs. Parrish?"

"I know they were opposed to his career choice, but other than that, I don't know."

"That's fine, Mrs. Summerfield. From his cell phone records, we know that your son was in Rosedale the day he showed up at the ER. Did he contact you that day?"

"He was? No, he didn't call or come to the house," Cara's voice was pained. "How I wish he had," she started to cry again.

D'Angelo cast a "help me here" look at Dory and Billie Jo. Handling female tears was obviously not D'Angelo's strong point. Stoneman gave an exasperated snort.

Dory intervened saying, "Danny's cell phone was turned in anonymously to Sheriff Bradley's office in Rosedale today. My partner said that there were only two calls on the phone that day. One was to Austin Cantwell, the owner of the horse Danny trained. The second was a call from Danny's girlfriend, Tracey. Since Danny didn't call his mother, is there anything else you need to know from her?"

"Let's back up a moment here," Stoneman said. "Is your husband Danny's father?"

"No, I had Danny at seventeen. His father was my high school boyfriend, Rafe Marston."

"Are you and Mr. Marston in touch?"

"No. I haven't seen him or talked to him in many years."

"Was he in touch with your son?"

"I never even told him I was pregnant. He is unaware of Danny's existence."

"When was the last time you saw your son alive?" Det. Stoneman asked.

"It was ten years ago. I sponsored Danny's apprenticeship as a racehorse trainer. I haven't seen or heard from him since. I did get a letter recently from his girlfriend, Tracey, who said he owed money to a bookie and had been beaten up. That's what made me call Rosedale Investigations. I planned to give them the money to pay my son's gambling debts, but he passed away before I could get it to him." Cara swallowed and blinked back tears.

"Do you know Danny's employer, Austin Cantwell?" Det. Stoneman asked.

Cara hesitated a few moments before saying, "Yes. I met Mr. Cantwell and his wife a month or so ago. They sponsored a fund-raiser for my husband's political campaign at their home and stables. It was a very glamorous evening and quite a bit of money was raised. His wife's name is Debbie. She had a valuable piece of jewelry stolen and wondered if I had a picture of her wearing it. She needed it for an insurance report."

Dory shot Billie Jo a look and whispered, "Is that the jewelry theft I'm looking into?" Billie Jo nodded.

"At the time of this fund-raiser, or at any time before or after that, did you know that Danny worked for Austin Cantwell?" Det. Stoneman's eyes were laser-focused on Cara.

"Cantwell talked a lot about his stallion, Boyd's Boy, that evening and I've recently learned he was the horse Danny was training. Perhaps my son was in Rosedale to ask Mr. Cantwell for an advance on his pay to cover his debts."

"We'll look into that. That's all for now," Stoneman

said. "We may wish to talk to you again, Mrs. Summerfield. We'll come to your house next time."

Cara cast Dory a desperate look and she said, "Mrs. Summerfield doesn't want you to have to make a home visit. Her husband is very busy with his political campaign and she travels with him. If you have further questions, could you let me know? I'll get a time for you to talk on the phone or we can come back to the station."

D'Angelo rose saying he would escort them back to the parking lot. He, Billie Jo and Cara left the room but Dory lingered.

"Since Danny was in Rosedale the day before he died, I'm thinking this case should be investigated by our own Sheriff Bradley."

"The kid died here, in the hospital," Stoneman said forcefully. "It's in our jurisdiction." He clearly didn't want to give up...or share...the investigation.

"True, but the beating or poisoning that caused his death may have occurred in Rosedale. And the perpetrator could be a resident of our town, or the person who gave the kill order might be from Rosedale. Since Sheriff Bradley is already involved, having received Danny's cell phone..." Dory trailed off, looking meaningfully at Stoneman.

"I'll call him," Det. Stoneman said shortly, obviously irritated.

Dory said her good-byes quickly and left.

WHEN THE CAR pulled out of the parking lot, Billie Jo asked if anyone was hungry. It was nearly four o'clock in the afternoon and the snacks in the car were long gone. Cara looked at her watch.

"I don't think we have time for anything but a drive-thru. My husband gets back tonight and I've got to be there before he gets home."

"Drive-thru it is then," Billie Jo said and they proceeded to a local Wendy's. Dory had a burger and Billie Jo had a baked potato loaded with melted cheese and broccoli. Cara said she couldn't eat a thing.

Once on the freeway, Dory said, "I think we've successfully averted Detectives D'Angelo and Stoneman from thinking of you as a *person of interest* in the investigation."

"A person of interest?" Cara asked. Her eyes widened.

"Yes, they could tell by your demeanor that you knew nothing about Danny's death. I doubt they will even be back for a second talk."

"You think they suspected me?" Cara asked in an incredulous squeak.

"They always suspect family members and his girlfriend *was* asking you for money. They probably thought you would have had a hard time paying off your son's debts."

"I was planning on using the money I inherited from my father. Grant never needed to know. As far as what I asked you to do, you did find Danny, which was my initial request, but I must know who caused my boy's death. Can Rosedale Investigations find that out for me?" Cara asked.

"Whoever caused Danny's death committed a crime. It's a matter for the police now. However, since we work closely with the Sheriff's Office and they have worked with the Nashville Police Chief in the past, we can definitely inform you when an arrest is made," Dory said and Cara seemed to relax a bit.

Billie Jo turned on the radio and to Dory's surprise chose a classical station. They were playing Mozart's opera, "The Magic Flute." She looked at Billie Jo, who was clearly enjoying the music. Dory frowned and shook her head. Young girls who looked like Billie Jo didn't usually care for opera.

Two hours later, they arrived at the Summerfield residence. When Cara pulled the garage door opener from her purse and opened the four-car bay, she took a quick indrawn breath.

"That's Grant's car. He's home already," she said, despairingly.

The front door opened and Grant Summerfield came out on the porch. He was watching their car carefully.

"Do you want to introduce us?" Billie Jo asked.

"God, no, just drop me off please and go!"

As Billie Jo backed the car out quickly of the driveway, Dory looked back. Cara had reached for her husband's arm. He pushed her hands away and threw his hands up in the air. The couple were clearly arguing.

"Not going to be a pleasant evening in the Summerfield residence," Dory said and Billie Jo nodded.

THIRTEEN

"WHAT THE HELL is going on, Cara?" Grant Summerfield demanded, as color flared across his face.

"It's nothing, Honey. You said you were going to be away for the day and so I took a shopping trip with a friend to Nashville." She tilted her face up at him, trying to summon a smile.

"A shopping trip? With a friend? What friend?"

"Um… I don't think you know her. Her name is Debbie."

"Was it Debbie Cantwell?" He was frowning.

"No. It was… Never mind, it doesn't matter."

"What did you buy? I don't see any packages," his forehead was furrowed. "I have never heard you talk about this so-called friend, and there were two women in the car that dropped you off, a young white teen-ager and an African American woman." His frown deepened.

Cara looked down the street. It was after six o'clock and parents were walking beside their younger children on bikes with training wheels in the warmth of the autumn evening. "We should go inside, Grant," she said and opened the front door.

As Cara and Grant walked into the kitchen, he took a bottle of Pinot Grigio from the refrigerator and poured two glasses. Cara's stomach was quivering and her breathing was shaky. She had to think of a plausible story, but casting a glance at her husband, she saw he was stonily silent.

"Let's go to the great room," she said. Carrying the two wine glasses, Grant followed her into the spacious high-ceilinged space. Cara walked to the back wall of the room with its round-bouldered fireplace flanked by floor-to-ceiling windows. She gazed outside toward a long perennial flower border that ran across their back-yard in front of a split-rail fence. White phlox and yellow Black-eyed Susan's had been planted in front of a swathe of yellow oat grasses. Leading up to the back fence, grass paths meandered around three island beds filled with hostas in full bloom and the bright red circular blossoms of rose mallow.

You're going to have to tell him at least part of the truth, the voice in her head said. She swallowed and turned to face her husband.

"Well?" he asked.

"A child I knew a long time ago died recently and I went to see him. See his body I mean." Her eyes were starting to fill again, seeing her son's long body lying on the pathologist's table.

"Oh, Sweetheart, I'm so sorry," Grant said and took her in his arms. The mention of a child had dispersed his anger, their childlessness had been a profound loss for them both. They stood together, linked by a deep connection and twenty years of marriage. She felt his warm body and realized they had not been intimate for over two weeks. He had been too busy with the campaign. He pulled back and looked down at her, his eyes kind now.

"For Heaven's sakes, if it was a funeral you were attending, especially a funeral for a young boy, why didn't you ask me to go with you? I would have cancelled whatever was on my calendar to be there." When Cara didn't respond, Grant's frown reappeared. "I'm still confused though. Why did you need someone to drive you? Was it a long way away?"

Cara brushed her tears away and straightened her shoulders. "The boy's death was not caused by disease or by an accident. He died after a beating and the police are looking into it. They wanted to talk to me, that's why I went with the two women." She took a shaky breath.

"The cops? Was it the Sheriff's Office personnel here in Rosedale? That's why the black woman looked familiar. I met her once, she works for the Sheriff. Dory Clarkson, that's her name, right? Where did the boy die?"

"The boy died in Nashville. I talked to the police there."

"But why did the police want to talk to you? I'm sure you knew nothing that would help them. You said you knew the boy from years ago." He stopped speaking and with his finger tucked a piece of her dark hair behind her ear. It was an old familiar gesture and Cara felt shame rise in her heart. *Why did I never trust him enough to tell him the truth?*

"It all happened before we met, Grant. I didn't have anything to tell the police, but I knew you would want me to cooperate with the authorities."

"Yes, of course. After all, I've campaigned on a law and order platform," his voice trailed off and he turned to pick up the wine glasses he had set on the mantle. He handed Cara hers and, taking her hand, led her over to the couch. They sat together sipping wine in silence for a while. The sun was going down and the sunlight through the windows was golden.

"So, how was your event today?" Cara asked.

"It was fine. Lots of people attended. I acquired several more big donors. Austin Cantwell was there. He's become a good friend. He was telling me that he had a young kid training Boyd's Boy, his racehorse, but recently decided to switch to a more experienced trainer."

Cara felt her stomach contract at the mention of Cantwell.

Grant continued saying, "Did you know his wife lost a valuable necklace the night of the fund-raiser."

"Yes, Debbie called wanting to know if any of my pictures of that night would show her wearing it. Apparently the necklace has sentimental as well as financial value. It was her grandmother's."

"I hope you can help her. They are going to be powerful supporters for me in this campaign. Austin told me he was planning on starting his stallion, Boyd's Boy, in the races he would need to qualify for the Derby next year. The horse is two years old now and at the peak of his strength. There are only twenty positions available at the starting gate for the Kentucky Derby."

Grant finished his wine and asked his wife if she wanted another. She nodded and he picked up the glasses and returned to the kitchen. When he returned, a look of perplexity was on his handsome face.

"Cara, how exactly did you know this boy that died? What was your connection with him?"

She cleared her throat, playing for time. "He was a son of a friend, a man I haven't seen since I was a teen-ager."

"A man from your past," Grant said quietly. "Cara,

if this boy who died was this man's son, who was his *mother*?"

Cara knew she had made a drastic error. She needed to divert her husband from his far too perceptive questions. "I am sorry, Honey. I just can't talk about this anymore." She stood up, standing close to her husband, so close they were almost touching. "Set the wine down," she whispered and he did. She pressed herself closer to him, until she could feel the heat of his body. She laid her head on his chest and began to cry—for Danny, for herself and for the man in front of her—the man she loved so much but had never trusted with her secret.

Grant leaned down and kissed her forehead and when she looked up, she met his eyes. They were soft and his frown had disappeared. She took his face in her palms and kissed him slowly for a long time. When the kiss ended, Grant took her hand and led her through the great room, the kitchen and down the hall to the master bedroom.

FOURTEEN

Friday

SHERIFF BEN BRADLEY and former Detective Wayne Nichols were having coffee at their usual haunt, the Donut Den. They were seated in their regular booth in the back corner of the cafe. It was Wayne's choice; he liked to be able to see the whole room and didn't like having his back to the front door. His attitude came from years of being on alert and although he told himself he wasn't in law enforcement any more, his caution had served him well in the past.

"Have they called you yet?" Wayne asked. "The Nashville Detectives?"

"No, but they will. I'm sure of it," Ben said. "They can hardly avoid the fact that Daniel Parrish was in Rosedale the day he died. Or that he worked for Cantwell who lives here."

The waitress came up and poured more coffee. They chatted with her for a minute or two before Ben's cell phone rang. "It's them," he said, glancing at the number before answering the phone. "Good morning, Detective. Yes, in fact Detective Nichols is here with me now. Have you made any decisions yet?"

Ben paused and met Wayne's eyes. He quickly switched the phone to speaker, picking up Stoneman mid-sentence.

"…from the cell phone data, it's clear that the vic was in Rosedale, at least until about two o'clock in the afternoon the day he was found behind the hospital."

"Have you located his car?" Ben asked

"Not yet, but I've sent a Deputy out to the racetrack. Cantwell has his own stables at his home in Rosedale, but rents stable quarters here as well. The car might have been left here. I also want to find out if either Cantwell or the stable boy—his name's Harris Stephenson—saw Danny that day. The Pathologist isn't ready to give us a cause of death. She thinks he was poisoned, but can't find a likely injection site. The problem is that Vanderbilt is a teaching hospital and there are tons of medical and nursing students, interns and residents who could have given him pills or a shot, which should have been noted in his chart…"

"Unless the killer took some pains to cover his or her tracks," Ben said.

"I talked to the nurse at the ER again," D'Angelo said, joining in the conversation. "She spotted Danny on the ER loading dock at around 8 p.m. It was her impression that he'd been there an hour or so. It had rained an hour earlier, and she noticed his skin was wet. He was still alive at that point, but barely."

"Given that Parrish died here, I don't see the point of cooperating. I've done a couple of joint investigations in the past and they are always a pain in the backside," Stoneman said.

"Agreed," Ben said, calmly. "However, I can't get past the fact that the kid was in Rosedale the last day of his life. He called and visited his employer's stables here and learned that Cantwell was switching trainers. He was putting his stallion with a more experienced man.

It would have been a devastating blow to Danny, owing fifteen thousand dollars to a bookie with no possibility of continuing employment to pay it off. We're thinking that while Danny ended up dying on your patch, the order may have been given here in Rosedale."

Stoneman sighed volubly. "You could be right, however, it's also possible we don't even have a case to investigate. At present, we have no proof Parrish was murdered. He could have died of natural causes. We are going to wait until we have the pathologist's report before initiating any formal investigation."

"Understood," Ben said.

"Until then, our Captain Crawley said she doesn't have any problems with you looking into things in Rosedale. Hang on a minute," Stoneman said. "My Deputy is on the other line." There was silence before the Detective returned. "He's found Parrish's car. It was at the stables by the racetrack here. It's a white Saturn Vue, 2014. I'll get the lab techs to go over it. Looks like somebody from here drove Daniel to Vanderbilt."

"Is there any reason you wouldn't at least look into the assault? My guess is that the bookie and his thugs are on your turf," Ben said.

"At present there's nobody to make a complaint. The kid is dead," Stoneman said.

"True, but his girlfriend, Tracey, could make a complaint," Ben said.

"She could, but she hasn't yet."

"Have you had any other reports of assaults involving bookies and their arm breakers?"

"I'd have to check, but I doubt it. People tend to avoid reporting that sort of crime," Stoneman said drily.

After ending the call, Ben turned to Wayne. "What do you think?" he asked.

"I think they aren't going to do a damn thing," Wayne said, looking frustrated.

"I can probably get Captain Crawley to give us the name of the person who drove Daniel Parrish to the hospital. It's unusual to have a patient dropped off without checking him in."

"Likely someone with something to hide," Wayne said.

"I agree," Ben added. "Since Captain Crawley said it's okay for us to talk to people who live here, you can go out and talk to Cantwell."

"I'm on my way," Wayne said and finished the dregs of his coffee.

FIFTEEN

WAYNE NICHOLS HAD to consult his GPS to locate the residence of Mr. Austin Cantwell. It was over twenty miles outside Rosedale, on a private dirt road. He inched slowly down the overgrown lane, hearing the lick and scrape of tree limbs hitting against his truck. When he reached the end of the track, he saw the impressive Cantwell estate. It was located on a piece of property which stretched over many acres of mowed green grass. Raw countryside crept up behind and to the sides of the manicured and sprinkled grounds. The old farm house and out-buildings that had been there originally were long gone, except for the barn itself which had been remodeled to become a stable. Wayne parked his car on the cement pad by the barn. All the horse's heads turned toward him as he walked up. He strolled over and reached out to pet an enormous black stallion who reared back, snorted and kicked the sides of his stall. Wayne backed away respectfully.

He looked up at the house which stood atop a nearby rise. It had been built in the style of a Mexican hacienda with a long exterior colonnaded walkway and bright magenta bougainvillea climbing the pillars in front of the main entrance. He hiked up flat granite boulders set into the hill as steps and rang the doorbell. A young Hispanic woman, dressed in a black dress with a frilly white apron opened the door.

"Hello," she said.

"I have an appointment with Mr. Cantwell," Wayne said.

"What is your name?"

"It's Nichols, Wayne Nichols. I called earlier."

"Come this way," she said, and gesturing for him to follow her, she led him through the expansive entry-way with its Mexican Saltillo tile flooring. The house was curiously silent and their footsteps echoed. Walking through an enormous sitting room, Wayne was surprised to see a full-sized sculpture of a horse. It looked like a replica of the Leonardo da Vinci's work cast in bronze he had admired in a large garden park in Michigan. Cantwell's statue was only a quarter the size of da Vinci's work, but still looked ostentatious in a private home. The maid took him on a circuitous route until they reached a set of carved walnut doors that came to a pointed arch at the top. She tapped on one of the doors and opened it, saying, "*Señor* Cantwell, your appointment, Mr. Nichols, is here."

"Show him in," Wayne heard the man say.

The young woman turned away and Wayne walked into an enormous office. It was a sitting room with sofas, chairs, and end tables graced with huge bouquets of red gladioli. The floor had been done in oak parquet. A conference table and chairs were placed on the right side of the room. Beyond the sitting room area, Wayne saw an alcove containing an enormous walnut desk. Behind it sat the man he had come to see.

Cantwell was a slender middle-aged man with salt and pepper hair, dark eyes and a dazzlingly white smile. His teeth were so perfect, Wayne wondered if they had been capped. He was wearing tan wool slacks, a striped shirt and brown loafers. It was a casual outfit but looked expensive.

Before he set off for this appointment, Wayne and PD Pascoe had talked on the phone about how he might handle the interview, including how to introduce himself. They decided it would be best for him to use plain, "Mr. Nichols," although he could say he was a former Detective, if his background came up.

Cantwell came around the desk, extending his hand. "Mr. Nichols, is it?" he asked.

Wayne nodded and they shook hands.

"What can I do for you? My secretary said you had some questions about my former trainer, Daniel Parrish."

"That's right," Wayne said in a conversational tone. He was trying to keep the interaction light, but inside he felt suspicion rise like a dark cloud. Already he wondered if he was facing a man who was involved in the death of Daniel Parrish.

"Please have a seat," Cantwell said gesturing to the living room area.

Wayne walked to the conference table and seated himself in the head position. He locked gazes with Cantwell who frowned, clearly uncomfortable relinquishing his normal head-of-the table seat. When Wayne didn't move or apologize, Cantwell took a seat at the other end of the long redwood table.

"Were you aware that Mr. Parrish died recently?" Wayne asked.

A look of frustration crossed the patrician countenance of Mr. Cantwell. "Yes, I learned that he passed away. Danny had been working with my stallion, Boyd's Boy. I plan to run the horse in the preliminary races he needs to win to become a Kentucky Derby entrant next year. The kid had done a reasonable job, but I thought it would be best to place the horse with a more senior trainer for this coming year."

Wayne looked down at his cell phone, trying to give the impression he was confirming information he already knew. "The day Daniel Parrish died, he called you. What did you discuss?"

Cantwell looked a bit discomfited. "I did speak with him that day. What are all these questions about, Mr. Nichols? I don't need to answer your questions unless you are with the police."

Wayne reached inside his jacket pocket for his police identification before remembering relinquishing his badge. His frustration with the situation rose. The role of private investigator felt like a set of handcuffs preventing him from finding out what he needed to know. "I'm working with Sheriff Bradley and the Nashville police. Please answer my question. What did you and Daniel Parrish discuss?"

"Are you still with the Sheriff's Office in Rosedale? I heard you had resigned."

Wayne clenched his teeth. He felt frustrated but wasn't particularly surprised that Cantwell had done a background search.

"In addition to cell phone numbers showing that you and Daniel Parrish talked, we have triangulated cell tower data indicating that he actually was on your property the day before he died." The temperature in the room felt like it had risen. Wayne's attempts to keep the conversation pleasant had been abandoned. He felt his old persona taking over. He wanted to nail the bastard who had likely colluded in the boy's death.

"If he was here, I didn't see him," Cantwell said. Although he had looked uncomfortable earlier, he now seemed to have hit his stride, sounding more confident.

"You're not denying he was here on the property? Or that you talked with him? If he didn't see you, why do you think he came?" Wayne asked.

Cantwell took a deep breath. "Perhaps he came to see Boyd's Boy. The horse was in my stables that day, although he was to be trailered to Nashville later to start training with the new man. As far as what we discussed on the phone, Mr. Parrish asked if I could advance him some money. I said I was letting him go as Boyd's Boy's trainer and would be sending his last check to his house, but would not give him more than he had earned, except for a week's severance pay."

There was a lot more to uncover here, but Wayne knew he was in an untenable position. He wasn't a Detective anymore and had no standing as an officer of the law. He couldn't force the man to come to the police station or threaten him with arrest. He felt a wave of conflicting needs—a powerful need to catch the bastard who was involved in the young man's death—and an equally potent urge to distance himself from violent crime. In the last few years, he had felt ready to leave the dirty business of murder. Now murder had found him again. He was caught between his past and his future.

"If that's all, Mr. Nichols, I'll bid you good-bye. I'm a busy man and have another appointment."

"Thank you Mr. Cantwell," Wayne said and without shaking hands turned and left the room. He would be back, but would not be unaccompanied. Next time, if there was a next time, Sheriff Bradley would be with him.

WAYNE WALKED ACROSS the lawn and descended the stone steps toward the stable. At one point he glanced back and saw Cantwell standing by the full-length drapes at his office window. When he reached the bottom step, Wayne walked directly to the barn entrance. He slid the huge stable door to the side, letting a slab of sunlight fall on the cement floor strewn with shards of gold straw.

"Hello?" he called. "Is anybody here?"

Emerging from the dusky back of the stables was a young African American boy. He looked to be about sixteen or seventeen. He was dressed in denim overalls and T-shirt with a baseball cap on his head. The brim of his cap was pushed back and Wayne could see he had the tight dark curls common to his ancestry. He had a friendly expression on his face.

"Can I help you, sir?"

"What's your name, son?"

"It's Frank Stephenson," the boy said.

"Any relation to Harris Stephenson, the stable boy who works for Mr. Cantwell in Nashville?"

"He's my big brother."

"I have a couple of questions for you about Daniel Parrish." As he spoke, Wayne could hear a phone ringing in an office at the rear of the stable. When the boy turned in that direction, Wayne said, "How about you don't get that just now, Son." He made his voice flat and authoritative. He knew it was Austin Cantwell calling, not wanting the kid to answer Wayne's questions.

"Okay, guess I can get it later. They'll leave a message. What did you want to ask me about?"

"First off, I'd like to thank you for dropping off Danny's cell phone to the Sheriff's Office in Rosedale."

Wayne was pretty sure Frank had been the person who found it. He could be wrong, but it was worth a shot.

The boy looked startled, but then shrugged. "No use denying it, I guess," he said.

"Since we think Daniel Parrish was *murdered*," Wayne paused, "The phone was helpful in knowing who he talked to before he died. Where did you find it?" As Wayne said the word, "murdered," the boy's eyes had widened and he swallowed.

"Boyd's Boy got upset by the sound of the phone so Danny didn't take it into the horse's stall. I found it on the gatepost after he left. I didn't want the phone to get lost or busted, so I nabbed it. When I learned Danny died, I dropped it by the Sheriff's Office."

"As I said, it's been helpful. I also have some questions about Danny as a trainer. Was he any good?"

"He was awesome, really amazing. Danny was totally committed to Boyd's Boy. He was always here, or at the track in Nashville, by 6 a.m. for the timed morning gallops. The stallion's jockey, Jordan Dane, complained about the having to spend time in both Rosedale and Nashville, but Danny got him on his side. He was using a stopwatch and the horse's times were getting shorter and shorter."

"So Danny was good," Wayne said.

"Better than good. The stallion has only been with Danny as head trainer for about nine months, but in that time he developed from a headstrong colt into a winning racehorse. He could run and he knew it. He was proud and scornful of the other horses in the stable. Danny told me once that when Boyd's Boy was a colt, he never socialized with the other foals. If you're looking for a future racehorse, that's a good sign."

"Why is that?" Wayne asked. This was a new world and he was intrigued.

"Because when the horse is running a race, you want him to pull away from the pack, not look to stay with them. Danny always said that Boyd's Boy was an aristocrat."

"How does an owner know if the trainer is any good?" Wayne asked.

"According to Danny, when a horse has been trained to the peak of his strength and fitness, you can see it in his legs and shoulders. It's visible in his tendons and in the muscle tone of his legs where muscle shades into bone. The legs are supposed to look carved, like a sculpture of a horse in marble."

"I've heard that sometimes racehorses are doped. Was there any doping going on here or in Nashville?"

"No, man. Nothing like that here," Frank shook his head, but Wayne noticed he hadn't denied doping happening in Nashville.

"What about the new trainer. If Danny was so good, why was Mr. Cantwell changing trainers?"

The boy looked away and shrugged. "No idea, man. Maybe something to do with the Syndicate. I thought it was stupid myself." The boy's voice trailed off as he heard a sound. He looked over Wayne's shoulder to see a thoroughly irritated Mr. Austin Cantwell entering the stable.

"I want you off my premises immediately, Nichols," Cantwell said.

Wayne raised his arms in surrender and left the barn. Walking out to his car he whispered, "Pompous prick," under his breath.

DRIVING BACK DOWN the laneway, Wayne reached for his phone and dialed Dory. She picked up immediately and asked him what he was doing.

"I just left Cantwell's house. I got nothing from him, but I did get a chance to talk with Frank Stephenson, the stable boy. He respected Danny as a trainer and I think they were friends. When I asked him why Cantwell fired Danny, since he was very good at his job, Frank said it might have something to do with the Syndicate."

"Syndicate? That sounds like the mob to me," Dory said.

"Not in this case. Racehorses are so expensive and their training, feeding and housing is so pricey that they are often owned by a Syndicates. Cantwell is a player but I'm not sure how big a one. I probably need Billie Jo to look into it."

"Did you remember we have a staff meeting this afternoon? PD wants an update on what everyone is doing. You can ask Billie Jo to look into the Syndicate when you get here."

"Right. What do you have on?"

"After the meeting, I'm going to Nashville to interview Tracey. I called D'Angelo and he agreed to meet me there. He made a point of towing the party line and saying they weren't investigating, but I prevailed on his instincts, which are pretty good by the way. He thinks Danny was murdered, just as we do. It's his boss, Detective Stoneman, who is stalling."

"You need to call Sheriff Bradley and tell him what you're doing, Dory. He absolutely must be kept in the loop. And keep in mind that if we eventually nab a killer and want it to stand up in court, we need to have all your reports turned over to a Sheriff's Detective."

"Would that be Rob?" Dory asked. "Sorry, now I'm the one having a hard time adjusting to my new role. Rob is just a *wet behind the ears* kid to me. I've been investigating murders since he was in diapers."

Wayne sighed. He felt the same way. Walking the minefields between his former career and his new one wasn't easy. "I know, Dory, but we have to be careful. I've had cases thrown out of court because of failing to dot the i's and cross the t's. I'll see you back at the office."

SIXTEEN

"JUST WANTED TO bring everyone up to date," PD said as the team entered the conference room at Rosedale Investigations. "Wayne, please tell us what you've been doing."

"I met with Sheriff Bradley who talked with Detective Stoneman. Police Chief Paula Crawley in Nashville has no problems with us looking into Daniel Parrish's death here in Rosedale. However, she is waiting for the pathologist to issue a cause of death before initiating an investigation there. We may end up working together, but if so we will have jurisdictional issues."

"Wayne could you explain that? I don't know much about jurisdiction," Billie Jo asked. She was dressed in a bright orange blouse and blue jean overalls. It looked like the outfit of a person who had recently discovered the world of the trans-gendered. Wayne mentally shook his head at her attire. He glanced at Dory. While she always wore weird clothes for holidays, including ugly Christmas sweaters, she normally wore dresses and high heels to the office. He wondered if Dory could do something about Billie Jo's style. *It could be good for Dory too*, he thought, she always needed someone to manage.

"Sorry, Billie Jo, I was distracted momentarily by your outfit," Wayne said and Dory chuckled. "Territorial jurisdiction is the authority confined to a geographic space, over all those residing there and any unlawful events which occur there. In this case, Sheriff Bradley has jurisdiction over crimes that occur in Rose County. He and Captain Crawley agreed that we can talk to the folks who live here."

"Thanks," Billie Jo said with a smile.

"What have you got, Billie Jo?" PD asked.

"I've been pounding the keys on my computer. As I mentioned in our previous meeting, I located Rafe Marston, Danny's father. I called Cara Summerfield and asked her if I could talk with Mr. Marston. She said no. Since he doesn't even know he had a son, she hopes he can be left completely out of this."

"Not likely," PD said looking at Wayne who nodded in agreement. "Go on."

"I also located the address for the Parrish's. And I found the new trainer Mr. Cantwell hired for Boyd's Boy. His name is James Walters. I looked into how lucrative a job it is, and good trainers make about twenty five hundred dollars per month per horse. Mr. Cantwell has ten horses so if James Walters works with all of them that would mean a quarter of a million dollars a year."

"Was Danny working with more of Cantwell's horses or only Boyd's Boy?" PD asked.

"Tracey said Danny wanted to start working with more of Cantwell's horses, but before he could start, he was terminated. Training just one horse, he would only have been making about thirty thousand dollars a year, as opposed to James Walters who would be making way more."

"I clearly chose the wrong job," Dory said. "With my

needs for a fashionable wardrobe, I should be making that kind of money." She grinned.

"Okay. Let's wrap this up, people," PD said. "Dory, I know you are leaving shortly to interview Tracey in Nashville. Billie Jo, you can leave now to talk to Mrs. Cantwell about her missing jewelry. Get a copy of her insurance claim and ask her how she thought she lost it. It's got to be an inside job. Necklace was probably taken by a maid. Pretty hard to get a necklace off a woman's neck in public."

"What are you going to be doing, PD?" Billie Jo asked.

"I am going to talk with my contacts in the gambling world. Hope to find out who Daniel Parrish was placing his bets with and the names of the guys who beat him up. Wayne, you can come along," PD said.

"Could you take a look into the Syndicate that owns Boyd's Boy when you get a chance?" Wayne asked Billie Jo. "I want to know how big a player Austin Cantwell is."

"Does this have to be done now? I am supposed to be going to the Cantwell's place this afternoon."

"Just get to it when you can," Wayne said.

As the group disbursed, Dory cast Wayne a look and whispered, "I need a word with you now."

"Just a minute, I have to visit the gents," Wayne said and headed down the hall. He entered and closed the bathroom door behind him. Standing at the urinal, he heard the door open and inhaled the scent of Dory's perfume.

"Wayne," she said quietly.

"I think this is taking the concept that you are *one*

of the boys a bit far," Wayne said. "Hang on a minute and I'll see you outside."

WAYNE FOUND DORY standing behind Rosedale Investigations. The house had a small fenced backyard with a painted picnic table and shrubbery that provided privacy from neighboring houses. The Rose of Sharon shrubs with their pink, white and blue flowers had grown very tall. The flowers were shaped like hollyhocks and had a subtle, pleasant scent. It was late afternoon and the thermometer had hit ninety degrees. The lawn and shrubs looked dry, like they needed watering.

"What's going on?" Wayne asked.

"Do you remember a weaselly jewelry fence named Clint Jay? He's the guy Sheriff Bradley eventually terminated for making off with petty cash every time he was in the office."

"I remember Jay."

"Anyway, he contacted me last night to say that he has Mrs. Cantwell's necklace. Wouldn't say how he came by it. It's antique, from a time that women's jewelry was made of 22 karat gold, much more valuable than the usual 14 karat used today. The necklace is gold filigree and authentic cabochon rubies. Lots of gems today have been heat-treated or are made in factories, not mined. These are the real deal. Clint thinks he can fence it for ten thousand. You'll never guess who he contacted asking to pay for the necklace."

"No clue," Wayne said. It was getting warmer in the enclosed small yard and the scent from the shrubs was cloying. He heard PD calling his name out front. "Stop playing games, Dory. PD is waiting for me."

"It's Austin Cantwell. Once they settle on a price, he's willing to buy."

"Hmmm. So, he's buying his wife's necklace back from the thief or at least the fence who is working with the thief. It happens," he said and shrugged. "It's not against the law."

"Right, but Mrs. Cantwell has filed an insurance claim."

"Hmmm. Now insurance fraud *is* against the law."

"Turns out she had the necklace appraised recently by a reputable jeweler and has paper to prove it is worth fifteen thousand dollars."

"You need to tell Billie Jo *before* she gets to the Cantwell home. Remember we're supposed to be a team here," Wayne said pointedly, looking at her askance. Dory had a tendency to keep details of a case to herself, until she found an opportunity to show off her knowledge. He had often criticized her attempts at grandstanding.

TWO HOURS LATER, Dory entered the coffee shop in Nashville where she and D'Angelo were meeting Tracey Dimond. She saw the girl standing in line waiting to pay for her order. Tracey was wearing pink scrubs, probably the uniform for beauticians working at her salon. It was called "A-Hair Affair" and from Dory's quick look on the internet offered medium-priced services.

She called the shop from the car and talked to the Manager who said Tracey was a contract employee who rented a station at the salon. Although the Manager wouldn't give her a specific dollar amount, she agreed when Dory guessed Tracey's income for the previous year was less than twenty thousand. Casting her eyes around the room, Dory spotted D'Angelo talking on his cell phone toward the back of the shop. He was dressed in a black suit with a flat-collared dark blue shirt. He raised his eyes and nodded.

"Hi Tracey," Dory said, touching her shoulder. She jumped.

"Oh, hello, Miss Dory. Do you want to order?" Tracey's demeanor eloquently revealed her recent loss. Her posture was slumped and her normally tan complexion was washed out. She wore no make-up and as she reached in her purse to pay for her order, her hands were shaking.

"I'll get it," Dory said and paid for Tracey's coffee and a sandwich combo for herself. The women walked toward Detective D'Angelo who rose to greet them.

"Hello, Tracey, Dory. There is a private dining room here and I reserved it for us. We can talk there without being overhead. Bring your food and follow me."

The three of them walked into the private room which had glass double-doors. Once closed, they could see the whole dining area from their seats at the table, but couldn't be overheard.

"Good idea to get this room, D'Angelo," Dory said, approvingly.

"I wanted you to be comfortable talking with us, Tracey," he said. "I don't know if you have noticed, but we have a squad car parked near your house in the evenings. We are doing everything we can to ensure your safety."

"I saw it," Tracey said quietly, but Dory thought she looked anything but reassured.

"Danny's cell phone was turned in to the Sheriff's Office in Rosedale, Tennessee and we saw that you made a call to him on the day before he passed," D'Angelo said. "What did the two of you talk about?"

Recalling the conversation, Tracey started to tear up.

Dory cast the Detective a raised eyebrows look and when he nodded, she took over. "Tracey, honey, I know this is hard for you, but you want to help find whoever hurt Danny, right?"

Tracey nodded, her face a study in sorrow.

"We want the same thing. We want to get the low-life thugs who beat Danny up. All Detective D'Angelo and I want is for you to tell us what you and Danny talked about. It could really help us, especially if he told you anything about who he was meeting that day."

Tracey took a deep breath and straightened her shoulders. "He was terribly upset. I've never heard him sound like that. He went to see that *worm* Cantwell who said he was letting him go. He'd hired a more experienced trainer, even though nobody could have been better than Danny with Boyd's Boy. He wouldn't give Danny any money beyond what he was owed. The horse was being trailered back to Nashville from Cantwell's house and Danny drove behind them so he could say good-bye to the horse. His voice was thick with tears when he told me about petting him. He had known the stallion his whole life. In fact it was Danny who picked him out for Cantwell as a newborn colt. It was awful, just awful." Tears trickled from her eyes. Then suddenly she looked panicked. "I'm sorry, I have to go to the bathroom, right now!"

Dory stood up to follow Tracey who practically sprinted toward the Ladies before D'Angelo stopped her.

"Not a word to Detective Stoneman about this, right?" he said. "I really shouldn't be here."

Dory nodded, putting a finger to her lips before heading toward the bathroom. By the time she walked in, Dory heard Tracey in a stall. She was retching again and again.

"Do you think you have the flu, Honey?" Dory asked her when Tracey emerged and bent over the sink to wash her hands and wipe her mouth.

"No," she said. "I think I'm pregnant. And I never got to tell Danny."

SEVENTEEN

BILLIE JO LEFT for the Cantwell estate after the staff meeting. Her phone rang when she was almost there.

"I have some pertinent information for you," Dory said. "A jewelry fence I know by the name of Clint Jay contacted me last night. He has Mrs. Cantwell's ruby necklace and already contacted Austin Cantwell about it. His plan is to sell it back to the owners."

"Thanks, Dory. That's good info," Billie Jo said. "Is it even worth me talking to Mrs. Cantwell then?"

"I think so, you can probably get more information. Remember, Danny Parrish worked there. You might pick up something useful. What are you wearing for this interview?" Dory asked, sounding distrustful.

"Jeans and a top," Billie Jo said shortly. She was getting tired of having to justify every wardrobe choice. It has been bad enough with PD talking to her about wanting her to look professional, but now Dory was sticking her nose in.

"You were seated at the meeting so I didn't get a look at your pants, Billie Jo. I hope there aren't too many holes in your jeans."

Billie Jo looked down and wondered what Dory would consider too many holes. "Hardly any," she lied.

"Appears Mr. Cantwell is willing to pay for the jewelry, which makes it unlikely he stole it for the insurance money," Dory said.

BILLIE JO THANKED Dory for her information and said good-bye. Shortly thereafter, she arrived at the Cantwell estate and parked her car by the stables. She doubted she'd learn anything helpful from Mrs. Cantwell, but PD always said when you were investigating you couldn't never get too much information. She hiked up the hill and rang the doorbell. A young maid with a nametag reading "Valentina" answered the door.

"Hi. I'm Billie Jo from Rosedale Investigations. Mrs. Cantwell is expecting me," she said.

"Follow me. She's in the kitchen," the girl said and led the way.

The kitchen for the house was enormous with walnut cabinetry, stone countertops, and an island that could easily seat eight. On one side of the room was an arched brick opening for a pizza oven. Despite every kitchen amenity known to man, the kitchen didn't look like anyone actually cooked there. And although it was only early afternoon, Debbie Cantwell was already drinking—a Margarita—in a glass with salt particles glistening on the rim.

"Mrs. Cantwell, this is Billie Jo Bradley," Valentina said.

"Thank you for coming, Billie Jo," Debbie said, standing up and setting her drink down. "Come with me to the Master Bedroom. I want to show you where I keep my jewelry." She was wearing a magenta cashmere sweater and narrow gray slacks. Her hair was long, shiny and perfectly straight. She looked like she had just emerged from the beautician's chair.

Billie Jo, wearing jeans with numerous holes in them, a midriff-revealing tight top and flip-flops felt distinctly outclassed. Usually, she didn't give a fig what other people thought, but Dory's recent questions and Mrs. Cantwell's outfit had made her more aware of her appearance.

The two women walked to an enormous master bedroom. It had its own locked entrance with a security camera. Mrs. Cantwell lowered her eye to the tiny screen and the big door swung open.

"That's a very good security system you have there, Mrs. Cantwell," Billie Jo said approvingly.

"It is and that's why I can't figure out how my necklace went missing. It was the night of the Summerfield fund-raiser."

"Did you leave it in the bedroom when you took it off that night?"

"That's the problem, I can't quite remember. Just a bit too much champagne that night," she giggled.

"Have you submitted an insurance claim for it?" Billie Jo asked.

"I certainly have. My agent was giving me a bit of a rough time, saying I had no proof of exactly when the necklace went missing, but luckily Cara Summerfield had a picture of me wearing it."

"May I have a copy of the insurance claim?"

"I'll have the insurance company fax it to you this afternoon."

"Did they ask how it went missing?" Billie Jo asked.

"They did and the only thing I could think was that the clasp was digging into my neck during that party. I removed it to adjust the metal section that was irritating. I think I put it back on then, but could have left it in the powder room. It's possible someone was using the toilet when I took the necklace off. There's a closed stall."

"If you left it in the powder room, any number of people could have taken it."

"I guess that's possible," Debbie said. "Although all the people attending were our friends. I would hate to think one of them took it. Otherwise, I think the only way it could have been taken was from my bedroom. And you saw the security for this suite. It's unbreakable."

She and Billie Jo walked from the spacious bedroom into a dressing room which was beautifully lighted by a chandelier that reflected all Mrs. Cantwell's expensive clothes in full-length mirrors. Debbie showed Billie Jo her jewelry case in a locked cabinet with lighted glass shelves.

"Does anyone besides yourself have access to this room?" Billie Jo asked.

"Only my personal maid, Valentina, and my husband."

"How long has Valentina worked for you?"

"Three years and I would never suspect her. She's loyal to a fault."

"Could I speak to her privately?" Billie Jo asked.

"Of course, but as I said, she would not have taken it. If that's all, I have other things I need to do."

"Does Valentina drive herself to work here?" Billie Jo asked. The house was a long way out in the country and she hadn't seen any cars in the driveway.

"No, she doesn't drive, so either my husband or someone from her family drives her. It's about forty-five minutes, too long for her to walk."

Billie Jo must have looked suspicious because when she asked, "How often does Mr. Cantwell drive her?"

Mrs. Cantwell's tone of voice was cold when she

said, "Several nights a week, but I told you before Valentina would not have stolen that necklace, and in case you were wondering, my husband would never hit on that girl."

WHEN BILLIE JO found Valentina in the kitchen, she was competently mixing another Margarita for her employer.

"I have a couple of questions for you, Valentina. The night of the big fund-raiser for Grant Summerfield, did you help Mrs. Cantwell get ready?"

"*Si*, I did. She wore her full-length silk gown. It's red and the necklace she inherited from her grandmother is gold with red rubies. She looked smashing that night."

"Did she have the necklace on after the party?"

"No, not then. When I asked her where it was, she said the clasp had been scratching her neck. She had gone into her bedroom during the party once and could have left it there, or she might have left it in the powder room by the front entrance. I went right away to look, but didn't find it either place."

"I'm surprised she can't remember where she left it, given its value," Billie Jo said.

Looking embarrassed, Valentina said, "She did have quite a bit to drink that night."

"Valentina, I need you to be honest with me now," Billie Jo's voice was gentle. "Did you take the necklace? If you did and you bring it back immediately, nothing needs to be said," Billie Jo watched the maid's face carefully.

Valentina's eyes widened and a shocked expression crossed her face. "Me? No, I never take anything from Mrs. Cantwell. She is a nice lady." Valentina's eyes started to fill. "I am not a thief," she said defensively.

"Sometimes Mrs. Cantwell gives me one of her old dresses. Once in a while she gives me jewelry, but not precious stones or gold. And I wouldn't take her grandmother's necklace. My grandmother died last year and I know the things they leave us are to be cherished."

"I believe you," Billie Jo said. "Who else is on the staff here?"

"Mrs. Hannah Slater, their cook, is the only one who is here every day. There is a service that comes in to clean, a landscaping firm, and of course the trainer and stable boys for the horses. Mr. Cantwell has a childhood friend who is here a lot. His name is Carl. Mrs. Cantwell calls him the rainmaker. And the Cantwell's niece, Justine, spends a lot of time in the stables. She likes hanging out with Danny, the trainer. I think she still has a crush on him."

"You said she *still* has a crush. Were they a couple once?" Billie Jo asked.

"I think so. Is there anyone else you want to talk to?" Valentina asked.

"Can you introduce me to the cook?"

"Yes, she's just pulling in the driveway now," Valentina said, looking out the window.

Talking with Mrs. Slater, Billie Jo learned that unless Mr. Cantwell drove Valentina home, it was her cousin, Marco Vasquez, who drove her to and from work. When she asked about Valentina's family situation, Billie Jo learned her mother was ill with cancer, her father had passed away recently and the only income in the family came from the girl's job with the Cantwells. When she asked how much Valentina made from her job, Mrs. Slater said she didn't know exactly, but the job paid well and the girl got a Christmas bonus each year. *Still, medical care and medicines were expensive. Supporting her mother well as herself on a job as a ladies' maid might not be enough.*

"This friend of Mr. Cantwell's, Carl, what is his role in the family?" Billie Jo asked.

"I'm not sure. All I know is that he's connected in some way with the horses," Mrs. Slater said. "They spend a lot of time in Mr. Cantwell's office talking about money."

DRIVING BACK TO the office, Billie Jo put on her CD of Mozart's "Cosi fan Tutte". She didn't know a lick of Italian, but from the first moment she heard opera, she was hooked. The tones of the arias were so pure, so lovely. She knew it was a slightly odd musical preference among her contemporaries, but didn't care. Listening to opera helped her focus.

It had been quite a fruitful visit to the Cantwell estate, she thought. If Mr. Cantwell drove Valentina home most evenings, the drive gave them a lot of time for private conversations. *Could Valentina and Mr. Cantwell be having an affair?* Billie Jo wondered. The idea might not even have occurred to her, had not Mrs. Cantwell been so fierce in her insistence that Mr. Cantwell wasn't making moves on Valentina. *Perhaps the lady doth protest too much*, Billie Jo thought. Valentina was a very pretty young woman and would probably do anything for her employers, but given the maid's loyalty to Mrs. Cantwell, it seemed pretty unlikely she was sleeping with her husband. Then there was Justine, the Cantwell's niece. If she and Danny were together and then broke up, would that give her a motive? Probably PD would dismiss it as one of her "girlie" conjectures.

She decided she would include Justine in her summary, but wouldn't point to her as having a motive.

Once back at her desk, Billie Jo checked the crime database and found that Valentina's cousin Marco Vasquez had a juvenile record for theft. He and a friend had held up a local 7/11 store and made off with a case of beer and the money in the register. Since Marco was only sixteen at the time, he served just a year in juvie. She also discovered that he currently worked for the catering company the Cantwell's had hired to do the food the night of the Summerfield fund-raiser. Marco was starting to look like the thief.

Another hour on the computer and Billie Jo found out that virtually all the money in the Cantwell family came from Mrs. Cantwell. She had inherited the estate and millions more from her late father. *So that's why she's confident her husband wouldn't be trying to get Valentina in bed*, Billie Jo thought.

As she walked upstairs to her small suite, several other ideas occurred to her. *Could Mr. Cantwell be less wealthy than his reputation suggested? Was Mrs. Cantwell starting to get antsy about all her money being spent on racing? It was a wealthy man's hobby and many a man had lost everything playing the horses. Was Mr. Cantwell's friend, Carl, the one Hannah Slater called the rainmaker, there to stop the erosion of her capital? And how did any of this possibly relate to the death of Daniel Parrish?*

EIGHTEEN

LEAVING THE OFFICE, PD Pascoe and Wayne Nichols drove to an area of Nashville, Tennessee near the race-track. PD was headed to a bar where he said he had spent many hours during his drinking days.

"Aren't you recovering?" Wayne asked. "Billie Jo told me you were."

"I still drink, but not often and I never binge. Billie Jo won't let me. There were times years ago when I wanted a drink more than I wanted to solve a mystery. In those years, I could taste the whiskey that waited for me driving home at the end of the day. Now though, I usually just have a couple of beers in the evenings. I think of it as brain food," he gave Wayne a cheeky grin.

"I'd always heard once alcohol got ahold of a person they had to quit completely or would be right back where they were. Isn't that true?" Wayne asked.

"It depends on how hooked you were. One of the VA counselors told me that if you were a binge drinker and cut way down, you could become a social drinker. If you were an everyday drinker, especially of a fifth of whis-key or scotch a day, you couldn't touch alcohol again. They cautioned me that it wouldn't be easy and it isn't, but so far I've managed to hold my drinking in check."

"Interesting. Tell me about the man we are going to meet."

"It's a guy called Billy Harding. He's a small-time

numbers man, a bookie who is not very good at it. He knows everyone in the business though. He's been pulling a meager living out of gambling for thirty plus years."

"Was he a Confidential Informant for you when you worked Homicide?" Wayne asked.

"He was, but now he's more of a friend. I don't usually give him more than fifties or hundreds for information. If you want a tip on a horse race, though, that will cost you five hundred."

"What does he think about Cantwell's stallion, Boyd's Boy?"

"Billy says he's going to sweep the field, make it all the way to the starting gate for the Derby."

Wayne chuckled. "You realize you just gave me a horse race tip for free, man."

"So I did," PD grinned. "You cleverly set me up for that, talking about Boyd's Boy so that I thought you were asking about the case. We're here."

PD PULLED INTO the dirt parking lot of a run-down café on the outskirts of Nashville. The building was low, flat-roofed and made from cement block. A neon sign above the dusty windows said, "Virginia's Victuals." Taped to the front door was a piece of paper reading, "Pulled Pork Sandwiches, Special $3.99." When the men walked in, the smell of grilled ribs was almost palpable. They could hear the cook in the back singing off-key to a country ballad playing on the ancient jukebox.

The restaurant had a linoleum-topped counter fronted by a dozen stools at the back of the dining area. Two of the vinyl-topped stools were occupied by heavy men in grass-stained Wrangler overalls laughing at some joke.

There were four tables in the center of the place and two booths, one on each side of the room. The middle-aged waitress behind the counter was filling salt and pepper shakers. When she finished, she took a seat on a straight-backed wooden chair by the register, sighing audibly and settling in as if she had lived her whole life there. Beside the register was a red plastic dish for tips and a half dozen mason jars filled with peaches or green tomatoes. Little handwritten price tags read "$2" each.

"All right if we take the booth, Ginny?" PD called and the woman nodded. She looked tired and it had taken a moment for her to even register the two new customers.

"Want menus?" she called out.

"In a minute." PD said, as they walked to a booth and took their seats. Turning to Wayne, PD said, "It'll be a while before Billy shows up. He's a law unto himself, has no idea of time when it comes to appointments, but can tell you to within a tenth of a second a horse's time on the track."

A LITTLE LATER, they called Ginny over and ordered two beers and pulled pork sandwiches. Billy Harding appeared as they were eating. He was African American, dark-skinned and short. His skin had that ashy look that many black men get as they age and his legs were like twigs. He wore denim cut-off shorts and a tee-shirt that read "I'm a Feminist."

PD got to his feet and shook hands saying, "Good to see you, man. Want you to meet my newest PI, Wayne Nichols."

"Nice to meet you," Wayne said, standing up and shaking hands.

"Have a seat, Billy. What will you have?" PD asked, waving Ginny over.

"I've just got to ask about the T-shirt. What makes you a feminist?" Wayne asked, amused.

"Far as I'm concerned a woman has a right to do whatever she wants with her body and if she wants to sell it to me, that's just fine," Billy said and both detectives chuckled.

When the waitress appeared, Billy said, "I'll have my usual, Ginny, hamburger, onion rings and a shot of bourbon." As soon as she was out of earshot, Billy said, "What can I do you for you today, PD? Need to get back to the track."

"I have a client whose son, Danny Parrish, died recently. Before he passed away, he was beaten up. Told his girlfriend it was because he owed a bookie a bundle and couldn't pay." As he spoke, both PD and Wayne looked closely at his expression. From the look on Billy's face, Wayne suspected he had already known about Danny's death.

"What do you want to know?" Billy asked.

"We want to know which bookie he bets with and whether the man employs any arm-breakers for debt collection," PD said.

Billy frowned. "Don't want to get no punter man in trouble," he said, shaking his head.

"We aren't interested in shutting down the numbers racket or hassling the bookie involved," Wayne said. "The problem is that the kid died in Nashville, so now there's a couple of Homicide cops from there who are looking into things. Plus, Sheriff Bradley is involved in Rosedale."

"What the hell does a PI shop have to do with murder?" Billy asked. He was on alert now, frowning and intent on what they were saying.

"The kid's mother hired us to find out what happened to her son," PD said. "She didn't want to involve the cops. This was just a missing person's case originally, but since the kid died there's no choice but to involve the law."

Ginny returned with Billy's hamburger, rings and beer. She had added a small ruffled apron with red apples over her uniform, but it was spotted with grease and did little to enhance her careworn appearance.

"Anything else, gentlemen?" she asked. "We have fresh peach pie today. Made it myself this morning."

"I'm good," Wayne said.

"I'll have a slice of that pie," Billy said.

"Make that two," PD added. "And a couple cups of coffee. One black, one white."

"You got money today, PD?" Billy asked when Ginny left. PD pulled a crisp fifty from his wallet. Billy nodded, pocketed the money and said, "The bookie is named Lyndon Aces Dockery. He employs two thugs who do his debt collecting. Both those guys are pretty careful. I'd be surprised if the kid died from the beating. They know their jobs. 'Nobody dies', that's Dockery's watchword."

PD pulled another fifty from his wallet and said, "I want their names."

Billy shook his head and PD added a second fifty. Billy reached across the table intending to add the extra money to his stash, but PD kept his hand firmly on the bills. The two men looked at each other across the table until Billy sagged back in his seat.

"It's the Tusk brothers, Mike and Rick. I'm really

taking a chance telling you this, PD. If Dockery finds out I told you, my life is not worth a plugged nickel. I wouldn't live through another beating. Too old to survive much of a scuffle now."

PD took his hand off the cash and Billy grabbed it. Not waiting for his peach pie, he scarpered from the café.

When Ginny appeared shortly with pies and coffees, she looked perplexed.

"Billy had an appointment, but I'll have that pie and coffee," Wayne said. "Smells delicious. Bet you're a good cook."

Ginny smiled wearily, thanked the men and returned to her seat by the cash register. She had become a fixture again, waiting her life out behind that counter.

"How do you propose we find the Tusk brothers?" Wayne asked. "They have definitely stayed off the radar of law enforcement in Rosedale."

"They are usually at the track on race days. Soon as we finish our pie we can run over there."

"You're talking about the track in Rosedale, not in Nashville, right?" Wayne asked. "Have to be careful about this jurisdiction thing."

"Yeah, they will be checking out all the horses, but particularly Boyd's Boy. He's an odds-on favorite."

Remembering the arrogant stallion who knew he could run, Wayne nodded.

NINETEEN

Saturday

CARA SUMMERFIELD WOKE to her husband coming back into their bedroom carrying a cup of coffee for her. She was wearing a silky nightdress and one strap had fallen off her shoulder. She sat up in bed and smiled.

"Thank you, Honey," she said sweetly—before noticing the critical expression on Grant's face. Her smile faded.

"Cara, you told me the boy whose body you went to view was the son of a kid you knew in high school, but when I asked you who the boy's mother was, you didn't really answer me. Who was it?"

Cara looked down, trying to collect her thoughts. Soon, she would have to tell Grant the whole story. When she looked up and met his judgmental eyes, however, she decided it wasn't the right time.

"I didn't really know her," she said. *It was true in a way. The girl who got pregnant so long ago seemed to be another person—from another life.*

"That's sort of odd, isn't it, Cara? Usually if a girl gets pregnant in high school, all the other girls know. Plus, everyone knows who is dating who in high school." The frown on Grant's face had turned deeply suspicious.

Cara took a deep breath and found herself unexpectedly in tears again. She just looked up at her husband. His face softened.

"Did the girl go to another school, maybe?" Grant asked. "Was that it?"

Cara nodded, hating herself.

"I'm sorry you had to go through that by yourself, viewing the young man's body, but next time something like this comes up, you really need to tell me. I'm announcing my candidacy for District Representative soon and that will mean the press will have their beady little eyes on both of us all the time."

Cara winced inwardly, knowing it wasn't likely that the person who took Danny's life would be arrested by then.

Grant continued saying, "So, I need your word, Honey. Anything odd or unusual that happens in either of our lives, we have to face it together. Okay?" He looked at her questioningly, still seeming a bit upset and Cara nodded, knowing her secret couldn't stay hidden much longer.

WHEN GRANT LEFT for the campaign breakfast on his schedule, Cara felt a desperate need to talk to somebody. Her entire world seemed to be collapsing and the only person she could think of was Billie Jo. It was just 8 a.m., but Cara got into her car and headed for Rosedale Investigations. The bell tinkled as she entered the business. In just moments, Billie Jo came out of the kitchen at the back of the house. Seeing the awful look on Cara's face, she put down her coffee cup.

"What can I do to help, Cara?" she asked.

"I want to talk to Danny's father, Rafe. It's all about

to fall apart and I need someone on my side. You told me you found him."

"I did, but *all* of us are on your side, Mrs. Summerfield," Billie Jo said.

"I need his phone number. Please get it for me."

Billie Jo retrieved the contact information from her computer and printed it out.

"Earlier you said you didn't want Mr. Marston to know about Danny, since he could never meet him," she said, but Cara Summerfield had already grabbed the slip of paper and was turning to leave.

"Wait," Billie Jo called. "There are other people you could talk to who knew Danny."

Halfway out the door, Cara stopped.

Billie Jo quickly added Mr. and Mrs. Parrish's as well as Tracey's phone number to her document and printed it off. "The Parrish's are back in town now and this is Danny's girlfriend's phone number at work. I'm sure she is just as devastated as you are, and would appreciate your calling. This is such a dire situation, Mrs. Summerfield, I'm wondering if you should get an appointment with a therapist?"

Cara nodded, took the little note and turned to go, tears falling.

ONCE BACK AT HOME, Cara pulled out her cell phone and found the office phone number for Dr. Roberta Jakes, the counselor she had been seeing a few years ago. She left a frantic message saying it was an emergency. While she waited for a return call, she looked down at her hands. They had a fine tremor. She had noticed this sometimes when she drank too much coffee, but today the trembling was not caused by caffeine. She could feel her carefully constructed world disintegrating. Two hours later, the counselor called. She could see Cara at after lunch. Cara sighed in relief.

Dr. Jakes was standing in the entryway of the small modern building where she had her office when Cara drove into the parking lot. The therapist held the door open for her.

"Thank you so much for seeing me so quickly, Dr. Jakes. I'm sorry but it really is an emergency," Cara said and followed the woman down the hall to her consulting room. It was a corner office with built-in bookcases below the windows on two sides of the room. Atop the bookcases, dark green trailing plants with a blue ginger jar in their midst, gave the office the feeling of a living room. The furniture consisted of two caramel-colored leather chairs, teakwood end tables and lamps. A blue teapot and two cups stood on a tray on the coffee table. The sun had gone under a bank of clouds and Dr. Jakes switched on the lamp beside her chair. The darkened sky and single lighted lamp made the room seem cozy and welcoming.

"Please have a seat, Cara. How are things going for you?" Dr. Jakes smiled, took her chair and crossed her long legs in tan wool pants. She leaned forward and her ash blonde hair curved against her cheeks.

Cara took a deep breath. "I'm sure you remember the day you told me I couldn't live a lie forever."

Dr. Jakes nodded. "So it's happened has it? The lie is about to be exposed?"

"My baby, my son Daniel is dead," Cara said, her eyes filling with tears.

"Oh Cara, that's awful. I'm so terribly sorry for your loss," Dr. Jakes said. She rose and walked over to the sideboard and poured Cara a cup of tea. She handed it to her and touched her shoulder gently. "Does this mean you won't tell Grant now," she asked, softly.

"You don't understand. Danny didn't just die, he was killed, murdered."

Dr. Jakes eyes opened wide in shock. "That's just terrible. I'm so sorry, Cara."

"He died in Nashville and the police from there and Rosedale are trying to identify his killer. I fear all this is going to spill over on me like acid. And when the truth comes out, Grant won't want to be married to me anymore." She brushed away tears and then continued, "I went to see Danny's body in the hospital morgue. The private investigators from the firm in Rosedale found him and took me. He looked so peaceful, almost like he was asleep. Except for the day he was born, I saw him only once, when he was sixteen."

"Tell me about that," Dr. Jakes said.

"At the time, he wanted money to become a horse trainer. I covered the costs, but how I wish I had said no. He got into gambling, and that was what led to his death. He was in debt to a bookie and got beat up by some thugs. When I went to see him at the morgue, I kissed his forehead, but he was cold, all the life in him was gone." Cara took a deep shaky breath, striving for control.

"Go on," the therapist said.

"When I got back home, Grant was waiting. I told him I had gone to see the boy. I didn't say his name, only said he was the son of a high school friend. He keeps asking who the boy's mother was. I can't bring myself to tell him."

"Oh, Cara, this has gone too far now," Roberta Jake's

face was grave. She shook her head slowly. "There's been a murder and this investigation is going to inevitably unearth your decades-long deception. I don't usually give patients advice. It is my practice to encourage them to find their own way out of their troubles, but this is different. I must advise you in the strongest possible terms to tell Grant the whole story. And you need to do it soon."

"I'm afraid he will hate me," Cara wailed.

"Regardless, you must do what is right. I'm sorry, Cara, but you simply must. Would you like to rehearse it, you and me? Do you think that would help?"

"I am simply not ready, Dr. Jakes," Cara said as she picked up her purse and rose to leave the room.

"Oh, Cara," the therapist said, sadly. "Please think hard about this. Come back when this is all over. I'll make myself available."

TWENTY

PD HAD SENT a text to the entire team. He apologized but asked all of them to come to the office. Dory arrived first and found Billie Jo in the kitchen.

"Why the heck are we meeting on Saturday morning?" Dory asked.

"PD probably just wants to prepare for the video conference later this afternoon. It was the only day everyone could be available, apparently. The Sheriff and the Nashville Detectives are all going to watch it with us. By the way, thanks for letting me know about Mr. Cantwell being contacted by your jewelry fence, Dory. I think I've figured out who stole the necklace. I had to listen to Mozart all the way back from the Cantwell place yesterday before I got the whole picture. Opera helps me focus for some odd reason," Billie Jo said, smiling. Dory smiled back, bemused by the girl's odd musical choice.

Filling the coffee carafe, Dory looked at her young compatriot. Since it was a Saturday, she herself was dressed in a business casual outfit, navy trousers, a blue V-necked sweater and silver hoop earrings. Billie Jo was in jeans and a tight red T-shirt. "Do you have a boyfriend, Billie Jo?" Dory asked.

"Don't know that I'd call him a boyfriend, exactly, but I date a young guy I met at the Romanov Club. He's a good dancer and cute, but not good for much else. He washes dishes at the Club, rides his motorcycle and hangs around with druggies most of the time," Billie Jo shrugged.

"Goodness, girl. Here you are, what, twenty? Twenty-one?" Billie Jo nodded. "You are at the peak of your physical beauty and attractiveness to the opposite sex. You are ambitious, going to school with the goal of becoming a private investigator. You have a good job. And you love opera—of all things. It just seems to me that you might like to meet a young man, unlike the *loser* you are currently dating, who might someday take you to go to the opera."

Billie Jo tipped her head to one side, obviously caught by Dory's idea. "I actually didn't know you could go to see an opera. Is it like going to a movie?"

"No, it's more like a play. Operas are given as live performances, with upscale staging, lighting and the music is stunning—if you like that sort of thing. The tickets are very expensive, hundreds, even thousands of dollars. Anyway, if you wanted to get yourself a boy-friend who could *afford* to take you to the opera, I would be willing to be a style consultant for you."

Before Billie Jo could respond, the two women heard PD and Wayne coming through the front door.

"Billie Jo, Dory, let's get started," PD's voice was gruff. "Conference room everybody."

ONCE SEATED AT the table, a general conversation broke out before PD called the meeting to order. "We've all been busy since yesterday so I thought it would be good to meet. Jewelry heist first. Dory, you start."

"First off, PD I want to officially protest a staff meeting on Saturday morning. I'm already working this afternoon and I need my beauty sleep."

"Sorry, Dory, but we could only have the video conference today and I wanted to get updates from everyone before then."

"Okay. Shortly before Billie Jo went out to meet with Mrs. Cantwell, I learned from a CI of mine that Mrs. Cantwell's necklace is now in the hands of Clint Jay. He's a ferret-faced jewelry fence well known to the Sheriff's Office. He contacted Mr. Cantwell and asked for ten thousand for the necklace."

"Good work. What did you find out, Billie Jo?"

"Thanks to Dory, when I went out to the Cantwell estate I already knew where the necklace was. I wasn't sure it was worth my time to talk to Mrs. Cantwell, but Dory told me to go ahead. She said something might come up about Danny Parrish. I got everything you asked me for, PD. The insurance claim form was faxed to us yesterday. Working on the assumption that it was an inside job, I checked the people who work for the Cantwells. They have several staff, none of whom live on the premises. They have a cook named Hannah Slater, a ladies maid named Valentina, a grounds crew, a professional cleaning service, and a stable boy. Mr. Cantwell has a niece, Justine, who spends quite a bit of time there hanging out with Danny in the stables and a childhood friend named Carl who is supposed to be helping him make money on the racehorses."

"Go on," PD said.

"The night of the fund-raiser, the Cantwell's had a catering service called 'Company's Coming' do the food and wine. Valentina's cousin, Marco Vasquez, works for that catering company. He is fully familiar with the estate as he comes to pick Valentina up often."

"Can we get to the point here, Billie Jo," PD asked.

"Sorry, PD. Just wanted you to have the whole picture. I believe Valentina's Cousin Marco could have stolen the necklace on the night of the party. Mrs. Cantwell must have left it in the powder room. Marco has a bit of a checkered past, including minor theft for which he served a year as a juvenile."

"Is there any connection between Dory's jewelry fence and Marco you could find?" Wayne asked.

"It's tenuous, but I did find that Clint Jay's grandson was in juvie with Marco."

"Good work, Girl," Dory said.

"Now, in order to get a fee for the jewelry exchange, it's critical that one of us handle the transfer, not Mr. Cantwell. Dory, can you get on that?" PD asked.

"Certainly can," Dory said. "I've already told Mr. Cantwell that meeting the jewelry fence could be dangerous. It wouldn't be, of course. Clint Jay is about as hazardous as a six week-old puppy. But I think he will feel relieved having me make the exchange. At some point, we will need to inform the insurance company that the necklace has been found and Mrs. Cantwell will have to recall the claim."

"I'll take care of that after the exchange goes through. Wayne, do you have an update for us on the insurance company embezzlement case?" PD asked.

"With the urgency of the Daniel Parrish matter, I haven't gotten very far," Wayne admitted. "The agency is owned and operated by a man named Penrose. The agency's bookkeeper hasn't returned to work since the theft, which makes me suspicious. I plan to meet with Penrose as soon as we get a break in the Parrish case."

"Let's move to Daniel Parrish then," PD said. "Wayne and I met yesterday with a CI of mine who gave us the name of the bookie Daniel owed money to, it's Lyndon Aces Dockery, and the thugs he uses to collect bad debts are called the Tusk brothers. We're chasing them down, but right now I'd like to take a step back. We don't have a cause of death and the pathologist is still waiting on lab results. I think it would be helpful to talk through the last two days of Daniel Parrish's life. That could pinpoint the time and place of the killing. Neither Wayne nor I believe Danny's death was accidental."

Wayne stood up walked to the whiteboard in front of the room and grabbed a marker. "For those of you who haven't investigated a murder, the single most important tool in understanding what happened is what the victim did and who he talked to on the last day of his life." At this point Wayne paused and made a grid on the board with a column for each of the critical days before Danny Parrish's death.

"I believe the key to this murder is the visit Danny Parris made to the Cantwell estate the day before he died. Although Cantwell says they only talked on the phone, Danny was definitely on-site. His cell phone was found by the stable boy who turned it into the Rosedale Sheriff's Office. Something happened around the time of that phone call that set the crime in motion. Later that evening, Daniel Kidd Parrish was found on the loading dock behind the ER at Vanderbilt hospital. There are six hours between 2:30 and 7:30 p.m. that day unaccounted for."

Saturday	Late afternoon	Evening	Midnight.
	Danny beaten up by Tusk Brothers	Danny goes to local Urgent Care, has broken wrist and cracked ribs	Danny arrives home, tells Tracey about owing the bookie $
Monday	Morning		
	Cara Summerfield gets letter from Tracey		
Tuesday	Cara Summerfield Hires Rosedale PI		
Wednesday	Morning	Afternoon	7:30 p.m.
	Danny talks to Cantwell on phone. Fired from job. Cell phone found by stable boy, Frank	Shows Danny in Nashville stables. His car left there	Danny is found on ER dock. Admitted to hospital
Thursday	Danny in critical care		Danny dies

"We can tie down some of that 5-hour gap. It takes almost two hours to drive from Cantwell's house in Rosedale to the stables on the other side of Nashville." PD said. "The critical hours are from 4:30 to 7:30 that day."

"Danny was already in bad shape from the beating he had been given. Perhaps he heard something in the stables he shouldn't have heard. Or saw something or someone he shouldn't have seen," Dory said.

There was a distinct pause after that while the group digested Dory's idea. In the brief silence, Billie Jo said, "Excuse me…"

Before she could make her point, Dory added, "We know that Cantwell fired Danny that day. I wonder if there was more to him firing Danny than just getting a more senior trainer."

"Pardon me. Could I just add something…?" Billie Jo said but PD talked over her.

"More importantly, we need the Detectives in Nashville to find out who drove Danny to the hospital. Since his car was left at the stables in Nashville, it's somebody from there. The cops can access the CCTV at the hospital's loading dock."

Several people started talking simultaneously before Wayne slammed his hands down hard on the table. Pairs of startled eyes looked at his furious glare.

"When I started with this firm, I agreed to us using a cooperative approach. I was a bit reluctant as all of you know, but that is what we all agreed to. Yet already we have violated that agreement. Billie Jo, our youngest colleague, has been trying to add to the conversation about this case for several minutes and has been talked over."

Silence greeted his remark.

"Go ahead, Billie Jo," PD said. "Sorry to ignore you."

"Me too, Honey," Dory said.

"I am well aware that all of you know more about this type of investigation than I do. Maybe I should just keep my mouth shut," she said, coloring.

"Go ahead now. You have the floor," Wayne said, nodding at her.

"I just think it's all about the *horse*," Billie Jo said, tipping her head to one side.

"So, the horse is what? A person of interest? A prime suspect?" Dory said chuckling.

"Here we go, another far-out theory from the peanut gallery," PD looked amused.

Wayne gave both PD and Dory cold looks before turning back to Billie Jo. "What about the horse?" he asked.

"Danny really loved Boyd's Boy and if somebody had planned to do something to the stallion, tried to drug or injure him maybe, Danny would have gone ballistic. And if there was a second fight, maybe with another trainer or jockey, it could have left Danny in bad enough shape that he died from his injuries in the hospital." Billie Jo's blush deepened.

"Well done," Wayne said. "We always say that the motives for murder are love, loathing and lucre. I'd personally dismissed the love motive—this isn't a sex crime—but Billie Jo has just reminded us that love isn't always between people. Love of animals can be a pretty powerful motivator too, for good or for evil."

"Dammit. This just looked so easy in the beginning," PD said shaking his head. "Daniel Parrish owed money to the bookie, Lyndon Aces Dockery. Dockery had him beaten up. Danny died in the hospital. I thought Nashville PD would have an arrest in hours. I'm beginning to think now that this is a far more complicated crime than it looked originally."

"And if we think of the big three that point to a killer, we always look for *means, motive and opportunity*. In our theory of the crime, we have to consider more that more than one person could have had a motive," Dory added.

"Or possibly we are looking at more than one crime," Wayne said, thoughtfully.

"Okay. That's it for now, people. Don't forget we have that video conference with the Nashville Detectives this afternoon. It's being transmitted to the Sheriff's Office," PD said and the small group left the conference room.

TWENTY-ONE

A YOUNG WOMAN was standing partially behind the television in the conference room of the Sheriff's Office when PD arrived. She was in profile to him, connecting cables to the back of the TV set. He didn't know her and assumed it was someone who worked for the Sheriff or that Billie Jo asked for help to make sure the internet connections were working. The girl was wearing narrow black trousers, a shell pink blouse and a black jacket. He was surprised by the shoes, as he didn't think pink high-top sneakers were usually worn with professional outfits, but then he wasn't exactly an expert on women's fashion.

"Excuse me, Miss. I'm Detective Pascoe, have you got everything working?"

The girl turned toward him. To his astonishment, it was Billie Jo.

"Not necessary to introduce yourself to me, old man," she said grinning.

"My God, Billie Jo. I didn't recognize you," he said, almost stuttering. "You must have changed your clothes since this morning. You were wearing sweats then."

"It's my consummate fashion consulting skill," Dory said, entering the room. "Billie Jo and I went shopping last night. What do you think?"

"You look great," Wayne said as he entered the room. "Nice job, Partner." He smiled to himself. Dory always needed someone to boss around and in this new office, Billie Jo was clearly going to be the recipient of her ministrations.

Billie Jo looked a tad embarrassed at all the attention. "I'm still getting used to it. My skater-chick style has sort of gone out the window. Dory says I can still dress like I used to, *unless I'm meeting with clients,* but I do feel the need to assert my personal style just a bit. Thus the sneakers," she said grinning.

"We bought five outfits last night and I had a friend cut her hair and do her make-up," Dory said.

"She's getting me all fancied up so I can meet a boyfriend who can afford my taste in music," Billie Jo smiled and took a slight bow to mild clapping.

Just then, Sheriff Ben Bradley entered the room. He was wearing his uniform and looked very official. "Hello all. Dory, that coffee smells delicious," he said.

"Morning, Cousin," Billie Jo said to Ben.

"Cousin," he returned, nodding. "Nice outfit by the way."

"Thanks for having the video conference here, Sheriff. Detectives Stoneman and D'Angelo insisted on it taking place at your Office. Their Captain wants any collaboration to be between police posts," PD said.

The group heard the phone dialing and saw the picture come and go on the television before the reception cleared and they could see Detectives Stoneman and D'Angelo sitting in the conference room in Nashville.

"Good afternoon, Detectives," Sheriff Bradley said. "Thank you for agreeing to this video conference. Around the table, I have Investigator Dory Clarkson, Detective Wayne Nichols, Detective PD Pascoe, Billie Jo Bradley and myself. Can you see and hear us?"

Detective D'Angelo gave the group a thumbs up.

"What do you know?" Wayne asked, thinking of all the times the Sheriff had asked him that same question when they worked crimes together.

"First off, Captain Crawley has agreed to a limited investigation into the *beating* Danny received. It's assault and we have had several reports of threats and intimidation, as well as another assault locally, all connected to the racetrack," Stoneman said.

"The Captain also gave us permission to visit the Parrish's, Danny's adoptive parents. They needed to be informed of his death and it was obvious they were devastated," D'Angelo said.

"They were on a cruise when he died and had not been in close touch with their son. They usually only saw him at Thanksgiving, Christmas and the mother's birthday. The mother feels terribly guilty that they pretty much cut off contact with the boy when he started working as a horse trainer," Stoneman added.

"I also talked with Danny's girlfriend, Tracey. She called Danny on the day before he died," D'Angelo said, looking directly at Dory. He was *willing* her to keep her mouth shut about them interviewing Tracey together. "Tracey said Danny sounded on the verge of tears. She was a bit worried he might even harm himself."

"What was the content of their conversation?" PD asked.

"Options for paying back what Danny owed the bookie. He planned to talk to the new trainer, James Walters, to see if he needed help with any of Cantwell's other horses or those from his previous stable."

"What do you have from your end?" Stoneman asked.

"We have the names of the muscle that work for

the bookie, Lyndon Aces Dockery. They are called the Tusk brothers. The last name is Tuskegee, but they go by Tusk. They cover a lot of territory but according to one of my CI's they're here in the Rosedale area for a few days. We're hoping to catch up with them later today," PD said.

"I talked to Cantwell yesterday and his stable boy, Frank Stephenson. Frank was the person who brought Danny's cell phone to the Sheriff's Office," Wayne said. "He noticed the phone sitting on the gatepost for the stallion's box and thought he should give it to law enforcement."

"Did the kid's wallet ever turn up?" Stoneman asked.

"Likely the Tusks took it, and what little money Danny had on him. We'll check," PD said.

"Let's summarize where we are," Sheriff Bradley said. "We have the bookie, Lyndon Aces Dockery. He had motive; Danny owed him serious money. Since he lives here, I'm going to have my people pick him up and bring him in for questioning. Then there's the gap in the timeline when we know Danny was in Nashville before he arrived at the hospital. Tracey called him there and his car was left there. I'm assuming you two, Stoneman and D'Angelo, will follow up and find out who took the boy to the hospital? Can you also put some more pressure on your pathologist? We need that cause of death."

"One other thing," Wayne said. "Billie Jo wondered about the role of the stallion, Boyd's Boy, in this crime. She suggested Danny could have discovered something the trainer was doing, or planning to do to the horse which could have sent him into a rage, resulting in a second fight."

Billie Jo raised her hand. "I'm afraid you're all going

to think I'm crazy, but I'd also like to know if there was a horse in the former stable of the new trainer who is a contender for a shot at the Derby."

"Where'd you get this one, Pascoe?" Stoneman said. "She has the right instincts. We had the same thought and you're right, Billie Jo. There's a horse in Walters' former stable he's been training since he was a colt. He's called Easy Money and is considered to be the horse most likely to challenge Boyd's Boy for a shot at the Derby. We even wondered if Walters, or the Syndicate, could be trying to control which horses qualify for the big race." Eyebrows were raised at this. The Derby was a near-sacred event in the entire country.

The group broke up then. Dory was leaving to meet with Clint Jay to get Mrs. Cantwell's necklace. Despite her protests that it was a *Saturday afternoon,* Billie Jo had been ordered to source deep background on the trainer, James Walters, including financials and cell phone data. PD and Wayne left in search of the Tusk brothers.

It was late afternoon when Wayne Nichols and PD Pascoe located the thugs employed by the bookie, Lyndon Aces Dockery, at the Rosedale track. The sun was edging down toward the horizon and the horses were being brought in and bedded down for the night. Stable boys were delivering their food and water.

"No need to be nervous, guys," PD said as they spotted the Tusk Brothers. "You're the Tusk brothers right? Mike and Rick? We just have a couple of questions for you."

The two men looked at each other. They were obviously related, having nearly identical broad Eastern

European faces, heavy-lidded blue eyes and muscular bodies. They glanced at each other, suspicious and sullen. Just looking at them, Wayne could tell they had no ability to feel empathy for anyone other than themselves. You couldn't be a thug and feel for the person you were hurting.

"Aren't you Wayne Nichols? Thought you were a cop," Mike said, looking directly at Wayne.

Wayne sighed, once more feeling the loss of his former identity. "Retired now," he said shortly and gave PD a go-ahead look.

"We know you work for Dockery, the bookie, but as I said we're not interested in getting in the way you make a living," PD said. "Can we buy you a drink? Sun's over the yardarm."

The foursome walked across the street from the track to a small pub that catered to jockeys, trainers and owners. They chose a booth and ordered beers. The waitress carried over the brews and asked whether they wanted to order food. Nobody did.

"As I said, we have a couple of questions. Last week there was a kid named Daniel Kidd Parrish your boss wanted you to talk to, right?" PD asked. "He died in the hospital a couple of days after your encounter with him."

There was no response from the Tusk brothers who were downing their beers in silence.

Finally, Mike said, "Yeah, Dockery asked us to pay him a visit. It was just a warning. Young guys can get into real trouble with gambling. We wanted to let him know he was getting into deep waters and should knock off the betting."

"Do you hear that, Wayne?" PD asked, giving him

an amused look. "These guys aren't thugs after all, they are a couple of social workers. Just trying to help a kid kick a gambling addiction. Pillars of society with a conscience. I can practically see them in flowered dresses, straw hats and purses." He gave the Tusk brothers an evil grin.

"A couple of real sweethearts," Wayne said, but his eyes were narrowed and his gaze was tight with anger.

"We know you damaged Parrish's wrist, broke a couple of his ribs and gave him a week to get Dockery his dough. Now that's against the law, as you know, but we aren't interested in the beat-down. It's not our business. However, Sheriff Ben Bradley here in Rosedale and two detectives in Nashville are looking into the death of Daniel Parrish," PD said.

"He didn't die, he was *murdered*," Wayne added, feeling the hot tightness he got in his chest around the lowest of criminals, the ones who took the lives of the young.

"Parrish was walking just fine when we left him," Rick told them.

"Couple of specialists, I'd say. They know exactly when to quit, don't you?" PD said with raised eyebrows, glancing at Wayne.

"Mr. Dockery fires guys who end up going too far. I'm telling you; it wasn't us," Mike said insistently. "We went pretty light on him."

"Did you take his wallet?" PD asked.

"Standard operating procedure. He only had a couple of hundred dollars. We turned it in to Dockery that afternoon."

Thinking about what it took to bring a man to make a living by beating up other people, Wayne envisioned the brothers as little boys. If they had been disciplined for some childhood offense, he could just see Rick running from the kitchen up to the attic, sitting there with his back to the wall brooding—envisioning the pain he wished he could deal out. Mike looked like he might have fought back, even against his parents. Wayne had attended a police seminar once and learned by their estimate that fifteen percent of the U.S. population were considered to be sociopaths, people totally lacking in empathy. These two fit the profile. Had they lived in a war zone, they would be torturers.

"Thanks for the information," PD said and shook hands good-bye. Wayne didn't offer to shake.

As the two men reached the parking lot, Wayne said, "Doesn't sound like that beating was the cause of death. It happened on Saturday night and the kid didn't die until the following Thursday."

"Unless there was a second beating, I'm beginning to think Billie Jo is right. We need to figure out how all this relates to the damn horse."

TWENTY-TWO

LEAVING THE SHERIFF'S OFFICE after the video conference, Dory drove to the Rosedale Community Park. The autumn light slanted through the yellowing leaves on the trees as she made her way to the bandstand. She was thinking about how to handle the exchange when she spotted the skinny, pimpled man she was meeting. Clint Jay wasn't looking good. His skin was blotchy and he was very thin. His ginger-colored hair had been cut short. The color had been one of the hallmarks of his appearance, but now white hairs were heavily interspersed with the red. She suspected he was using drugs again.

"How's it going, Clint?" Dory asked, walking up to him.

"Keep your voice down," he said sharply, looking around.

"Have you got the necklace with you?" Dory asked. She lowered her voice although it seemed silly to her. The park was deserted. Clint Jay was in one of his paranoid phases.

Clint nodded.

"Have you got the money?" Clint reached for Dory's purse but she pulled it out of his reach.

"Hang on there, Buddy, I'm not giving you a dime without seeing the goods."

"Follow me," Clint said looking around to see if anyone was watching them and led the way past the mowed area of the park into a brushy area nearby. Once they were standing behind a scrim of shrubs, he pulled the necklace from the pocket of his dirty jeans. "Here it is."

The sun hit the gold and rubies and Dory felt a pang of jealousy for the wealthy woman who owned this treasure. The gold setting encasing the stones was elaborate and the rubies were rounded cabochons. Dory knew enough to be certain the necklace was absolutely authentic, probably around a century old. She took it in her hand, feeling its coolness.

"I only have eight thousand with me," she said. She actually had twelve thousand, but wanted to lessen the hit if he would take less. She could add the remainder to the coffers of Rosedale Investigations and it would give Clint Jay less to use for drugs. "Okay?"

Clint nodded and Dory opened her wallet and counted out they money. "You didn't steal it, did you?"

"Not telling you. You're a cop."

"Actually I'm not with the Sheriff's Office now, so you can tell me," Dory said.

"Once a copper, always a copper," he said. "Won't tell you how I got it, but you know I don't steal stuff."

"Except when you were a kid," Dory said, coolly. She knew Clint Jay's juvenile record by heart.

"Long time ago, almost a different life. When the necklace was brought to me, I thought about having a jeweler melt it down, but he said it would be a real crime. Too old, he said, too beautiful." Dory and Clint exchanged a quiet look, acknowledging the point. Then Clint took the bills and melted into the brush.

TWENTY MINUTES LATER, Dory walked into her favorite jewelry emporium called Sundance. It was located in a storefront on the main Rosedale square.

"Afternoon, Betty," she said as she entered the store. She and Betty were old friends, having close family connections in the black community.

"Dory, I haven't seen you in ages, how have you been, Girl?" the proprietor said, smiling and giving her a hug. She was wearing a short gray tent dress and was absolutely bedecked with jewelry. She wore a big necklace, giant gold earrings and diamond rings on virtually all of her fingers.

"It's been a while, that's for sure. I have a necklace you're going to love to see," Dory said pulling the piece from her purse.

"Wow, is that ever something," Betty's eyes widened. "Looks antique. It's obviously 22K gold. I can tell from the color. Is it Russian?"

"I think so. What do you think of the rubies?"

"Fabulous. Not even heat-treated is my guess. That's how they bring out the color in gemstones these days. Most of the time what's left in the mines is pretty poor quality and heating enhances the color. That's why the labs are starting to create gems from scratch. Probably better for the earth, although I miss the days of high-quality mined gemstones. How did you come upon this treasure?"

"It was stolen recently, and I brokered a deal that will return it to the owner. Just thought I'd come by and get it polished and buy a nice case for it." She handed the necklace to Betty who turned to fire up the professional ultrasonic cleaning machine. While the necklace was bombarded with soundwaves, Betty opened several drawers behind the counter before coming up with a black velvet case. Inside there was a white satin lining with a raised oval for the necklace. Once in the case, it would be presented beautifully.

"What do I owe you, Betty?" Dory asked as the woman placed the bright gold and ruby jewelry inside the case and closed it reverently.

"Nothing, Kiddo. You buy things here all the time and we black folk need to stick together. Don't charge my good customers the same as the local riff-raff," Betty grinned. "I was going to ask if you had seen your Aunt Delphine recently."

"It's been a couple of months, why do you ask?"

"She was in the store a week or two ago and had her grandson Tyrel with her. Good looking kid. He's going to UT, a business major apparently with a music minor of all things. Delphine wondered if I might have a job for him. I figured I could put on more staff. He's going to start arranging stock ahead of the Christmas season. She said she wished he'd get a girlfriend, bad breakup last year and the boy has yet to rejoin the social swirl. Just wondered if you knew anybody for the kid."

"Thanks for the info, Betty. I'll get over to see Delphine soon," Dory said and carrying the black velvet jewelry case as if it were the Holy Grail, left the store. *A well-educated, good looking African American boy, heir to a family business, with a music minor,* she thought. *Just needs a girlfriend—maybe one who likes opera.* She found herself humming the "Pretty Woman" song, remembering the Julia Roberts and Richard Gere classic movie.

AN HOUR LATER, having presented the necklace to a very appreciative Mr. and Mrs. Austin Cantwell, and saying Rosedale Investigations would send them a bill for their services, Dory called Billie Jo.

"How's the profile on James Walters coming along?" she asked.

"Funny thing, there's lots of stuff about this guy for about five years back. He trained horses in Santa Anita and Del Mar, California before moving to Nashville. He works closely with this one particular jockey. Looked jubilant in the shots at the end of the races putting the rose blankets on the winning horses, including Easy Money."

"What about earlier?" Dory asked, and deciding she just had time to go visit her aunt Delphine, flicked on her turn signal. She swung her car around toward Nashville.

"Nothing. Not a thing. It's baffling. Starting to wonder if I'm losing my touch. It's like until five years ago this guy didn't even exist. No social security number, no bank accounts, not even an address. I'll keep looking, but it's pretty much a dead end for now."

"Tell Wayne about that. He might have some ideas. What are you wearing, by the way?"

Dory heard Billie Jo's embarrassed voice say, "I changed back into sweats. Don't worry. Nobody came in."

"Go upstairs and get yourself fancied up, Girl. I might just return to the office with the opera swain."

TWENTY-THREE

Monday

THE PENROSE INSURANCE AGENCY was located in a newly-developed commercial area of Rosedale that had been a family farm in previous decades. The developer had constructed three office buildings scattered across the hilly site. All the buildings were one-story structures with white clapboard-siding and red roofs. Wayne called to set up the appointment and on arrival was greeted by the man's receptionist.

"Mr. Penrose will be with your shortly," the woman said and asked if he wanted coffee. He did. Penrose himself walked into the waiting area moments later. Wayne took a long look at the man who was in his fifties. He had a receding hairline, but looked very fit.

"Mr. Nichols?" Penrose asked, holding out his hand.

"Is there somewhere private we can talk?" Wayne asked as they shook hands and Penrose led him down the hall to a nicely-appointed conference room. Around the room were a gallery of framed pictures of the agency in all its earlier incarnations. The old black and white pictures showed the businesses which had been headed by Penrose's father and grandfather. "It's a family concern, I assume?" Wayne asked.

"Fifty years we've been in the insurance business," Penrose said with a proud smile. "I'm the third generation and have two children, so I'm hoping there will be a fourth. Have a seat."

Wayne pulled out his notebook and said, "Mr. Penrose, I understand your agency has been embezzled to the tune of nearly half a million dollars. That's major crime and I'm wondering why you would hire a private detective agency, rather than going to the police?"

Mr. Penrose looked slightly embarrassed. "It's because I know who took the money and if we can arrange to have it returned, I don't want that person to face criminal prosecution."

"I see. Who was it?"

"My bookkeeper, Miss Geraldine Gerard."

"How long has Miss Gerard worked for you?"

"About three years."

"What evidence do you have for her being implicated?" Wayne asked, writing her name in his notebook.

"Wasn't hard. I traced the movement of the money from my office account to hers. Rosedale Citizens Bank was very helpful, but I didn't really need them, I knew she took it."

Wayne frowned. "This sounds personal to me. What was the nature of your relationship with Miss Gerard?"

"As I said, she was the office bookkeeper."

Wayne looked critically at Penrose who shifted in his chair and tapped his pen against his lower lip. The man was lying. "Mr. Penrose, you are a terrible liar. No bank is going to tell you about the movement of money from your account to another without a subpoena. How long had you been sleeping with Miss Gerard?"

Penrose flushed, but managed to say, "About six months. I ended it recently. It was complete madness. I must have been out of my mind. I really love my wife.

We have just learned that she has breast cancer. She's now undergoing radiation," he cleared his throat. "I couldn't be an unfaithful husband given that situation."

"But you could cheat on her *before* her diagnosis," Wayne said dryly and Penrose looked ashamed. "Had you promised to divorce your wife and marry Miss Gerard?" Penrose hesitated but then nodded. "I see, and when you reneged on that promise, she decided to make you pay. Are you willing to make a financial settlement on your former girlfriend?"

"Yes, but *not* from office monies. I am also willing to give her an excellent reference, provided she returns the money and agrees to get another job, preferably not in Rosedale."

It was obvious to Wayne that Mr. Penrose had thought a lot about how to resolve the issue. He'd probably talked with the woman and made her an offer. She hadn't accepted the amount they discussed though, or he wouldn't have called Rosedale Investigations. Wayne would have some negotiating to do. "I'll need her contact details and a photograph."

Penrose opened his desk drawer and pulled out a silver framed photo. The good-looking woman had been photographed in front of a background of hills and trees. She was smiling and the wind had blown her hair back from her face. "I presume you have told Miss Gerard about your wife's diagnosis? And that you love the woman you married and gave you children," Wayne said, raising his eyebrows.

Arthur Penrose nodded, coloring.

"I'll handle things from now on. Do not contact Miss Gerard again. Rosedale Investigations will send you a bill once the agency's money is returned and she is paid.

And, if you don't mind a little advice, Penrose, don't *ever* do anything that stupid again."

"Believe me, I won't," Penrose said.

Walking out to the parking lot Wayne thought about fidelity. He and Lucy hadn't discussed it, but he would never cheat on her. *I still can't believe I've been lucky enough to have her in my life.*

AN HOUR LATER, former Detective Wayne Nichols walked into the Rosedale Sheriff's Office trying to look nonchalant, but feeling his stomach tighten. He was still having trouble adjusting to his new role and the investigation into Danny Parrish's murder wasn't helping. He felt naked without the privileges he had enjoyed for decades as an officer of the law.

The Sheriff's Office receptionist and dispatcher, the oddly-named Mrs. Coffin, was on the phone clearly trying to put off the caller. She nodded at Wayne and rolled her expressive eyes.

"Yes, Mrs. Dubois, if you insist, we will send a Deputy out. Usually, escaped kittens climb trees and the fire department comes to get them. They have the long ladders you know," she said. There was a brief pause in the conversation and Wayne could hear the volume of the caller's voice rise in frustration. "Of course, the Sheriff's Office is responsive to residents who have lost animals. I'll get someone out this afternoon if the Fire Department is unable to help. Please call me back if the kitten reappears, will you? Yes, Thank you for calling," she hung up the phone in exasperation. "Good Morning, Detective."

"Mrs. Coffin," Wayne said, nodding. "Just wondering if Ben is interviewing Lyndon Aces Dockery, the bookie. If so, I would like to observe."

"He is. George brought him in first thing. Surprised he was up to it at eight o'clock. He's not exactly a morning person. There's fresh coffee in the break room and donuts. If you're seeing Dory later, I got her a separate bag of blueberry."

"I'll make sure she gets it," Wayne said and made his way down the hall, remembering all the days he and Ben had worked crimes together. He passed his former office and noted Under Sheriff, Rob Fuller's nameplate on his old desk. He felt a brief pinch of resentment.

Continuing down the hall he spotted George in his office on the computer. He was in uniform, his pudgy belly hanging over the belt of his brown uniform pants. His hat was on the desk, together with a bulging sack lunch, an apple and a cooling cup of coffee. Deputy George had a look of complete concentration on his round face. He was facing the computer screen with one finger touching his mouse.

"Morning, George," Wayne said and the Deputy quickly shut down the solitaire game he was playing. "Hear you got to bring in a bad guy this morning. Lyndon Aces Dockery was it? How did that go?"

"No problem. He said he was happy to help the law. His business is registered here in Rosedale and he lives in that new subdivision called Pine Knoll. Ben is talking to him now. He said you might come by."

Wayne nodded, and George walked with him to the observation area outside the interview room. George flipped on the audio switch and Wayne could hear Sheriff Bradley say, "I wanted to let you know that my office and two Nashville Detectives are looking into the death of Daniel Kidd Parrish. He was one of your clients, I believe?" The Sheriff's blue eyes had turned steely.

"As you know, Sheriff, I run a legal business," Mr. Dockery said.

"Legal in Tennessee, I believe. Kentucky's legal gambling bill is still working its way through the system. I asked you if Daniel Parrish was a client."

"Yes. He was and before you ask, I am aware that he passed away recently. A shame for such a young man."

Butter wouldn't melt in that mouth, Wayne thought.

"Passed away?" Ben's voice hardened. "*Passed away*? The kid was murdered. And we are well aware that you sent the Tusk brothers to pay Parrish a visit a couple of days before he died. That's suspicious in my book."

Mr. Dockery squirmed slightly at the mention of the Tusk brothers, but rallied quickly. "Yes, I did. Parrish owed me some money. The Tusk boys were going to help Mr. Parrish work out a payment plan."

Ben snorted. "We know the Tusks boys sprained Parrish's wrist, busted two ribs and bruised him badly enough that he went to the Urgent Care for treatment." He focused a hard glare on Dockery who shifted in his seat.

"Parrish went home that night alive and well and showed up on Monday morning at the track. He didn't die until Thursday. It wasn't because of my men." Watching from behind the one-way view window, Wayne knew it was time for the Sheriff to turn up the heat.

"Daniel Parrish did indeed live through the beat down on Saturday night and was alive on the subsequent Wednesday morning when he went to meet with his boss, Austin Cantwell, and found out he had been fired. He was being replaced by a new trainer, James Walters, and that put you in a really bad position didn't it? At that point, Parrish had no prospects. He was a fired ex-trainer who was deeply in debt. I'm thinking you got your arm-breakers to make a second visit to the kid, before he appeared on the loading dock of the ER at Vanderbilt. He died the following day, and you just became our prime suspect in his murder," Ben's voice was rock hard.

"No. You've got that wrong, Sheriff," Dockery was starting to sweat. Wayne could see the sheen on his forehead. "I have no past involving violent crimes. No record of assault, or GBH. And I would never kill any-one!"

"Perhaps you are unaware, Mr. Dockery, of the stat-ute covering Conspiracy to Murder? You would only have to give the order to be convicted. You could have kept your hands nice and clean and still go down for it. And the Tusk brothers wouldn't have had to kill Par-rish then, just beat him badly enough that he died later. The Pathologist is doing more studies to determine if there was evidence of a second beating on Parrish's body," Ben sat back in his chair, calmly watching the effect of his words.

WHEN LYNDON ACES DOCKERY left the office, Ben joined Wayne in the break room. The Sheriff munched gloom-ily on one of Dory's blueberry donuts.

"Too bad you didn't have enough to arrest the bas-tard," Wayne said.

"I only had circumstantial evidence," Ben's mouth quirked in irritation.

"Good idea about a second beating. Maybe they gave him a head injury. A nice slow subdural hematoma. Something like that would have caused the boy's death."

"Listen to you with the *subdural hematoma* vocabulary," Ben grinned.

"Hanging around with an ER doc will do that for a man," Wayne said.

"Unfortunately, the post-mortem didn't show any head injury," Ben said. "What do you and PD think at this point?"

"Without any evidence of a second beating, our current theory of the crime is that James Walters, Austin Cantwell's new trainer, is involved somehow. Billie Jo is doing a complete background. Have the Nashville detectives called about the CCTV at Vanderbilt?"

"Yes, they already have it. Going to take a while to go through it, but they caught a break yesterday. They interviewed the Nashville stable boy whose name is Harris Stephenson. He admitted to taking Parrish to the ER. They asked him why he left Parrish on the dock, rather than take him in and get him registered. The kid said just as they reached the loading area, he got a call from the stable. Boyd's Boy had been delivered to the track earlier and was playing up. Other than Parrish, Harris is apparently the only person who can settle the animal. Daniel Parrish told Harris to leave him and take care of the horse. He must have passed out just after that."

"Okay, but what happened to get Parrish sufficiently messed up that he needed to go to the ER in the first place?" Wayne asked

"Ah, the trenchant question. That's exactly what the Nashville Detectives are planning to elicit this afternoon. Their forensics people went over everything in the stable. They think something was added to Danny's coffee mug. It's distinctive, showing a picture of Danny and Boyd's Boy. My guess is that he was doped with Rohypnol."

"That will narrow it down."

"Only if there are fingerprints on the cup beside Danny's and they match somebody in the system," Ben said, gloomily.

TWENTY-FOUR

WHILE WAYNE NICHOLS was commiserating with Sheriff Ben Bradley, Dory was handling the jewelry exchange and Billie Jo was searching for information on Cantwell's new trainer, Cara Summerfield was making a serious effort to mend fences with her husband. She had slipped from bed early, leaned across and kissed Grant on the forehead.

"Breakfast in twenty minutes," she murmured. Walking into the bathroom, she ran a brush through her hair, touched her wrists with perfume, applied her peony-colored lipstick to her mouth and put on a fresh white Spa robe. Checking her appearance in the mirror, she nodded at her image and walked down the hall into the kitchen.

Twenty minutes later, Cara opened the oven door and withdrew a half dozen large lemon muffins. They were just crisp on top and the scent was lovely. She placed the hot muffin pan on the granite countertop and sprinkled powdered sugar on the tops. While the muffins were baking, she had sliced red peppers, onions and diced cheese to make omelets. The omelets were sizzling in the frying pan and the coffee maker was guiding the lovely scent of hot coffee down the hall toward the bedroom when she called her husband saying breakfast would be ready in five minutes.

Cara stepped out onto their rear porch and picked a

cluster of white autumn anemones growing beside the steps. They were sweet little flowers with yellow petals and green centers. Putting the flowers into a silver vase and adding blue dishes and silverware to the table, she called her husband to the table.

Grant came into the kitchen freshly showered, looking very smart in his charcoal suit, a pink shirt and a tie that said "Just Vote."

She walked across the kitchen, gave him a quick kiss and said, "This is such a big day for you. Couldn't send my man out into the world to storm the castles with an empty tummy." She grinned, gesturing to the table.

"Thanks, Honey," he said. "I woke up this morning with a good feeling. I'm making the official announcement that I'm running for District Representative from the steps of the courthouse. The staff at my campaign office have managed to arrange press coverage. A small group of well-wishers and a bunch of high schoolers will be passing out buttons and little American flags. It's going to be at 3:00 today."

"I'll be there with bells on. I bought a new pink dress, cute shoes, a silver gray jacket in case the weather cools and I'll be bringing your staff boutonnieres. Blue carnations for the girls and pink for the boys. Decided people would be more likely to notice if I switched the usual blue for boys, pink for girls thing."

"Thanks, I really appreciate your support. I was up late last night preparing the speech to announce my candidacy. I'm going to focus on jobs, more support for public education and some changes I hope to make to TennCare. It's designed to provide health care insurance to low income children, pregnant women, low-income parents of minor children, the elderly and people with disabilities, but there are some glitches in getting people covered, especially children with pre-existing conditions," Grant's face was glowing. Cara felt his passion and her love for him bloomed. He continued talking about infrastructure, bridges and roads that needed repair. He said he had thought quite a while about his closing shot. "I deplore the partisanship between the parties and so I've decided my final words will be *Vote for me, my fellow Tennesseans, I'm more about potholes than politics.*"

After breakfast, as Grant was heading out the door to the garage, Cara stopped him. "You aren't still upset with me, are you? About me going to see my friend's poor son?"

"Can we talk more about this once the announcement is made and the campaign is officially underway?" he asked and clicked the garage door opener. At that moment, her husband of twenty years turned toward her and seeing the confused, almost betrayed look on his face, Cara knew it was time for the truth to emerge.

"I'll tell you the whole story soon," she said and took a slow shivering breath.

"Promise?" he asked, looking at her with a winsome expression, his face tilted.

"Promise," she said and watched him get into his car. She had loved Grant for so many years. He deserved the truth. *So why haven't you told him in twenty years?* Her conscience asked.

WATCHING HER HUSBAND's car pull out of the driveway, Cara grabbed her purse from the kitchen desk and pulled out the pieces of paper Billie Jo had given her. Seeing Rafe Marston's name on the top slip, she sud-

denly recalled a day from the year she and Rafe had
been a couple. They had absconded from school with
their packed lunches and a blanket Cara had wadded
up in her backpack.

*It was a bright blue October day and a light breeze
was blowing; golden leaves fell through the air and skittered across the parking lot. They met up behind the
school and ran—hunched down below the level of the
windows. Laughing they made it to the student parking lot unseen. Rafe had an old red clunker of a car.
They drove to a local woodland park and walked down
the path with splashes of sunlight falling on the grass,
hand in hand.*

"Should I call Rafe?" she whispered to herself. "No.
It wouldn't be fair." She looked again at the slips of
paper, dismissed the idea of calling the Parrish's for the
time being and dialed Tracey's number at work.

"A Hair Affair," the woman's voice said. "Make an
appointment. We can make you beautiful."

"Is Tracey there?" Cara asked and heard the woman's
voice call, "Trace, phone for you."

"Hello?" Tracey's voice was low and husky—no
doubt from the tears she had shed—and Cara's heart
went out to her.

"Tracey, this is Danny's mother," Cara said realizing
she had never called herself that before.

"Mrs. Parrish?" Tracey asked. "It doesn't sound like
you."

"No, I'm Cara Summerfield, Danny's birth mother,
and I wonder if we could talk." Before the girl could
end the call, citing the pressing needs of her job, she
said, "I want to know Danny, to see him through your

eyes. I need to understand the dear person I know he must have been."

Tracey cleared her throat and Cara knew the girl was trying not to cry. "I can take a break in about twenty minutes. Give me your phone number and I'll call you back."

Cara used the time to get dressed for Grant's announcement. She put on her pink dress, slanted-sole pink heels (her husband really needed the female vote) and was searching for earrings and repairing her make-up when the phone rang.

"Tracey, hello. Thank you for calling me back. Tell me about Danny, will you?"

"He was such a great guy, Mrs. Summerfield, smart, cheerful, kind, dedicated to the horses, and he loved me." Cara could hear the girl swallow. "He really loved me and I loved him…beyond all reason."

They talked about Danny for over half an hour, both of them crying from time to time before Tracey said, "I'd like to have a funeral for him. Could you help me with that?"

Cara hesitated a long time before she said, "I don't know anybody in Nashville that I could ask to perform the service. Do you?"

"No, I'm not a church-goer but Danny was a very spiritual person. Could you arrange a funeral if the service is in Rosedale?" Tracey asked.

There was a long silence before Cara was stunned to hear herself say, "I'll see if they will do a private service here at the Congregational Church in Rosedale."

"Thank you. I'd like the Parrish's and Danny's father to be there. I don't think they ever met. Danny's adoptive parents told him his father left before he was born, but I'd like to meet him and tell him about his son."

"Please call the Parrish's and make sure it's okay with them that we do this, will you? As far as Danny's biological father is concerned, I know how to reach him," Cara said and looked down at Rafe Marston's contact details.

"I have something important to tell you when we meet in person," Tracey said softly. "Good-bye Mrs. Summerfield."

TWENTY-FIVE

Monday

A THOROUGHLY DISCOURAGED and disgruntled cohort assembled in the conference room at Rosedale Investigations for the morning staff meeting. The weather had clouded up and rain was smattering against the office windows. Long rumbles of thunder could be heard in the distance and the trees outside thrashed in the wind.

"Morning everyone. We are going to see the CCTV footage of when Danny was dropped off at Vanderbilt today. Before then, I wanted to review where we are with the case. We are positive he was murdered, but the Nashville PD is still waiting for the pathologist to give them a cause of death before they will investigate. Until then, they are only looking into the assault and we already know the beat-down didn't cause Danny's death. We are also hampered by the fact that Danny died in Nashville and without their willingness to work together, we can't get access to the people and information we need," PD said, sounding frustrated.

"Jurisdiction problems," Billie Jo said, nodding sagely.

"Plus, we are not the cops and can only investigate on behalf of our client, Cara Summerfield. I was thinking of dropping the whole thing, but there's something about this case that reminds me of an old one of mine that wasn't solved for a decade. Bottom line, I'm not ready to give up," PD said. He rubbed his hands over his face, seeming older than he had just the previous day.

"Neither am I," Wayne said. "I feel in my gut that Danny was murdered. I'd like to run through our suspects again. Maybe we have missed something." Solving a murder was always harder once the first days had passed. He wondered if he was past it, too old to see the solution. It was fear of failure that always drove him, beyond his fatigue—and past his fears—to track the killer and bring him to ground. *Would his last case be his first failure since he came to Rosedale?*

"I'll write the suspects on the board," Billie Jo offered. She stood up and walked over to the whiteboard holding the marker in her hand. She was wearing a blue shirtwaist dress but noticing a frown on Dory's face, Wayne glanced at her footwear. To his surprise it was a totally appropriate pair of black flats. He looked again and grinned. The girl had bejeweled her belt. She obviously wasn't willing to give up every aspect of her former style. Wayne was starting to get a kick out of the kid's persistence.

"Our first suspect has to be Cara Summerfield," PD said. Dory protested and Billie Jo shook her head, but at his insistence reluctantly wrote her name.

"Justification?" Wayne asked.

"Cara Summerfield's husband Grant is running for political office. She never told him about her son. She could have killed Danny to prevent the likely destruction of her marriage. And let's not forget that Danny's girlfriend, Tracey, was pressuring Mrs. Summerfield for money. That request could easily have turned into blackmail."

The ugly word hung for a moment in the quiet air.

The rain hit the windows and the wind moaned around the house.

"Add the bookie, Lyndon Aces Dockery and his muscle, the Tusk brothers," PD said and they could hear the scratching noise the marker made on the board as Billie Jo wrote. "If Dockery ordered a *second* beating after Danny survived the first, it could have been the cause of his death."

"Austin Cantwell," Wayne said. "He fired Danny at his most desperate and may have ordered someone to kill him. I doubt he would get his hands dirty. I can't quite pin down why I sense he's involved, except to say that I got that itchy feeling around him. We know Cantwell recently hired a new trainer, James Walters, and Billie Jo can't find any background on him prior to the last five years. He likely has access to drugs, all trainers treat horse ailments, and some of those drugs are powerful."

"Write both names," Dory said and Billie Jo did so.

"This investigation would be a helluva lot easier if Dr. Llewelyn Jones gave us a cause of death. Coffee, anyone?" Seeing Wayne and PD nod, Dory walked over to the sideboard and turned on the coffee machine. She was starting to realize she was the only person in the office who made coffee. That would have to stop.

"Danny's girlfriend, Tracey Dimond," Wayne said.

"Wayne," Dory whirled around, "No! Do *not* write that, Billie Jo. Tracey was devastated about losing Danny. And she was at work during the day when he ended up at the hospital. I don't want her name listed."

"Okay, okay," Wayne said as Billie Jo grabbed the eraser. "Just want to include everyone. We're supposed to be brainstorming here."

"I had an idea," Billie Jo said, and this time all three of her colleagues turned toward her. "You remember when you said Danny was probably injured or doped *before* he showed up at the hospital?"

Wayne nodded, looking intently at Billie Jo. He had always respected female intuition and often relied on it in the past. And the kid had an off-beat and interesting mind. "Go on," he said.

"The pathologist said someone could have given Danny pills or a shot and her idea made me wonder if something happened to Danny not *before* but *while* he was in the hospital."

All three listeners' eyes narrowed.

"Interesting thought. If Billie Jo is right and Parrish was killed in the hospital, we need to look closely at anyone who has a medical background," Dory said.

At that moment, the group could hear the phone ringing at Billie Jo's desk. "I'll get it," she said and put down the marker.

Walking over to the whiteboard, Wayne put numbers before the names. "At present, we are considering six suspects. 1. Cara Summerfield, 2. Lyndon Aces Dockery, (the Bookie), 3. Rick and Mike—aka Frick & Frack—our Tusk brothers, 4. Austin Cantwell, and 5. Walter James, the new trainer."

"It's James Walters, not Walter James," Dory said.

"Right you are," he paused. "My God, Dory, you're a genius. You just gave me an idea. When Billie Jo comes back, I'm going to ask her to look up Walter James instead of James Walters. Possibly he transposed his name for some reason."

"We need to do more checking on the other patients in the hospital the day Danny died, just to be sure that someone else wasn't the intended victim," Dory said as Billie Jo came back into the room.

"Who was it on the phone," PD asked.

"It was Detective Stoneman. They have agreed to show us the CCTV from when Danny was dumped behind Vanderbilt. It's going to be available at the Sheriff's Office. We need to get going."

AN HOUR LATER, after everyone had gathered in the Sheriff's Office conference room, Billie Jo walked over to the television set and flicked it on. The video wavered and then steadied. They could see two men walking up to the rear of the ER from the parking lot. The shorter man was practically carrying the taller man who leaned on him heavily. He seemed only partially-conscious.

"That's Danny Parrish who is leaning on the other guy," Dory said.

"And that looks like Frank Stephenson who is helping him," Wayne said.

"No, I think that's his brother Harris. Harris is the one who works in Nashville," Billie Jo said.

They could see Harris virtually carrying Danny to the rear ER door which slid open and then closed again. The boy set Danny down and he sagged against the wall. Then Harris pulled his phone from his pocket, answered a call and said something to Danny who waved him away.

"Damn it, I wish CCTV had an audio track," PD said, as the video continued.

They could see Harris leaving and Danny slumping over on the loading dock. The video flicked off and Stoneman and D'Angelo's faces appeared.

"There's more on the CCTV but nothing happens

for about an hour before the nurse appears," D'Angelo said. "She checks Danny's breathing, runs back inside and returns with two orderlies and a gurney."

Wayne felt the first rush of success. He was invigorated by the data on the CCTV. They knew who had taken Danny to the hospital. It was Harris Stephenson. And Harris must have seen something or heard something. Now all he had to do was question him, although that might be the most difficult thing of all.

"We are sending a deputy out to bring Harris Stephenson into the office for questioning. We want to know who called him and why that call was sufficiently urgent that he left Parrish on the dock without even checking him into the ER," Stoneman said.

"Have you learned anything else?" PD asked.

"Forensics discovered traces of Rohypnol in Danny's coffee cup at the stable in Nashville. The drug was probably intended to render him unconscious, although we don't know why. We'll be back in touch after interviewing Stephenson," Stoneman said and the television went black.

"I'm beginning to think we're not going to solve this one looking at suspects," PD said in a thoughtful tone. "We think the *opportunity* to kill Danny was before or possibly during Danny's hospitalization—thanks to Billie Jo—but we lack the *motive*."

Wayne nodded. It was always motive that most intrigued him, the 'why' that could cause a person to take another's life. Despite decades working as a homicide cop, violent death still surprised and saddened him, especially when a young person was the victim.

"I agree," Sheriff Bradley added. "Motive is our big missing piece. I'm wondering what happened during the period of time between Daniel Parrish drinking the Rohypnol-doped coffee and Harris taking him to the hospital."

"Rohypnol, that's the date rape drug, right?" Billie Jo asked. "It wipes out memory, doesn't it?"

"Yes, it causes both anterograde and retrograde amnesia, which means if Daniel Parrish survived his hospital stay, he wouldn't have remembered a thing that happened at the track that day," Sheriff Bradley said.

"Somebody was making damn sure that Daniel Parrish *couldn't* remember what happened," PD added.

"Which leads me to think that Billie Jo has been right all along. This crime is about both Danny and his horse, and Harris Stephenson is going to lead us to Danny's killer," Wayne added and Billie Jo gave him a grateful smile.

TWENTY-SIX

SHERIFF BEN BRADLEY took Wayne aside as the meeting broke up saying he had something he needed to talk with him about urgently and in private. He asked Wayne to meet him at a nearby hole-in-the-wall Vietnamese restaurant located on the way to Nashville, as soon as possible. He had to run to his house first to get a change of clothes. He was staying overnight in Nashville, the Sheriff said, leaving Wayne completely perplexed.

Walking into the place, filled with the scent of garlic and hot oil, Wayne spotted his friend sitting in a booth at the back. He raised his arm in a wave, but taking a second look, he noticed Ben's distraught expression. As he walked up he asked, "What's wrong?"

"The babies are sick. They both have pneumonia," Ben bit his lip. "They have been admitted to the Children's Hospital in Nashville. Mae is already there, she's waiting for me. They are so little, it's just killing me to see them like this. Baby Joy was starting to pull herself up to a standing position and little Noelle was crawling all over the house. But this morning all they could do was lie listlessly in their cribs. Mae took them to the doctor who made the diagnosis and had them admitted."

"Get on the road, my friend," Wayne said. "Go now."

"I am going, but there is something we have to do first. The Daniel Parrish investigation is not progressing, and I'm getting pressure from Detective Stoneman to drop it. Because of my personal situation, I am tempted, but it's not right. Something happened here in Rosedale, I can sense it."

Wayne nodded. "Agreed. So what do you want to do?"

"I've decided to grant you authority to head the investigation on behalf of the Sheriff's Office while I'm on family leave—just until the babies are discharged."

"Do I get my badge and gun back?" Wayne asked. The day he handed them to the Sheriff he felt a dissolution of selfhood.

"You certainly do," Ben said and Wayne felt a surge of relief.

"Do you have them with you?"

"No. Both your weapon and your badge are in the safe in my office. Mrs. Coffin knows the combination. I'll text her and tell her to give them to you."

"What about Rob? Isn't he going to resent this?" Young Detective Rob Fuller had been made Under Sheriff while Ben was on his honeymoon and would certainly begrudge Wayne being put in charge of the murder investigation.

"I already told him. He was none too happy, but knows he has little to no experience investigating homicides. When I told him about the babies being in the hospital, he fell on his sword and said he would stand aside for you," Ben swallowed, looking at his watch.

"He's a good guy. It couldn't have been easy for him."

"It wasn't," Ben said. His pager rang and he said, "I have to go."

"Keep Lucy and me up to date will you? And if Mae

has any questions, Lucy will want to help. In fact, I'm sure she would come to the hospital."

"Thank her," Ben said. "But Mae's whole family are already there. I'll have Mae call Lucy," and grabbing his uniform jacket, Sheriff Ben Bradley hightailed it out of the smoky little restaurant.

SINCE CHILDREN'S HOSPITAL had a fine reputation, Wayne trusted that Ben's baby daughters would be well enough to return home in a few days. It didn't give him much time to find Daniel Parrish's killer. Mentally switching gears, he wondered if the Sheriff had taken the time to phone Det. Stoneman and D'Angelo to tell them his decision to make Wayne the lead Detective in the case. If not, it was going to be an uphill struggle to stay involved. He experienced a moment of paralyzing doubt. Maybe it was time to let someone else take the point position. Maybe he should let this one go. Wayne tapped his finger on the table as he considered the voice in his head. A waiter, misunderstanding the signal, came over.

"What do you want to drink, sir?" the young Asian man asked.

"Just water," Wayne said curtly and the waiter disappeared.

No, damn it, I can't let it go. A young man has been murdered and it's been long enough since he died that Stoneman and D'Angelo will be pressured to put the case on the back burner. Plus without a cause of death, they haven't even investigated the murder, only the assault. It's down to me. I have to find Danny's killer.

He took a deep breath and dialed Detective Stoneman's number.

"Stoneman," the Nashville Detective answered.

"It's Detective Nichols," Wayne responded. "I just met with Sheriff Bradley. He's going on family leave due to illness. I've returned to working for the Sheriff's Office. He told me you want us to relinquish the Parrish investigation—to turn it over to you."

"That's right. The kid lived here, died here, and we've already picked up Harris Stephenson. We're planning on charging him with intent to distribute drugs and possibly murder, if we can get enough out of him during the interrogation."

"Harris Stephenson?" Wayne tried to keep the incredulous note out of his voice. "What would his motive possibly be? Don't forget it was Harris who took Danny to the ER."

"We found out there's a single CCTV camera at the Cantwell stables in Nashville. Harris admitted to catching a glimpse of someone doctoring Parrish's coffee," Stoneman said and a note of weary finality entered his voice. "You know what that means, I assume. It's like the teen-age girl who lies to her mother saying one of her *friends* is having sex with her boyfriend and needs birth control, when she's the one who is having sex. Harris Stephenson is our guy. He just isn't admitting it yet."

"Then he knows who you *should* be talking to," Wayne said. "I'm telling you, Stoneman, Harris isn't your man. He doesn't even have a record! We checked. If you and D'Angelo arrest him for a capital crime, you're going to look like complete blockheads." He clicked off his cell phone and rage owned him. Walking out of the restaurant, he dialed Dory's cell.

"What are you doing?" he asked.

"Shopping with Billie Jo," she said cheerfully.

"God dammit, Dory. Things have changed. Stoneman and your little conquest D'Angelo are trying to cut us out of the Parrish investigation. Mae and Ben's twins are in the hospital and he's turfed the investigation to me. I'm back working for the Sheriff. The numbskulls in Nashville are about to arrest Harris Stephenson. We have work to do."

"Arrest Harris Stephenson? Whatever for?"

"For distributing drugs and assault."

"Unlikely, the kid had never been in trouble. Did you say that Mae and Ben's twins are sick?" Dory asked.

"Yes. Ben is a mess. I'm sure Mae is too. Stoneman and D'Angelo only have circumstantial evidence on Stephenson, but he admitting seeing someone adding something to Parrish's coffee. Unfortunately, he didn't give them this information when they first talked to him, only after they threatened to bring him in for questioning. Withholding that information puts him in a bad light."

Silence greeted this remark before Dory added, "Little nincompoop. What do you want to do?"

"You and Billie Jo need to meet me at the office now."

"She's in the dressing room, trying on a purple dress to wear to the opera. I'm not sure it's the right dress," Dory said, but Wayne knew she was going to give in.

"Just buy the damn dress and meet me at the office." Wayne clicked off the phone.

He then dialed PD who answered promptly saying, "Pascoe speaking."

"PD, I just got a call from Stoneman. They're planning to arrest Harris Stephenson, the stable boy in Nashville. Apparently he saw someone adding something to Danny's coffee cup. And further, they want us to butt out."

"Oh they do, do they?" PD's voice was deep and gravelly. "Fat chance. Mrs. Summerfield hired us to find her son. Since then she's added to her original charge wanting to know who caused his death. Did you tell them to go to hell?"

"Pretty much. We need to meet at the office and put together a plan. What are you doing by the way?"

"I was on my way to the dentist, but I'll happily cancel. They said I had to have a root canal! Even the words make me sick to my stomach. See you at the office," he said cheerily and the phone clicked off.

TWENTY-SEVEN

CARA SUMMERFIELD WAS trembling after saying good-bye to Tracey. She tried to control her rapid breathing and reached for a drink of water. "Whatever made you agree to arrange a funeral here in Rosedale?" She asked herself, as the small sarcastic voice in her mind said, *Could it have been your better self?*

Standing in her kitchen, Cara opened the cabinet door above her phone and consulted the list of frequently dialed numbers. Taking a deep breath, she dialed.

"Congregational Church, Mrs. Moffit speaking"

"Hello, Mrs. Moffit, it's Cara Summerfield calling."

"How can I help you, Mrs. Summerfield?"

"I am calling to ask for a favor. Would Reverend Andrews be willing to conduct a funeral for a person not a member of the church? It's for a young man who died unexpectedly. He was…family. His girlfriend asked me to arrange it."

"I'll have to ask, but she will usually conduct services for family of people who are members of our church. Just let me check the schedule," Mrs. Moffit said. A few moments later she returned to the phone and asked, "Would Friday work? In the early afternoon?"

"Yes," Cara said. She was still shaky, but knew having the ceremony was the right thing to do. "That will work perfectly. Let's say 1:30?"

"I'll put it on her schedule. However, Reverend always wants to meet with the guardians or parents before such a service, to learn more about the person. When could you come by?"

She's assuming I'm his parent, Cara thought and felt a little curl of happiness. "I'll come over tomorrow morning, if she has time to see me."

"She can see you at 10:00," Mrs. Moffit said. "Was there anything else?"

"No, but thank you, Mrs. Moffit," Cara said and ended the call.

Grant didn't arrive home until past midnight. All afternoon and evening Cara thought she was ready to tell him about Danny, but when he came inside looking exhausted and shattered, she decided to wait.

Just one more day, she told herself.

You have been telling yourself that for decades, her conscience responded. *When are you going to act?*

CARA ARRIVED AT the Congregational Church a ten o'clock. It was a small stone church with a tall spire. The building was unremarkable from the outside except for the carefully done split-stone work but the interior was perfectly proportioned and the fragile stained glass windows had recently been cleaned. When the sun shone, it threw blue, green and red splashes of color down on the stone floors that echoed as Cara's high heels clicked toward the altar. Entering the first pew, she bowed her head and prayed for a few moments, asking for the courage to confess to Grant. When she lifted her face, Reverend Sara Andrews was standing by the altar. She wore black trousers and a black shirt with the usual white clerical collar.

"Hello, Mrs. Summerfield. Let's go to my office," she said and Cara followed, dreading the disclosure she had to make.

Once in the Reverend's quiet office, with a cup of hot tea in her hands, Cara told her minister everything.

"Now that you know the whole story, do you feel right about doing a funeral?" Cara asked.

"Of course I do. Our ministry is for the support and comfort for all, we are an inclusive faith community. In fact, the Congregational Church/United Church of Christ is one of the most welcoming and affirming of Christian denominations. We celebrate same-sex marriages and ordain LCGTQ ministers. The only question I had was whether you had spoken to Danny's adoptive parents about the ceremony?"

"Danny's girlfriend, Tracey, is taking care of that. It's going to be a very small group, probably just his adoptive parents, hopefully his biological father and Tracey, in addition to me. He and Tracey weren't married, but I am certain Danny would have married her in time. Call it a mother's intuition," she said and managed a small smile.

"Would you like a traditional service?" Reverend Sara asked.

"That would be lovely," Cara said.

"I'd like to speak with Tracey before the service, can I have her phone number?" Reverend Andrews said.

"Certainly, that's a good idea," Cara said and held out her phone so the Reverend could enter the number into her contacts.

"Everything that you told me today—the fact that Danny was your birth son, that you didn't tell Grant about your pregnancy before you married, or that Danny would have married Tracey in due time, does any of it have to be kept confidential?" the Reverend asked with a slightly worried look.

"No, it doesn't matter now," Cara said, feeling the walls falling all around her. "I intend to tell Grant everything before the funeral."

"Then I will emphasize forgiveness in my remarks in the hope he can forgive you," Reverend Andrews said.

"As do I," Cara said and getting up to leave, was pleased when Reverend Andrews hugged her.

Nonetheless, she felt the hours she had left before her marriage came to an explosive termination were counting down—like the hours chiming in a tall clock—the secrets from decades ago were walking out of darkness into the unfeeling sunlight.

DRIVING FROM THE church to the grocery store, Cara dialed Tracey. There was no answer, so she left a message saying the funeral would be held on Friday at 1:30. She asked if Tracey had anyone to drive with to come to Rosedale. "It's over an hour's drive, Tracey, and it's going to be very emotional for you. I think it would be best to have someone come with you. Please call me back so I know you got the message." She quickly added the address of the church to her message and clicked the call off.

Tracey called back as Cara was putting her groceries away.

"Mrs. Summerfield, it's Tracey," she said.

"Thank you for calling. Can you come to my house before the funeral?"

"Yes, I'll ask for the week-end off. Thank you for arranging it."

"Did you contact Mr. & Mrs. Parrish?"

"Yes, they have planned a Memorial service in Nashville a month from now that will include all Danny's friends from the track. I told them you were planning a service in Rosedale and they said they would come. I just have to call them with the time and date. Did you get ahold of Danny's father?" she asked.

"Not yet, but I will, Tracey. As I said in my message, I'm a bit worried about your driving here by yourself. It's such a hard time for both of us. Can you have a friend come with you?"

"No. I'll come alone. I have to get used to it now... Being alone."

"You are so young, Tracey. It's going to take a while, but I don't see you alone for the rest of your life," Cara said. She hoped her voice sounded hopeful, and not like she was telling the girl what to do.

"I will not be alone, but there will be no other man in my life. Not for decades," Tracey said.

"What makes you say that, Tracey?"

"Do you remember me saying I had something else to tell you when we talked before?"

"I do," Cara said, putting the last of the fresh fruit and vegetables in the refrigerator drawer.

"I'm pregnant, Mrs. Summerfield. And no other man is going to raise Danny's child. No one but me." Her small voice sounded so determined, Cara felt her heart breaking.

"Oh, Tracey, how will you manage? Can you even afford to stay in your apartment?"

"I don't know, but I will figure something out. The baby is the one thing Danny left me. I will not fail him," she said and Cara heard a sad good-bye.

AT DINNERTIME, GRANT CALLED. He wasn't going to be home until late. "Don't wait up for me, Cara. I'm just exhausted and need to get right on the computer as soon as I arrive," he said.

"How are things going?" Cara asked.

"My opponent for the race has pulled out the big guns. He's trying to poach my staff and is offering lots more money. So far nobody has defected, but I fear it's only a matter of time. I have another 16 hour day tomorrow. Lots more before it's all over."

When Grant ended the call, Cara took the slip of paper with Rafe's contact information and before she could think of another way to stall, dialed his number.

"Hello," the strong male voice answered and Cara knew him instantly. She hesitated, trying to find her equilibrium.

"Hello? Is anyone on the line?" Rafe asked.

"Rafe, it's Cara Kidd, your high school girlfriend."

There was silence at the other end until at last Rafe said, "I've been dreaming that you would contact me." His voice was so warm, Cara's breath caught in her throat.

"It's been a long time," Cara managed. She was holding on to her kitchen counter so tightly that her fingers had turned white.

"More than twenty-six years," he said. "Why now, Cara?"

"I presume you married, did you?" she asked.

"Married and divorced," he said, shortly. "Did you marry?"

"Yes, I married Grant Summerfield over twenty years ago."

"Has he made you happy?" His voice was gentle.

"Yes, we've had a wonderful marriage, but I have a tragic thing to tell you, Rafe. You probably need to sit down." She heard the sound of a chair being pulled out. "Are you ready?"

"I am," he said. "Go ahead."

"Do you remember moving away before your senior year?"

"Of course," he said, sounding frustrated. "That's when we broke up. I tried everything to contact you, Cara. I must have written you a hundred letters. Every time I called, your father said you were out. We didn't have email or Facebook then and you never responded to a single one of my letters. You obviously stopped loving me, but I never did," he sounded utterly miserable.

"I never knew," she said feeling tears sting her eyes. "My father must have destroyed your letters. I never saw any of them. I just thought you didn't care that much about me."

"Didn't care that much… How can you say that? My God, I was so in love with you. Sometimes I think I never stopped loving you."

"Oh, Rafe," she swallowed. "This is so hard for me to tell you." She hesitated for some moments, cleared her throat and said, "I was pregnant when you left. I had a baby boy," she managed through her tears.

"I have a son? Oh, Cara that's just wonderful news. You have no idea how wonderful. I have no other children."

"It's not wonderful, Rafe. It's not wonderful at all because our son died a week ago. I am so, so sorry," she said.

She heard nothing but harsh, broken sobs at his end before a bitter voice came back on the line. "Never call me again. You have destroyed what was left of my life," he said.

"Rafe, no," she wailed in anguish. When the line clicked off, Cara put her face down on her kitchen island and sobbed inconsolably.

AN HOUR LATER, she picked up the phone and called Rafe again, knowing he wouldn't answer, but feeling the need to tell him about the ceremony, she left a message.

"Danny's funeral is going to be Friday at 1:30, at the Congregational Church in Rosedale. Come and say good-bye to our son. I never knew him either because he was adopted at birth, but there will be people there that knew him, his adoptive parents and his girlfriend. Please Rafe, please come. I want you standing beside me."

Late that night, slipping into bed, Cara wondered if she should have told Rafe about Tracey being pregnant. *A baby might help him. A baby might help us both*, she thought.

That night she dreamed she was standing a totally white room. It had white walls, a white ceiling and a white floor from which tendrils of mist curled upwards. She stood opposite Grant. She had told him about Danny and he was furious. His face was thunderous, suffused with rage.

"I want nothing further to do with you," he said. "I'm moving out and we're getting a divorce, campaign or no campaign." Then her husband's image blurred and he turned into Rafe.

"You gave away our only son," he said.

Suddenly the walls of the room dissolved and all three of them were standing outdoors in a snow-drenched pine forest. Rafe and Grant faced each other—old honorable combatants—like male elk squaring off to fight each other for the female they both desired.

Rafe spoke. "She didn't deprive you of your son, you bastard. That baby was mine. You got to be married to Cara and I lost her a long time ago. I'm the one that has a right to be angry. You have nothing to forgive," he said.

"She kept a secret from me for twenty years," Grant said. "She never trusted me enough to tell me about her son."

The snow swirled around them and Cara stepped forward to stand between the two men. She stood with her red-mittened palms resting on their chests and could feel their hearts beating.

"We have a grandchild coming," she told them. "We must live for what tomorrow will bring, not for what yesterday took away."

Her eyes snapped open. The dream, and the coming baby, had made her stronger. For the first time in decades, Cara Summerfield felt she was going to be able to survive the coming confrontation with Grant.

TWENTY-EIGHT

Tuesday

WHEN THE ROSEDALE INVESTIGATIONS team assembled at the office that afternoon, Wayne reminded them that it had already been a week since Cara Summerfield hired Rosedale PI to find her son's killer. They had all been working practically around the clock and hadn't unearthed a single solid suspect.

As everyone took their seats at the table, Wayne said, "I wanted you all to know that Sheriff Ben Bradley is on family leave. He's dealing with the illness of his baby daughters. They are at the Children's Hospital in Nashville. Because he feels strongly Daniel Parrish was murdered and that his killer will be found here in Rosedale, he had reinstated me as a Detective for the Sheriff's Office. This means I now have the power to detain and arrest a suspect. However, I can't and won't bring people in for interrogation on a hunch. We need evidence."

The team was quiet for a few moments before PD said, "The one thing we didn't get back to at our last meeting was motive. Without a compelling motive, or a murder weapon, we're no further along than Stoneman and D'Angelo who aren't even investigating. Let's review our suspects again, this time looking at motive."

"I don't see that Cara Summerfield has a motive. She

was heartbroken to learn about Danny's death," Dory said. "I'd like to see her eliminated."

"Agreed," PD said and Wayne nodded. Billie Jo erased her name from the board.

"I think Lyndon Aces Dockery, the Bookie, and the Tusk brothers can be eliminated as well," PD said. "With Danny dead, they couldn't possibly collect the money he owed them and according to the pathologist there was no second assault."

Billie Jo erased the names. "And none of us think that young Harris Stephenson had a motive to want Danny dead. Plus he doesn't have a record."

"Which leaves James Walters, Cantwell's new trainer, as the person who could have motive. We know he wanted his horse, Easy Money, to win the Derby. With Danny gone, he might be able to ensure that outcome by doping or injuring Boyd's Boy. I'm troubled by the fact that the man changed stables at this precise time. I'd like to know how Austin Cantwell lured him away from a horse he'd raised from a colt and a stable he'd been with for years. We need to know more about the man," Wayne said. "When you're doing your background check, Billie Jo, be sure to also check under the transposed name, Walter James."

"I will be back on the computer ASAP," Billie Jo said.

"Wayne, you just talked to the Nashville detectives on the phone. Fill everyone in on what you learned, will you?" PD asked.

"Stoneman and D'Angelo are planning to arrest Harris Stephenson, the stable boy from Nashville for drug distribution, assault, and murder. He's the older brother of Frank, the stable boy here in Rosedale. Harris told them he saw someone dope Danny's coffee mug, but the Detectives believe he was the one who did it. They hope to break him in interrogation," Wayne shook his head.

Dory shook her head murmuring, "Those idiots," under her breath.

"We have to find something we can use to spring Harris Stephenson from jail." PD said. "That will be the only way we can talk to him."

"I've been thinking if Harris confided in anyone, it's likely to be his younger brother. I'd like to question Frank to see what he knows. I can have one of our Deputies pick him up tomorrow, but I don't want to wait around," Wayne said. "I'm going to try to locate him today."

"Need a partner for this mission?" Dory asked.

"Oh, I sure do," Wayne said, smiling.

"Harris Stephenson is going to need a good lawyer. I'll stay here with Billie Jo and work on that," PD said.

"Who were you thinking of?" Wayne asked.

"What do you think of Levi Stevenson?" PD asked.

"Also known as *Loop-hole Levi*?" Dory said, narrowing her eyes. "He hasn't got a great reputation."

PD frowned and said, "I'll keep looking."

DORY AND WAYNE arrived at the Cantwell stables just as the sun went down in a flare of gold and red. They had checked every other possibility before going to the stables, including Frank's apartment, his parents' place, his grandmother's home and all the local eateries. They parked behind the stables, out of sight of the Cantwell home.

"He might have left the stables already," Dory said as they exited the car.

"Man, I hope not," Wayne said as the twosome slipped around the back corner of the stable and found the exterior office door. Dory peeked in through the window.

"Office is empty," she said and tried the door. It was unlocked and they walked in. On the other side of the office, an interior door opened to the long row of horse boxes. When Dory opened it silently, they could hear the clip clop of a horse's hoofs as a stallion was being brought inside from the paddock to a loose box. Whoever was bedding him down talked to the animal in a low sing-song voice. They could hear a soft swishing sound as someone groomed him.

"I'll see if it's Frank," Wayne whispered. "See what you can find in these office records." He walked soundlessly down the cement path between the horse boxes. One horse whinnied suddenly at the scent of a newcomer.

Frank's voice called out, "Who's there?"

"It's Wayne Nichols," he said in a low voice that carried well in the large open space. "I'm here because I want to get your brother released."

Frank opened the gate of the horsebox and looked up at Wayne.

"Can you really help him? I haven't told our parents about Harris being in trouble yet." He tilted his baseball cap back on his head and rubbed his forehead.

"Are you finished for the night?" Wayne asked. He wanted to get the kid out of the Cantwell stables as soon as possible. "My partner and I want to talk to you in private."

"One more horse to go. I can do him quickly. Where are you parked?"

"In back of the barn. It's a pick-up truck. Come out as soon as you can."

Frank nodded and moved to bed down the final horse.

WHEN WAYNE WALKED back to the stable office, Dory's face wore a triumphant smile.

"I found the payroll records *and* both boys' job applications. Took pictures of everything on my phone. Frank's only sixteen, apparently dropped out of school. He lists his brother as his contact person and here's the best part. Harris is also underage. He doesn't turn eighteen for three months. If they interviewed him without a parent present, Stoneman and D'Angelo are screwed."

"Excellent work, Partner. Well done. Frank is joining us in the truck shortly. Where do you want to take him that we can talk privately?"

"My house. He's got to be scared and my place is homey enough to reassure him."

"Good plan."

Ten minutes later Frank Stephenson emerged from the back door of the barn, locked up and walked across the parking lot. The floodlights on the eaves of the barn gave him a long shadow.

Wayne rolled his window down. "Hop in the truck, Frank. This is Miss Dory, my partner. We're taking you to her house so we can make a plan to get your brother out of jail."

"Are you hungry, son?" Dory asked when Frank got in the back seat of the truck. He nodded. "I believe I can do something about that while you and Wayne talk. I know what young black men like to eat." Her smile was radiant in the darkened cab of the truck.

On the drive to her house, Dory kept up a constant stream of questions—asking Frank about each of the horses, his family and what plans he had for the future. Wayne found himself smiling, knowing Dory's gentle technique had been known to sooth even armed sociopaths holding people hostage. He glanced in his rear view window from time to time seeing Frank's tight shoulders begin to come down.

Once inside Dory's small comfy home, she asked Frank what he would like to drink.

"Do you have Coke, or Pepsi, Miss Dory?"

"I sure do, son. Now you just have a seat here and talk to Wayne. He looks sort of crabby, but he's actually a marshmallow. Crusty on the outside, soft and melty inside."

Wayne cast her an irritated glance which she ignored.

Frank sat down on Dory's flowered couch and Wayne took a seat in a nearby chair, saying, "First off, I need to confirm your brother's exact age."

"He's seventeen, won't be eighteen for another couple of months," Frank said.

"Good to know. Now, I've never had a brother, but if I had one, I'd tell him everything. I wonder if that's the case with the two of you…"

WAYNE'S VOICE TRAILED off as Dory walked into the kitchen. It was separated from the living room by a Dutch door. Her dog was kept in the kitchen during the day, minimizing damage to the rest of her house. True was a chewer and Dory had already lost the upholstery on the seat of a chair in the living room as well as an expensive pair of leather boots to her sharp little canine teeth.

"You can go outside now, True," she said opening the back door and releasing the desperate animal. While the dog did her business in the backyard, Dory thought about what to feed Frank Stephenson. She knew the African Oldways diet and opened her spice cabinet seeing curries, peppers, coconut, dried herbs, garlic and onions. All of these spices were low-sodium ways to add flavor to grains, beans, vegetables, and meats. Opening her refrigerator's vegetable drawer she spotted okra, cabbage, green beans and eggplant. Above the veggies, she spotted a refrigerator dish of left-over Jambalaya rice flavored with beans and hot peppers. In the cheese and meat drawer was a lean beefsteak.

Hearing her dog scratching to come in, Dory opened the back door. Once True was in the kitchen, Dory opened her treat canister. "Sit," she said and the pup obediently sat, although not for long. She was a busy little thing. "You're just like me, aren't you," Dory said and bending down to pet the dog, suddenly realized that she still was wearing her office clothes, an expensive navy suit she had just purchased. No way was she cooking dinner in a suit.

However, getting to her bedroom would require walking through the living room and Dory didn't want to disturb Wayne's efforts to elicit information from Frank. She quickly opened her apron drawer and donned a white bib apron. Turning on her cooktop, she added some vegetable oil to a frying pan. When it sizzled, she seared the beef on both sides before turning down the flame. She started dicing the vegetables.

Fifteen minutes later she called Wayne and Frank to the table. She had decided to serve them in her eat-in kitchen, since it was cozier than her formal dining room. She clicked on her favorite blues radio station. She had set the table with her yellow and red Fiesta ware, dishes. The scent of the good food, the colors of the dishware and the music coming from the radio were all intentional, ways to help the boy relax and feel at home. When the men walked in, Dory handed Frank a Pepsi and told him to take a seat.

"This is nice," Frank said smiling at the table and Dory felt her efforts had all been worthwhile. "Oh, I see you have a dog. What's her name? Can I pet her?"

"She would love it. Her name is True. I named her that because working as an Investigator is all about finding the truth. She's the determinedly friendly type," Dory said and the boy got down on the floor to play with the dog before rejoining them at the table.

"I take it you've figured out a way to spring Frank's brother," Dory said.

"It was your lead that got us there, Dory. After I confirmed his age with Frank here, I called Stoneman and D'Angelo. They were horrified to find out that Harris was only seventeen. They kept blaming each other for not checking and finally agreed to let him go first thing tomorrow. They hadn't actually arrested Harris, he was just being held overnight, so there won't be anything on his record," Wayne said.

"I'm grateful I won't have to tell my mom," the boy said, shoveling food into his mouth.

"What else did our hungry guest help you with?" Dory asked Wayne. Sometimes she thought interrogation only consisted of listening and saying "what else" enough times that the suspect finally told them what they needed to know. Frank wasn't a suspect, of course, but it worked on everyone.

"Frank said his brother, Harris, saw someone dope Danny Parrish's coffee cup at the Nashville stables. During the interrogation, Stoneman and D'Angelo showed Harris the CCTV tape from the stable. They were trying to get him to confess that he was the one who doped the coffee. He continued to insist on his innocence."

"When Harris called me after it happened, he said the person who doped Danny's coffee was very small," Frank said.

"Sounds like a jockey to me," Dory said.

"Sound like a suspect to me," Wayne added.

TWENTY-NINE

Wednesday

IN AN EFFORT to repair his fractured relationship with Detectives Stoneman and D'Angelo, Wayne placed a phone call the next morning.

"Hello, Detective Stoneman, it's Wayne Nichols," he said.

"Hello," Stoneman responded gruffly. "When you told us Harris Stephenson was a minor we had to release him because we interviewed him without a parent present," he said and Wayne could tell Stoneman felt resentful that they had learned the kid's age from him.

"No choice," Wayne said. "We talked last night with Frank, Harris Stephenson's brother. He works at the Cantwell stables here in Rosedale. Didn't get anything you didn't already know," he said, although he was pretty sure there was more to get from both Stephenson brothers.

"We looked at the CCTV from the Cantwell stables in Nashville and it looks to us like the person who doped Danny's coffee might have been a jockey. Pretty small to be anyone else," Stoneman said.

"Harris told his brother the same thing," Wayne said. "Trouble is we don't know if the jockey came from the stables in Rosedale, or your stables there. I also wanted you to know I've been reinstated as a Detective with the Sheriff's Office. Sheriff Bradley is away on family sick leave."

"I presume you aren't on salary in two places. I could arrest you for that," Stoneman said sternly.

"Detective Pascoe officially removed me from the payroll at Rosedale Investigations yesterday. It would be helpful if you guys would talk to the jockeys at your end," Wayne said. He was trying hard to be gracious even though if he had free rein to both locations, he knew he could crack this one without them. Still, there was a grain of truth in what he said. Having both teams of detectives talking to the jockeys would be a better use of time.

"We'll start working through the jockeys here at this end. There are only two that ride for Cantwell. Shouldn't take long," Det. Stoneman said.

"It might be worth your while to talk to the jockeys who ride for James Walters' previous stables too, especially any jockey that rides the horse named Easy Money. He's apparently the number-two-rated stallion."

"This damn case," Stoneman said in a depressed tone. "We're getting pressure to make an arrest and having to release Harris Stephenson this morning wasn't making my Chief happy, but you're right, we'll talk to all of them."

"We'll talk to the jockey here. His name is Jordan Dane. It's unlikely Dane was the doping perp since he's Boyd's Boy's jockey, but we'll talk to him anyway. And I wanted you to know that Harris Stephenson agreed to come to Rosedale today. We will see if we can get anything more out of him. I'll call you later today with what we learn."

"I'm sure you won't learn anything more," Stoneman said abruptly and hung up.

Wayne looked down at his hands. They were clenched. *Condescending sod*, he thought. He knew full well when cases lacked a clear leader they often deteriorated into testosterone-fueled verbal slugging matches, but he couldn't help it. He would be damned if he would tell Stoneman another thing now, no matter what they learned.

SEVENTEEN YEAR-OLD Harris Stephenson arrived at the offices of Rosedale Investigations by early afternoon. Billie Jo brought him into the conference room. Dory had asked his younger brother, Frank, to be there. The two brothers were clearly happy to see other, hugged and clapped each other's backs.

"This is Miss Dory. She's the one who figured out since you are only seventeen they had to let you go," Frank told his brother.

"Thank you so much, Miss Dory," Harris said. "Glad to be out in the fresh air this morning."

"Nice to meet you, Harris," Dory said, shaking hands with the boy.

"I'm Detective Nichols and this is Detective Pascoe and our associate, Billie Jo Bradley. We are all hoping you saw or heard something that can help us solve Danny Parrish's murder."

"We know you saw the CCTV tape at the police post in Nashville yesterday. When you saw the person who put the Rohypnol in the coffee cup did you notice anything new?" PD asked. "We assumed from the size of the guy that he could have been a jockey. Was he wearing jockey silks?"

"No. Whoever it was wore a hooded sweatshirt and jeans," Harris said.

Frank frowned at his brother. "You told me there was something funny about the way he ran out of there," he said.

And there it was, Wayne thought. *All of last night's time with the kid has paid off. We can start looking for someone small who has a funny walk.* He glanced at Dory. She gave him a little self-satisfied nod.

"Do you think you could duplicate that walk?" Wayne asked.

Harris Stephenson nodded. "I think so, but it would be easier if I were outside."

The whole team watched from the lawn as Harris Stephenson ran up and down the sidewalk in front of the building that housed Rosedale Investigations. He did it three times before he was satisfied he had duplicated the gait. Walking back inside, Wayne noticed that Billie Jo had a thoughtful frown on her face.

"What did you notice?" Wayne asked.

"He took such small steps," she shook her head in confusion. "Reminds me of something, but right now I can't remember what it was."

Probably only a kid who worked with horses all his life could have been able to duplicate that mincing gait, Wayne thought

TWO HOURS LATER, Wayne and Dory were on their way to the track in Rosedale. Billie Jo had pleaded to go with them, but they declined the pleasure of her company. She hadn't finished doing the background on Walter James (or James Walters) and they needed her fingers on the keyboard. She had, however, found Jordan Dane's phone number and called him. He would meet them there.

"Sounded way too accommodating," Dory said. "I can already tell he isn't the doping perp."

"It was always a long shot, but I wonder what he might know about another jockey with a funny walk," Wayne said.

Jordan Dane was waiting in the stable office when they arrived. He was bandy-legged, about four foot, eleven inches tall and whip-cord thin. Despite his "archer's bow" legs, when he walked toward them he had a normal gait.

"Thank you for seeing us," Wayne said. "This is my partner, Investigator Clarkson. We are looking into the death of Danny Parrish."

A careworn expression crossed the jockey's face. "Danny and I were good friends, compatriots really. Between us, we thought we had a winning thing going with Boyd's Boy. I was furious with Mr. Cantwell for firing him. Almost decided to quit myself in protest, but I couldn't have the stallion lose both the people who cared the most for him. Horses are very sensitive creatures and easily upset when things change," he said.

"I'm not sure if you know, but apparently the day before Danny died, a small person in a hoodie and jeans put Rohypnol in his coffee."

"Wasn't me," Jordan Dan said, shaking his head. "And I don't know any jockey who would do such a thing. It's reprehensible."

"You're right about that," Dory said.

"The guy who doped Danny's coffee had sort of a funny walk. Does that bring anyone to mind for you?"

Wayne looked acutely at the jockey. He felt respect for the small man who had clearly found his niche in life.

"Nobody comes to mind, but I will keep my eyes open and let you know." Just then a bell rang. "Sorry, but the afternoon gallops are starting. Boyd's Boy is running against Easy Money today. I need to get him into position."

"Here's my card and Dory's too. These are our personal cell numbers. If you see anyone, or hear of anyone around the track with a mincing gait, please call," Wayne said.

"Will do," Jordan Dane said and darted off. Watching him from behind, Wayne saw a perfectly ordinary run.

THIRTY

Driving back to the office, Dory got a phone call. After she said, "Hello," she was quiet for a long time before saying, "Thank you for letting us know."

"Who was that?" Wayne asked.

"That was the pathologist, Dr. Llewelyn Jones. We have a cause of death for Danny Parrish."

"Finally," Wayne said in exasperation. "Danny died almost a week ago. It shouldn't have taken this long. So, out with it, Woman. What did he die of?"

"You're not going to like it," Dory said, glancing covertly at Wayne.

"I'm about to stop this car right now and strangle you if you don't tell me," Wayne said taking his eyes off the road briefly and glaring at his partner.

"The death certificate lists it as natural causes."

"What?" Wayne pulled the car abruptly off the road and parked on the shoulder. "Tell me you didn't say what I thought you said. Natural causes?"

"With one caveat. She noted that Danny had received morphine for pain. It was ordered by his doctor. And he had Rohypnol in his system."

"And that was it? No other drugs? No poisons?" Wayne's voice was incredulous.

"Except for the Rohypnol, and the Narcan that was prescribed in the ER to treat the overdose, not another blessed thing," Dory said. "All this angst, all this work!

And the kid died of natural causes. In the notes Dr. Jones wrote that his death was secondary to a beating, but her final conclusion was natural causes."

All the way back to Rosedale Wayne maintained a furious silence. They parked the car and walked inside without exchanging another word.

"PD and Billie Jo, get in here," Wayne called in a thunderous tone as he and Dory walked into the office.

It took the foursome an hour of bitter remarks and multiple threats to do bodily harm to the pathologist before PD wondered if Stoneman and D'Angelo knew the cause of death.

"We have to tell them if Dr. Llewelyn-Jones didn't," he said and seeing nods, dialed the number for the Nashville police post.

"Dr. Jones called us first," Stoneman said when he answered the phone. "Of course our Police Chief, Captain Crawley, is happy, it's one less case to investigate. But I find myself fighting it. It doesn't sit right with me."

"All of us here feel the same way," PD said. "Did you talk to all the jockeys yet?"

"D'Angelo did. None of them even gave him an eye flicker. All of them had iron-clad alibis for the day in question. He even made them run up and down the stables. Not a funky walk in the batch," his voice was clipped.

"Wayne and Dory interviewed Jordan Dane on this end. He didn't dope Parrish's coffee either and didn't know anyone with the walk. Wish we could have at least nailed the doper, but since Parrish is dead, it seems there's no point."

"Looking into this was a total waste of time," Stoneman said bitterly. "Wish I'd never listened to your guys." He rang off.

"All that is left to do now is inform Mrs. Summerfield. I'll take care of that later on," PD said and hung up the phone.

"I don't know about the rest of you, but I think all of us should go to Danny's funeral," Dory said.

"When is it and where?" PD asked.

"It's Friday at 1:30 at the Congregational Church here in Rosedale," she told them. "Mrs. Summerfield let me know it was taking place."

"I'm planning on going," Billie Jo said, looking intently at the two men until both Wayne and PD nodded.

"I will, of course, need to buy you a suitable little black dress beforehand," Dory said and tried to raise a smile.

"I guess we can call it a day, then," PD said.

"Hold on a minute. What about James Walters?" Billie Jo asked. "Doesn't anyone want to know what I found out about him?"

"It's kind of anti-climactic now, but tell us anyway. What did you find?" Wayne asked.

"Dory was right. The guy's name was originally Walter James. He changed it five years ago to James Walters. He was born in Montana to a cattle-ranching family and worked on the big ranches out west. When he was a kid, some of the grain wagons were still pulled by large draft horses and he got interested in them. He married a girl from the area. When the marriage ended in divorce, he changed his name legally and started in a new direction, training racehorses."

"I'm sure it was a lot of work, Billie Jo, and it's good to know," PD said, kindly. "I'm not hearing anything suspicious though. Lots of people change their names and careers, especially after a life-altering event like a divorce."

"I still don't like him transferring stables during the pre-Derby season," Wayne said.

"I agree. There are always loose ends, but some cases are like that. Unless someone comes up with something new, I guess we're done. Billie Jo, can you get Mrs. Summerfield on the phone for me?"

Billie Jo sighed but flipped her phone to speaker and dialed.

"Hello, Billie Jo," Cara said in a whisper. "I'm going to walk outside to talk to you. Grant's home."

"I'm handing the phone to PD, Mrs. Summerfield. We have some information for you."

PD took Billie Jo's phone and said, "Mrs. Summerfield, are you okay to talk now?"

"Yes," she said softly.

"We heard from the pathologist today. She gave us a cause of death for your son."

There was silence on the line.

"Danny died of natural causes," PD said.

"He did?" Cara asked in a confused tone of voice.

"Yes, the beating and the Rohypnol were contributing causes, and the doctors at the hospital had given him morphine for the pain, but I hope it will help you to know that Danny wasn't murdered."

"I'm sorry, Detective Pascoe, but I hadn't been informed about the drug you mentioned. Not morphine, I know they use that for pain, but the other one."

"I'm the one who is sorry then, Mrs. Summerfield. One of us (he flashed a quick angry look at Billie Jo) should have told you. The drug is called Rohypnol and it produces a sudden unexplained loss of consciousness which can be complete or partial, depending on how much of the drug is ingested. Someone added it to Danny's coffee at the stable in Nashville. Danny's near-comatose condition was what led the stable boy to take your son to the hospital. Unfortunately, we don't know who did it or why it was done."

"Does this mean you are giving up now?"

"We don't have much choice. All of us are feeling unsettled about it and wish we knew why your son was drugged, but it seems we are at a dead end."

There was a long silence before Cara said, "Perhaps it is for the best. At least he wasn't killed and wasn't in any pain at the end. Do I owe you anything more, Detective Pascoe?"

Despite Billie Jo making wild eyes at him, PD said, "No. Nothing more. I wish you luck. Thank you for contacting us. Good-bye," he said, pushing the "end call" button and handing Billie Jo back her phone.

"I thought we were going to be charging all our clients a bit more for our services," Billie Jo said, looking confused. "Did I get it wrong?"

"We didn't really give her an answer to the second assignment she gave us, so I didn't feel right about it," PD said.

The group started to pick up their used coffee cups and papers before Dory said she had an announcement. "I need both of you men here on Saturday night by 7 p.m."

Wayne and PD raised nearly identical confused eyebrows.

"I have a date to go to the opera," Billie Jo said,

beaming. "And I'd like all of you to meet my beau and see me off in my fancy purple gown."

"Don't worry, I'll check her outfit first," Dory said grinning. "I want to make sure Miss Billie Jo Bradley hasn't replaced her purple heels with pink high tops."

"As if I *ever* would do such a thing," Billie Jo said and smiles spread around the room.

THIRTY-ONE

CARA AND GRANT SUMMERFIELD were getting ready to attend a campaign breakfast at Rosedale General Hospital. Grant was wearing his navy blue suit, a shell pink shirt and his "Just Vote" tie. Cara decided to wear navy as well, and pulled a freshly dry-cleaned blue dress with a Princess waistline from her closet. She put her dark hair up in a French twist and added earrings and a pink and blue neck scarf.

"Do we have any carnations left?" Grant asked.

"In the refrigerator," Cara said. She had taken to buying them by the dozen and keeping them cooled until they were needed. The fluffy pink and blue flowers as well as Grant's "Just Vote" tie had been commented on favorably in the "Suzanne About Town" column in the local paper. Women were the majority readers for column and Grant was counting on the female vote.

"We should drive separately to the hospital, Grant," Cara said. "I know you have to get right to the campaign office after the breakfast."

"You know me too well," he said, smiling. "Come here, Sweetheart, give me a kiss for luck."

WHEN A REPORTER from the Rosedale paper was dispatched to meet with Rosedale General's CEO, to ascertain which candidate the hospital would be endorsing in the upcoming election, he said he hadn't decided.

He wanted to have his VP's meet the candidates before announcing the hospital's position. They invited Grant Summerfield and his opponent, attorney George Hopkins, to speak to the hospital leadership. Each candidate was given fifteen minutes to speak on the topic of "Health Care in the Community," prior to a Q/A session. The CEO tossed a coin to see who would speak first. Grant won.

Listening to her husband's passionate defense of the uninsured and the need to provide follow-up health care after ER visits, Cara was charmed. He cared so much about the causes he supported. Looking carefully at each of the VP's, especially the Chief Medical Officer, she could tell Grant had impressed them. Concluding his remarks, Grant introduced his opponent graciously and took his seat next to Cara.

"How did I do?" he whispered and Cara smiled and squeezed his hand. She was warmed by his always considering her opinion important. Following Grant's opponent's presentation, the hospital CEO asked both men to come to the podium to answer questions. In response to the question of whether the hospital should become a teaching hospital, which would require an affiliation with the medical school, Grant's opponent was opposed. He said that the income for Rosedale General would decline if it became a teaching hospital because doctors would not see as many patients due to time spent teaching. He insisted that most of the doctors in town were on his side because they feared their patients would be given sub-standard care by interns and residents.

Grant supported the idea of Rosedale General becoming a teaching hospital, reminding the group of the large infusion of Medicare funds that would accompany such a decision, the hospital's historic commitment to the poor and the need to train doctors for the future. Cara was watching the Chief Medical Officer who nodded several times during Grant's response. She felt he had acquitted himself well.

AFTER THE PHOTOGRAPHER from the local paper got shots of them shaking hands with the hospital leadership, Cara and Grant walked to the elevator that took them up to Doctor's parking lot located on the top floor of the hospital. A cool breeze was blowing and the trees below them in the meditation garden were mostly bare. Cara pulled her red coat tightly around her as she gazed down on the small town of Rosedale. The spire of the Congregational Church was the tallest structure in the village. Danny's funeral would be held there on Friday. *Grant has to know about Danny before then. It's now or never*, her conscience reminded her.

"I have to get going, Honey," Grant said cheerfully. "I think it went well. Betcha I'll get the hospital nod. Thanks for coming."

"Grant," she said, as he reached in his pocket for his car keys. He was inserting his key into the door lock, but paused to look at her.

"We have to talk," she said. In that instant time folded and she was seventeen again, cuddling in the back seat of his car with Rafe. It seemed to her as if every single day since she became pregnant with Danny had led to this moment. She knew she was about to destroy her marriage but could wait no longer. *I must do this for my son*, she thought.

"Every married man knows those words," Grant said. "If he wants to *remain* married, that is." He was still smiling but looking at her face, Cara saw his jaunty demeanor fade. "Shall we go back in to the hospital coffee shop?"

"No, I think it's better if we talk here. It's a private matter between the two of us and I don't want to be overheard," she said. "Let's get into your car."

"Okay," he said, frowning uncertainly and walked around to open the car door for his wife. When he got into the driver's seat, he turned on the car's heater saying he didn't want Cara to get cold. "What did you want to talk about?" he asked.

"The boy who died," she said and the silence in the car turned dense, as if the cold air outside pressed down on both of them. All sound vanished, as it does underwater. Cara could no longer hear the swish of cars driving past on the rainy street below them. "We agreed to talk about him once your campaign was underway."

"I had nearly forgotten about it," Grant said and Cara almost stopped breathing. Did she need to tell him after all? *Yes, you do*, her conscience said.

She took a deep breath and began. "When I was seventeen, I dated a high school classmate named Rafe Marston. We fell in love," she paused, hearing Grant breathe more quickly and seeing a wounded look on his face. Cara swallowed and said, "I became pregnant."

"What the hell? You got pregnant? I knew you weren't a virgin when we got together, Cara, but pregnant?" There was a ferocious frown on his face.

"Just listen, please, Grant. I need to say this." He said nothing, his eyes piercing hers. "I gave birth to a baby boy. It was the boy who died in Nashville. You kept asking me who the boy's mother was. I was his mother. I was Daniel's mother." She felt tears starting and cleared her throat.

"You've had more than twenty years to tell me and you never did," Grant said, in a dark voice that seemed to come from far away.

"I never told his biological father, either. Rafe's family moved away at the beginning of our senior year. I never heard from him again, until day before yesterday when I called him."

"So you told him before you told me," Grant said with an outraged expression. "You kept this big secret for all these years and then you tell him, your high school lover, before you tell me, your husband of twenty plus years."

Cara hung her head, not knowing how to respond. *It's true*, the small critical voice in her head said, *you told Rafe before you told Grant.*

"I'm sorry," she said. "Very sorry, but there's more. The Sheriff in Rosedale believed Daniel was murdered."

"The boy was murdered?" Grant looked stunned, as if he couldn't believe what he was hearing. He gave a harsh bark of a laugh. "That doesn't surprise me. He was obviously a low-life. Probably a junkie. People aren't murdered unless they are into crime."

A flare of rage rose in Cara's body. She gritted her teeth. "That's what the police believed at the outset, but it turns out it wasn't true. Daniel died of natural causes."

"When the reporters find out about this, and you can bet they will, I can kiss my campaign good-bye," Grant's voice was bitter.

"I'm so awfully sorry, Honey. I was actually trying to protect your candidacy. Rosedale Investigations has a reputation for complete confidentiality."

"You went to a PI firm about this?" His voice was dead cold.

"I wanted them to find Danny, so I could give him the money to pay off his gambling debts."

"Oh my God, this just keeps getting worse and worse," Grant said, shaking his head. "Gambling debts? The kid was in debt because of gambling and you decided to pay it off? I don't suppose it's important in lieu of all this, but how much was it?"

"Fifteen thousand, but you don't understand, Grant. Danny had been beaten up by some thugs that worked for the bookie he placed his bets with. I was just so scared for him."

Grant shook his head. "Bookies and thugs. I can't believe I'm even hearing this, Cara. I'm running a family values campaign and you were going to pay off a bookie. Where were you going to get that much money? What funds were you going to use?"

"I still had the inheritance from my father. There is something else," Cara said.

"Go ahead then. You've already destroyed my political ambitions," his voice was devastated.

Cara took a deep breath. "I have arranged a funeral for my son. It's Friday at the Congregational Church. I'd like you to come. That's it. You know it all now." She collapsed back into the car seat like a ragdoll.

"My God. You couldn't even have this service out of town? We are members of that church. The funeral will be posted in the church bulletin. All our friends, all my supporters, or should I say *former* supporters, will read it. If you have set out to torpedo me, you couldn't have done a better job."

Cara started to cry. "I didn't think about that, Grant. I'm so very sorry."

"Sorry isn't good enough, Cara. You have lied to me for two decades."

Then, to her surprise, Grant reached across the car seat, grabbed her shoulders and kissed her—hard. Almost a biting kiss.

"Have you forgiven me?" Cara asked when the kiss ended.

"No. I have not. Our marriage is over. That was me kissing you good-bye."

She just looked at him, as hurt and despair flooded her heart remembering the day Grant proposed.

All those long summer afternoons on campus when they were courting, the hum of bees. The lazy sound of the river rippling past. The day he knelt before her and asked her to be his wife. Someone was burning leaves and the smell of the bonfire was forever linked in her mind with the moment Grant slipped the cool ring on her finger.

"Oh no, Grant, please no," she cried.

"You can keep the house, but I'm leaving you. There is a crappy student apartment above my campaign headquarters I can use. I'll talk with my lawyer tomorrow and get the divorce papers drawn. Now get the hell out of my car and my life."

Cara felt like she had been punched in the stomach. Sobbing, she managed to open the car door and walk unsteadily toward her vehicle. Grant wheeled out of the parking lot, screeching past her with his phone to his ear. To her surprise, she found she was unable to take another step and sank to the cement by the wheels of her car. A spitting petulant rain had started and her feet felt ice cold. Looking down, she realized she was sitting in a puddle, too miserable to move.

She had no idea how much time passed before she heard two people talking as they exited the elevator looking for their car. The male voice was laughing, teasing the woman, saying it was typical that she couldn't remember where she parked.

"Me?" the girl said. "What about you Mister Big Wig doctor? We drove to work together and you can't remember either."

Cara, you have to get up now, her inner voice said. *If you are ever going to be able to even be in the same room with Grant, you can't be found by hospital personnel sitting in a puddle in their parking lot.* She managed to pull herself up, get the car unlocked and slide inside before the couple came by. They were holding hands.

Remember, you consented to this, even knowing he would probably leave you, the voice in her head said. *You could have told him it was his fault you couldn't get pregnant, but you didn't. You protected Grant's pride all those years. You finally did the right thing today by telling him the whole story.* Cara put her head down on the steering wheel and the tears came down.

THIRTY-TWO

BOTH WAYNE AND his girlfriend, Lucy, arrived home late that night. Wayne pulled in after midnight and Lucy drove into the driveway a bit later. She was coming off a twenty-four hour shift. Wayne had a glass of wine waiting on the counter when she came into the kitchen.

"Thanks, Wayne," she said, gratefully taking a swallow of the wine. "It was a long day. There was a car crash on the interstate. A trucker swerved to avoid a car full of kids and tipped over in the median. Unfortunately, he clipped the car the kids were in and it flipped too," she shook her head. "The kids are okay. The trucker's in the ICU. How's your case coming? I know it's been a week since Daniel Parrish died."

"Well, the pathologist finally gave us a cause of death for Danny," he said.

"What was it?"

"Natural causes," Wayne's shook his head. "It's infuriating. I don't believe it. Neither do PD, Dory or Billie Jo. I need your expertise to figure this one out. Can we sit down and talk for a bit?"

"Just for a little while. I've got about half an hour before I fall asleep standing up," she said pulling off her lab coat. "I'm going to change and then I'll be back." Five minutes later, Lucy, wearing comfy jeans and a soft green sweater, returned to the living room. "Okay, I'm all yours," she said.

"As I told you before, I think somebody killed Daniel Parrish by giving him a fatal dose of a drug while he was in the hospital. I know in the past that people took sleeping pills to kill themselves, but I'm thinking you'd have to take an awful lot of today's pills to commit suicide, right?"

"That's right. The newer generation of sleeping pills are far less potent than the old types. It's more common these days to have a person end up in the ER very much alive after an attempt to end their lives with sleeping pills. An injected drug would be more likely and more lethal," Lucy said.

"That's what the pathologist originally told Dory. She said someone could have injected him with a lethal substance. She went over his body minutely with magnification but found only two injection sites, one in the inner elbow of each arm. The one in the right arm was the site of the IV they inserted in the ER. If that one was used to provide the morphine dose prescribed in the ICU, what would the second one been for?"

"The other IV could have been for glucose, or it was a dummy IV, just there in case it was needed."

"Could the killer have used an existing IV site to kill Danny?" Wayne asked.

"As you know, Wayne, my job is keeping people *alive*, not killing them," she said, raising an eyebrow. "However, in this *hypothetical* scenario, if I were going to commit murder and get away with it, I'd use an intravenous injection site already present. It's called 'Intravenous Push' and it's the rapid administration of a small volume of medication into a patient's vein via a previously inserted IV catheter. It's usually done with a syringe."

"And continuing with this hypothetical scenario, what drug would you inject?"

"Morphine," Lucy said. "Enough morphine stops the heart within minutes."

WAYNE GOT UP at 5 a.m. the next morning, having lain awake most of the night thinking obsessively about the case. If the pathologist was right about Danny dying of natural causes, all of them had been completely off track, but Wayne didn't think so. His antennae for killers had been honed over decades. Talking with Lucy last night had at last given him a solid working theory of the crime, but he needed more information.

His girlfriend was sleeping beside him, dead to the world. He knew he was taking his life in his hands, but he spooned against her and put his arm around her shoulders. She made an inarticulate sound of rage before suddenly sitting up, brushing her long brown hair back and peering at him blearily.

"What," she said, crossly.

"I just wanted to ask you one question," Wayne said, wincing a bit at her tone.

"Coffee," she said and flopped back on her pillow.

He got out of bed, put on his robe and walked to the kitchen. He had put coffee and water in the pot the previous night and set the timer for four-thirty, knowing he never slept more than a few hours a night when investigating a murder. Reaching for Lucy's favorite coffee mug, he added cream and sugar. Walking back to the bedroom, he wondered if Lucy would have fallen back asleep. Opening the door he was relieved to find her still sitting up. She held out her hand for the mug.

"You, my friend, have just taken your life in your

hands. I am very adept with scalpels you know," she said grouchily, taking sips of the coffee. Wayne sat down warily on the edge of the bed.

"Thanks for helping me last night, but our conversation left me with a question."

Lucy set the coffee cup down on her nightstand and laid back. She closed her eyes. "This had better be important," she said.

Wayne walked over to the window, he was reaching for the cord to pull up their blinds when Lucy said, "Stop right now. Do not, I repeat, do NOT, open those blinds." He went back to sitting on the bed.

"If a young person is found passed out near the ER, a patient with no i.d. on him, who is the first person to take care of him?"

"Whichever ER attending is available," she said, still sounding groggily pissed.

"One more thing, Lucy and then I'll leave you to sleep."

"You said one question. This is two. And I am on the verge of dumping this hot coffee in your lap."

Wayne shifted uneasily before saying, "Could you please find out the name of the ER doctor who saw Daniel Parish? And the hospitalists name? They both work at the Vanderbilt hospital in Nashville."

"Go away," she said darkly and he waited, watching her. She rolled her eyes before saying, "I'll text you."

Wayne grabbed his jeans from the previous night, a clean shirt, underwear from the dresser and tip-toed from the room.

DRIVING TO ROSEDALE INVESTIGATIONS, Wayne's phone chirped with the incoming text sound. Lucy had found the names. The ER doc was Rob Stuart, M.D. and the Hospitalist's name was Alan Harding, M.D. Even practically asleep, Lucy had come through for him. She always did. Nonetheless, he wondered if he would return home to find a symbolic pillow and blanket placed on the couch. It had happened before, letting him know he wasn't welcome in the bedroom, usually after he woke her up too early.

Walking up to the front door of the Rosedale Investigations, Wayne suddenly remembered when the team learned Danny died of natural causes, PD had closed the business for the day. Billie Jo would probably be asleep. Knowing he was about to piss off another important woman in his life, he rang the doorbell. Nobody answered. He continued to push the doorbell at one minute intervals. Ten minutes later a disheveled Billie Jo came thumping down the stairs. Dory would definitely not have approved of her outfit. She was wearing only a long T-shirt and as far as he could tell absolutely no underwear.

"Wayne?" Billie Jo asked opening the door. She looked mystified. "What are you doing here? We're closed."

"Can I come in? I need your help."

Still frowning, Billie Jo opened the door. "I'll leave you to it," she said once he was inside. "I better get dressed."

Indeed, he thought, taking a seat at her computer station. He didn't even know how to turn it on. Nonetheless, he eventually managed to find the power button and was pushing keys at random when she returned.

"Stop, stop. Stop!" she said. "Do not *touch* another thing."

In the time-honored tradition of suspects everywhere, Wayne raised both his hands in the air.

"For pity's sake, Wayne," she said as he rose from her chair. "What were you trying to do?"

"Remember me telling you that the doctors had prescribed morphine for Danny?" he asked. Billie Jo nodded. "I have the names of the doctors who treated him. All I need now is to find out who ordered the morphine and how much was ordered. My current theory of the crime is that Danny died of a morphine overdose."

"That's *all* you want? You do realize that even I, computer genius of the Western World, can't access patient records. Are you *trying* to land me in jail?"

"No, no. All I need is for you to say you're calling from the Sheriff's Office and get the doctors on the phone for me. Be sure to tell them that it's a police case and tell them the patient's name."

"And the reason you couldn't ask your girlfriend, who is I believe *works* in the ER, to do this?" she asked, raising her eyebrows ominously.

Wayne knew the unvarnished truth was his only hope. "It's because I'm sleeping with Lucy and if I had asked her even one more question, I would be sleeping alone for the foreseeable future," he gave her a wry grin.

Billie Jo sighed. "And since you are clearly NOT sleeping with me—and never will be by the way—you figured I was a bit less dangerous."

"You have that right," he said and they both laughed.

"Leave," she said waving him away.

HALF AN HOUR LATER, Billie Jo had Dr. Rob Stuart, the Emergency Room doctor on the line. She handed the phone to Wayne.

"Good morning, Doctor. I have some questions about a patient, Daniel Parrish, a young man you cared for recently in the ER. After his ER stay, he was admitted to the hospital and died the following day. I wondered if he was given morphine in the ER?"

"Hang on just a moment. Let me think. There might be some HIPPA issues about this. Do you have a subpoena?"

"No I don't, but it is my understanding that health care personnel may provide information to law enforcement in response to an official's request for information about a victim or suspected victim of a crime. We suspect Daniel Parrish of having been murdered."

"You're right, I remember now. We just had an in-service program on HIPPA given by the hospital HR people and our lawyers. Hang on and I will pull up the electronic medical record for the patient." Wayne waited on hold almost ten minutes before the Doctor returned to the phone. "Here it is. Mr. Parrish was found unconscious by one of our nurses on the back dock. When a patient arrives at the ER unconscious, it is often an overdose and controlled substances are contraindicated," he said. "He wasn't prescribed morphine in the ER."

"What did you do for him?" Wayne asked.

"Upon arrival, we immediately inserted an IV line. The plan was to give him Narcan to reverse a possible overdose. We got his vitals, temp, bp, drew blood and did a tox screen. We also checked for a head wound but there wasn't one. We did a finger stick to check for hypoglycemia in case he was a diabetic. He wasn't."

"You said you inserted an IV to give him Narcan. I believe you can use an IV to deliver other medications?"

"Yes, it's the normal method of delivering whatever medications the patient might need."

"Who could have prescribed morphine for him?"

"As I said, it wasn't ordered in the ER, but once the patient was admitted, the Hospitalist could have ordered it and nurses, pharmacists and/or pharmacy techs would have given it to him."

"Thank you doctor. This is all very helpful," Wayne said. "I'll be back in touch if anything else is needed."

BILLIE JO THEN called the Hospitalist who was on duty. She left a message saying that police suspected a recent patient, Daniel Kidd Parrish, had been killed during his stay in the hospital. Detective Nichols had some questions about the use of morphine in the case and would appreciate a return call.

"I see your problem, Detective," Dr. Harding said when he called back to talk to Wayne. "You're thinking someone tried to murder the kid by giving him an overdose of morphine?"

"That's our current theory of the crime," Wayne said.

"Before I returned your call, Detective, I checked with the hospital attorney. He approved me answering your questions. There are no HIPPA issues when there's a crime suspected. I also talked to Danny's nurse, Margo. While Danny was on our service, he woke up and pushed the button for the nurse. When she came into his room, he said his wrist and ribs were hurting. I ordered a low dose of morphine which she administered. The dosage was never increased beyond the initial level."

"I am trying to figure out how Danny could possibly have received a higher dose. When I spoke with

Dr. Stuart from ER he said that nurses, pharmacists, pharm techs and even paramedics are allowed to administer morphine. It's critical that we find out who did," Wayne said.

"There are several different systems that automatically dispense controlled substances. In our hospital we use the Pyxis system which requires an access code. The Pyxis system identifies every employee accessing the drug for each shift, at the time of inventory. The Nurse Administrator for that area reviews the use of the system monthly. If there are any anomalies, she flags them."

"Were any anomalies found during the period Danny was in the hospital?" Wayne asked.

"Unfortunately, the monthly review was completed just before Danny was with us. If it is critical, I could ask for a check on those dates. However, you face another problem in trying to find your killer, Detective. It's not just *who* gave him the morphine, if that's what happened, it's also *how* would they get the drug in the first place. Morphine is a controlled substance and must be stored in a securely locked cabinet and only fully-credentialed nurses and/or pharmacists have the codes and are permitted to remove drugs from the machine— once prescribed by a doctor."

"So our killer must be one of those people then," Wayne said, thinking it through. "Nobody else would be able to get the drug, much less figure out how to give it to Danny. I have another question for you. Is there Closed Circuit Television, CCTV, in the patient rooms?"

"No. It would be an invasion of patient privacy," he said. "There is, however, CCTV in the hall outside the

ICU. Maybe you could see someone you suspect by viewing the tape."

"I have to say, Doctor, you are clearly *lost* on medicine. You would make a great detective."

Dr. Harding chuckled. "I have to caution you that lots of people, nurses, doctors, interns and residents could be walking in the hall during that period of time."

"Can you get permission for me to view the CCTV video from the night Danny died?" he asked.

"We will probably have to consult the hospital attorney and the Nashville police, but I'll start the process."

"I'm not looking forward to looking at eighteen hours of looking of poor quality black and white video," Wayne admitted.

"I might be able to cut the time down for you, Detective. Patients in the ICU are checked on every 30 to 60 minutes during their time with us. We can isolate the period just before Danny died because he had a heart monitor. An overdose of morphine would cause the patient to stop breathing. Shortly thereafter his heart would stop beating and the monitor would sound an alarm."

"That's extremely helpful, Dr. Harding, but this case is complex and could involve more than one person. We will certainly focus on the period around the time of Danny's death, but I'm afraid we will still have to watch the whole darn thing. Thanks to your help, however, we now know the nurse or pharmacist in Danny's room just before he died is likely to be our killer."

"Good luck with it," Dr. Harding said and rang off.

THIRTY-THREE

By THREE O'CLOCK that afternoon Detective Stoneman had approved the Rosedale Investigations team watching CCTV tape showing the hall outside the ICU from the night Daniel Parrish died. Hospital administration agreed and provided the access codes. Wayne could hardly believe it had been so easily accomplished. He called Stoneman to thank him.

"We already looked at the whole tape and saw nothing," Stoneman said. "Spending eighteen hours watching it again is a fool's errand, especially when this is not now, *and never has been* a murder case. You will recall that Dr. Jones said he died of natural causes."

"You're probably right," Wayne said, gritting his teeth and forcing down his irritation.

"If you're determined to waste your time, it's yours to waste. Call me back if something turns up," Stoneman said and Wayne caught the condescension in his voice.

I already know more than you do, Wayne thought. After talking with Lucy and then the doctors at Vanderbilt, he was convinced Danny had died from an overdose of morphine. Plus, he had narrowed down the time considerably. His phone buzzed with a text and he walked into the conference room where the Rosedale PI team had assembled. He said, "I just got a text from Sheriff Bradley. Baby Joy was discharged from the hospital and is back at home. Mae's sister July is watching her so Ben can come over and watch the CCTV with us."

"We may as well hold off until he arrives. In the meantime, we need to make up a viewing schedule," PD said.

"In the interests of full disclosure, the Hospitalist who took care of Danny told me that they could isolate the time of Danny's death down to within a few minutes," Wayne said.

"Exactly why are we watching the whole damn thing then?" Dory asked, darting him a look.

"Yes, why look at hours of tape when just looking at the period before Danny died will find our killer," PD said.

"Sorry, but I want to see the whole she-bang," Wayne said. "It's possible more than one person was involved. Or that a slower acting drug was given earlier."

"Fine, but you are going to owe us all dinner and drinks in the most expensive restaurant in Rosedale and the business isn't paying for it," PD said, looking at Wayne meaningfully.

"Agreed," Wayne said.

The plan was for all of them to watch the video together from the time Danny was discovered outside the ER. Then they would split up and each person would watch four hours from the time Danny was in the ICU before handing the viewing over to the next person. Billie Jo scratched out a schedule on the blackboard.

When Wayne looked it over, he noticed he was on the midnight to 4 a.m. slot. It was always the hardest time to stay awake. "Have I been assigned the *graveyard shift* because I woke you up early this morning?" he asked.

"You bet your sweet bippy," she grinned.

Ben Bradley breezed into the conference room a bit later. He looked windblown but thoroughly happy. "I am pleased to announce that baby Noelle is coming home tomorrow," he said and the room erupted into applause. "I can stay for an hour or so and I'll take a stint later watching if that would help."

"I don't suppose you would like to take my slot, would you?" Wayne asked gesturing to the schedule Billie Jo had put on the blackboard.

"No way, my friend. I need to be in Nashville to pick up my wife and number-two daughter at eleven o'clock tomorrow morning and before that I have to get some sleep. I could take the 4–8 p.m. schedule today."

"Thank you," PD said. "I'm sure you realize, Sheriff, that the majority of the people we are going to see on the tape are not associated with this case. What we are particularly interested in is whether any of you notice a man…"

"Or a woman," Dory added.

"Right. Or a woman, with an unusual gait. Billie Jo, please demonstrate the walk for the Sheriff, will you?" PD asked.

Billie Jo removed her high tops before trotting around the conference table. She was starting to be pretty good at imitating the gait.

"Excellent mincing, Girl," Dory said, approvingly.

"Okay, now let's watch the first part of the tape where Danny gets rescued by the ER nurse," Wayne said.

The group watched as the ER nurse came outside, saw Danny and raced over to him. Although there was no audio track on the tape, her actions were perfectly clear. She knelt down and put her fingers on his neck to check for a pulse and used her stethoscope to check his breathing. Then she dashed back inside and returned with two orderlies and a gurney. Once they were inside the hospital, the screen showed only a view of the empty ER dock before the screen went blank.

"The next part is going to be the really boring segment," Wayne said as the tape started up showing a long hospital hall. People were walking toward the camera, mostly alone, but sometimes in groups of two or three. Most of them were talking to each other or on their phones.

They had watched about an hour of the tape before Wayne noticed that everyone around him was half asleep. It had started to rain and water sluiced down the windows outside giving the room a soft gray light. The near-silent room with only a slight whirring from the video and the gentle rainfall had made it hard to stay awake. Ben was audibly snoring when Wayne asked Billie Jo to stop the tape.

"Okay, people, that's enough for now," Wayne said, turning on the overhead lights and seeing everyone rouse.

"It's four o'clock," Dory said checking her watch, "I'm sorry Sheriff, but you are clearly not up to watching the next four hours."

"I was awake," Ben said defensively.

"People don't usually *snore* when they are awake," Dory said, caustically. "Go home. Get some sleep. I'm sure Mae is exhausted too. Caring for the twins at home is likely to be your job for the next few days while she catches up."

Ben nodded sheepishly and said his good-byes.

The group looked over the schedule and made some adjustments. PD was going to take the 4–8 p.m. slot, followed by Billie Jo covering the four hours until midnight, before Wayne started on duty. They knew Danny died around 2 a.m. which meant Wayne's shift was the one most likely to catch the killer. He would turn off the video when he left at four o'clock in the morning. Dory would start the tape up again at eight o'clock the next morning.

"I'm going to make a pot of coffee," PD said and Dory smiled. "We have a long night ahead of us and I was recently reminded that real men make coffee and don't always rely on *women* to do the job."

WAYNE KNEW IT was going to be a difficult slog watching the CCTV during the hours Billie Jo had assigned to him. He decided to drive home to ask Lucy if she would prescribe an amphetamine for him, to keep him awake.

"Sometimes I think I've got an *idiot* for a boyfriend," she told him. "The answer is no. Always and forever, the answer is no. And I've put a pillow and blanket on the couch so you can catch a few hours sleep before you go back to work."

"Why not our bed?" he asked.

"You know why," she said, giving him a meaningful look. "I'm leaving for my shift in an hour."

Wayne set his alarm for 11 p.m. and laid down on the couch. He planned to drive to a gas station when he got up and get one of those Five Hour Energy drinks. He would have to be sure to throw away the bottle before Lucy saw it. He was exhausted and didn't think he could sleep, but fell almost instantly into a dreamless dark space. When the alarm rang, he had a momentary disorientation, wondering where he was and what he was supposed to be doing before he remembered. Sometime in the next four hours, he was going to catch Danny Parrish's killer. He got up, washed his face, drank a cup of leftover cold coffee and left for the office.

TWO HOURS LATER, he called upstairs to Billie Jo. She came to the top of the stairs in shorty p.j's and frowned down at him without speaking.

"I found it," he said and she practically flew down the flight of stairs.

"Show me," she said.

Wayne rewound the tape and stopped it. "Watch this," he said.

When the tape started again, they could see a person with short blonde hair wearing hospital scrubs open the door to Danny's room. It wasn't possible to tell whether it was a man or a woman. Ten minutes later, the same individual came out into the hall again. Looking quickly from left to right, the person scampered down the hall.

"It's the mincing walk," Wayne said. He felt a surge of pride fill his body. He wasn't going to fail. He had found Danny's killer. "You agree, don't you?" he asked Billie Jo.

"Not only is it the mincing walk, but it's a girl," Billie Jo said, sounding euphoric. "I am surprised I didn't see it before. A girl's hips swing when she walks. And she's pigeon-toed."

"In case I haven't mentioned it before, my young colleague, you are stellar. Absolutely brilliant. I plan to ask PD to give you a raise."

Billie Jo grinned. "I could certainly use it. Dory's taste in clothes is costing me a mint."

"I'm going to call Dory and PD right now," Wayne said. He couldn't wait to tell them.

"Perhaps it would be better if you waited a bit," Billie Jo said gently. "It's two o'clock in the morning, my friend, and we still have more work to do. We don't even know who *Mincing Walker* is. Finding her is going to take time. Why don't you lie down on the couch in the waiting room? I'll bring a pillow and blanket from my apartment for you."

Wayne nodded, "Getting used to sleeping on couches," he said feeling the fatigue come down on him hard. Just before he closed his eyes, he looked up to see Billie Jo standing over him.

"You're smiling," she said.

He nodded, already half asleep with that triumphant smile still on his face.

THIRTY-FOUR

CARA WOKE SLOWLY that morning. She vaguely remembered she was scheduled to attend Grant's campaign event scheduled at the high school that day. In the next instant, reality crashed down around her like a blade cutting through her heart. Her marriage was over. Grant had left her the day before. He didn't want anything more to do with her. She winced thinking of the harsh kiss he gave her before he told her to get out of his life.

He had sent one of his campaign staff to the house to pick up some clothes the previous evening. When the young man rang the doorbell, he had a besieged look on his face. She could tell the boy hated Grant's decision. It seemed cowardly to her, when she had been so brave, that her husband would send a student to get his things, rather than coming himself.

Not wanting to make it any more difficult for the boy, she quickly assembled some outfits, underwear, pajamas and Grant's bathrobe. When she handed them to the boy, he could not meet her eyes. "I'm sorry," he muttered and turned to leave.

As he was loading the clothes into his car, she called for him to stop and ran out the front door. "I can't give you his bathrobe," she said and grabbed it. She bundled it up and lowered her face to take in the scent of Grant.

"I'm really sorry, Mrs. Summerfield," the boy said as he got into his car.

As am I, she thought, knowing it was her own fault, knowing she should have told Grant before they married. *I wonder if he would have married me if he had known*, she wondered. Now she would never know. She brushed the tears from her wet eyelashes, straightened her shoulders and walked into the house. There was something she needed to do before Danny's funeral that afternoon. She called Grant's cell and left him a message. "Please join me at the Church at 1:30 today. Sweetheart, I fell in love with you at first sight. And I've never stopped loving you in all these years. I don't know if I can do this without you."

AFTER GETTING DRESSED, Cara decided to call Tracey and ask her to come by the house before the funeral. They could go to the service together. She was feeling unsteady and having the girl with her would help, especially since she feared Grant wouldn't appear.

"Tracey?" she said when she answered the phone. "It's Cara. I wanted to make certain you knew that the investigation into Daniel's death is over and that the pathologist decided that he died of natural causes. Did the officers call you?"

"Yes, and I was glad. I hate that he died alone, but at least we know he wasn't murdered."

"That was my exact thought. I wanted to invite you to come to my house before the service tomorrow. My address is 1778 Blacksmith Trail. Will you have enough time to stop by? I know you met the Rosedale Investigations team when the investigation started but you and I have still not met."

"I know your husband wasn't Danny's father, but I hope I can meet him while we're there."

Cara found it hard to breath. "I hope you can too," she said crossing her fingers. "Are the Parrish's coming?"

"They are. What about Mr. Marston? Danny's father?"

"I invited him to the service, but I'm not sure if he will be able to make it."

"Could you call again?" Tracey asked.

"Yes, I'll give him another call. I'm so looking forward to finally meeting you. I know you met the Rosedale Investigations team when the investigation started but you and I have still not met."

"Will Billie Jo and Dory be there?" she asked. "I'm afraid it's going to be an awfully small group."

"I think they'll come, but in any case the most important people will be there. Danny's adoptive parents, his mother and girlfriend."

"And the baby," Tracey said. "Danny's baby will be there."

Saying good-bye, Cara hung up the phone and called Rafe again. He picked up the call but didn't speak. "Please come to Danny's funeral in Rosedale tomorrow," Cara said into the silence. "I have good news for you, for both of us." Then she listened to him breathing for a few moments, remembering the last night they were together before Rafe's parents told him they were moving away.

They had sat together at the school assembly, holding hands secretly under Rafe's varsity jacket. It was the night they were playing their historic rival, a nearby high school. Later they walked to the football field together...a cool October night with red leaves swirling in the dark air, the scent of raked leaves burning, the sounds of the cheerleaders practicing their chants, the laughter as they walked past other athletes making jokes about how Rosedale High was going to crush the opposition. Rafe had kissed her just before joining his teammates who were teasing him mercilessly about needing to get his mind on the game.

The phone clicked off and Cara brushed the tears from her face.

TRACEY RANG THE doorbell to Cara's house the following day at noon. Seeing the slender girl with an expectant face standing on the front step, Cara reached out to hug her.

"Thank you so much for coming," Cara said, feeling grateful for her presence. Tracey was wearing a chocolate brown sweater dress with black trim that zipped up the front and a brown velvet cloche that emphasized her dark expressive eyes. "Please come inside. I see you didn't wear black. I had a hard time deciding what would be appropriate."

"This was Danny's favorite outfit. That's why I decided to wear it," Tracey said, trying hard to smile.

Cara led the way into the kitchen and poured the girl some coffee.

"I'm sorry, Mrs. Summerfield, but coffee makes me nauseated for some reason," Tracey said pushing the cup away.

Cara smiled. "I remember coffee making me nauseated in the early days of my pregnancy. I should have remembered. And Tracey, please call me Cara."

Just then the phone rang. It was the number for Rosedale Investigations. Cara reached for it and said, "Hello, Billie Jo."

"Hello, Mrs. Summerfield. I wanted you to know that all of us will be attending Danny's funeral today. Sheriff Bradley is coming too."

"Thank you. Both Tracey and I really appreciate it. After the service I've arranged to have a buffet meal in the church basement. All of you are invited." Hanging up the phone she told Tracey that all four principals from the agency would be attending as well as Sheriff Bradley.

"That's so nice of them," Tracey said. "Did you reach Mr. Marston?"

"I left him a second message," Cara said.

CARA AND TRACEY arrived at the Congregational Church half an hour before the ceremony. On either side of the church's front door were dark blue ceramic pots filled with yellow mums. Walking up the sidewalk, Cara looked around for Grant. He wasn't there and she reached for Tracey's hand. Although it was the day to bid farewell to her son, she found herself remembering her wedding to Grant.

Dressed in her long white gown, she and her father had walked down an alee of trees that bordered the stone walkway leading to the back door of their church. It was autumn and the ginkgo trees were releasing their bright yellow leaves, shaped like Asian fans. Most of the tree's branches were bare, but some leaves were still falling in the quiet air. Cara lifted her long veil and wrapped it around her arm so it wouldn't touch the ground. The ginkgo's golden leaves fell on her veil-wrapped arm like a blessing. She left them lying there— amid the soft white folds—thinking she had never been so happy.

Entering the church, Cara saw the whole team from Rosedale Investigations already seated. In the first row, she spotted an older couple. The woman's white hair was tightly permed in ringlets. She was wearing unrelieved black and had her arm linked tightly through her husband's. The man looked up as they came in.

"Are they the Parrish's?" Cara whispered to Tracey.

Tracey nodded and quietly introduced the couple to Cara.

"Thank you so much for coming," Cara managed, just barely keeping her tears under control. They took their seats in the second pew. Looking from left to right, she saw neither Rafe nor Grant. The organist began to play "Canon in D" by Pachelbel.

"Did you call and ask them to play that?" Tracey asked. At Cara's nod, she told her it had been one of Danny's favorites.

"I talked with Reverend Andrews. I told her quite a bit about Danny and that I'm carrying his child," Tracey said, a bit of a proud smile on her lips.

Just then Cara heard the back door of the church open and felt the autumn breeze as the organist concluded the first piece. She hoped it was Grant who had come, but didn't turn around as the organist began to play, "Oh, God, our help in Ages Past."

Reverend Andrews entered the sanctuary from behind the altar and walked to the pulpit. Dressed in a long white robe with gold embroidery. She said, "Great is the Lord and greatly to be praised." She then greeted the assembled and thanked them for coming. "We gather here today to mourn and remember the all too short life of Daniel Kidd Parrish. Danny, as he was usually called, meant many things to each of you. He was an unprecedentedly talented racehorse trainer, a devoted son to Mr. and Mrs. Parrish, his adoptive parents, and a birth son to Cara Summerfield. He was husband-to-be to Tracey Dimond and a friend to all who knew him."

At the words, "a birth son," Cara's breathing quickened. Anyone who hadn't known of Cara's relationship to Danny prior to the funeral knew now. The minister had also said Danny was Tracey's "husband to be". Turning toward the girl, Cara saw a dawning smile. Her intuition must have resonated with Reverend Andrews and talking with Tracey had convinced her to include the words in her ceremony. *Once he knew the baby was on the way, I know my son would have married the lovely girl sitting here with me.*

The ceremony continued but Cara had mentally wandered away, again recalling the day of her wedding to Grant. *She remembered his courtly courtesy as he asked her elderly grandmother to dance. They swirled slowly around the floor, her grandmother's flowered dress billowing out to the music. She recalled her father's words when he said he was so proud of her for marrying a lawyer. Her mother was already very ill with breast cancer, but helped her dress for the ceremony and kissed her, saying she looked lovely.*

As the Reverend said, "Let us pray," Cara bowed her head and the words flowed around her, soft as petals. "Now is the time to let all bitterness and anger go. It is a time to be kind and tender-hearted. It is a time to forgive ourselves and to forgive one another as God forgives us. We have a fundamental responsibility that we now assume, a responsibility to ourselves and our God, to remember Daniel Kidd Parrish. As we go forward with our busy lives, let us never forget him standing by his glossy black stallion that he loved so much. Now he awaits us all at the gates to the Kingdom of Heaven. Amen."

Car raised her head and smiled at Tracey who was in silent tears.

"Everyone is invited to attend an informal meal on the lower level," Reverend Andrews said. "I'm looking forward to meeting you all."

As they exited the pew, Cara turned to see a number of people she didn't know. Walking down the church aisle, Tracey whispered their names.

"That's Jordan Dane, Boyd's Boy's jockey," she said, smiling at the small man who wore his green and white racing silks. "You already know Austin Cantwell," she said with a tight face. "His wife, Debbie, is with him. That's his childhood friend, Carl, sitting there. And those are the stable boys, Harris and Frank Stephenson."

As they passed the Rosedale Investigations team, Cara introduced Tracey to PD Pascoe since they hadn't met and to Sheriff Ben Bradley.

When she raised her eyes to look toward the back of the church, she saw him: it was Rafe. He was decades older, but he had aged well. His hair was pepper and salt, but he smiled widely. He reached out a hand to Cara and she took it.

"Thank you, Rafe. Thank you so much for coming. This is Tracey, Danny's girlfriend. Tracey, this is Danny's father."

"I'm so pleased to meet you."

"I'm so happy to meet you too, Mr. Marston," Tracey said and as he lowered his face to kiss her cheek, she added, "I want you to know that I'm carrying Danny's child. I hope you and Cara and the Parrish's will be my baby's grandparents and will always be involved in his life."

The smile on Rafe Marston's face told Cara everything she longed to know. He had completely forgiven her.

Passing through the narthex and turning toward the stairs that led to the lower level, Cara looked around desperately for Grant. He hadn't come. Then she caught a glimpse of a small young woman dashing out the side door. Her hair was mostly hidden by a black scarf. Turning back to Tracey, intending to ask her who it was, Cara saw a look of fury overtake the girl's beautiful features.

"What the hell is that woman doing here," Tracey said, her lips compressed into a grimace.

"Who was that?" Cara asked.

"I'll tell you later," Tracey said and they continued down the stairs.

After getting cups of pink punch, Cara and Tracey walked over to a table decorated with flowering plants and several condolence cards. Tracey picked one up.

"Who was that girl who left the church," Cara asked. "She had a funny walk."

Billie Jo was walking toward them, drawn by their conversation and heard the telling phrase.

"That was Justine Cantwell, Austin's niece. She's his brother's daughter," Tracey said.

"Why were you angry that she came to the funeral?" Cara asked.

"I guess it doesn't matter now, but she was Danny's girlfriend before me. When he broke up with her, she couldn't accept his decision. She stalked us for a year, always showing up in places where we were eating out or attending functions. I found it in very bad taste, her appearing at his funeral," Tracey said.

Then the Parrish's walked over and Cara turned to talk with them. Tracey fell into conversation with Rafe, but Billie Jo moved away, a tiny mischievous smile on her face.

THIRTY-FIVE

Friday

THE ROSEDALE INVESTIGATIONS team were riding back to the office in PD's old Lincoln. Dory and Billie Jo were in the back seat. Wayne was riding shotgun in the front. Dory kept looking intently at Billie Jo who couldn't stop smiling.

"All right, out with it, girl. You look like the cat who ate the canary," she said.

"I know who Mincing Walker is!" Billie Jo covered her mouth with her hand, obviously trying to suppress a wild giggle. "And, I know the *motive* for the murder."

Wayne turned to look into the back seat. "How did you figure out who it was?"

"I overheard Cara Summerfield ask Tracey why she was upset at seeing a woman at the church. She mentioned that the woman had an odd walk." Billie Jo was wiggling in her seat like a puppy; she could obviously hardly contain herself.

"Name," PD demanded.

"It's Justine Cantwell, she's Austin Cantwell's niece."

"Well done," Dory said, clapping Billie Jo on the shoulder. "Wayne, do you think we have enough to pick her up?"

"Hang on. What else did you hear, Billie Jo?"

"Justine was Danny's girlfriend before he met Tracey.

He broke up with her because he fell for Tracey and Justine took it hard. She apparently stalked the couple for months. Tracey was disgusted that she came to the funeral. Justine is also short, so she was probably the person who doped Danny's coffee."

"Loose ends," PD said, thoughtfully. "There are just too many loose ends."

"What are you thinking?" Wayne asked, turning toward PD.

Before PD could answer, Dory said, "You would think Mincing Walker would have wanted to kill Tracey, not Danny. If Tracey were dead, she'd have had a shot at the man she was obviously crazy about. Even now, if she killed Tracey, she would have her revenge."

"Billie Jo, do you know where Mrs. Summerfield and Tracey were going after the service?" Wayne asked. He was trying hard to keep his voice neutral but as he made eye contact with Dory he saw her expression grow fearful. The murderer could be after Tracey next. He felt his breathing quicken.

"I'm pretty sure they were going back to the Summerfield's house."

"Turn the car around now!" Wayne said and PD yanked the steering wheel hard and whirled the car around in a wide screeching arc. Other drivers honked furiously as the old Lincoln headed toward the Steeplechase subdivision.

WHEN THEY PULLED into the Summerfield's driveway, Cara came outside to see who had arrived. PD rolled down his driver's side window and said, "Is Tracey with you, Mrs. Summerfield?"

"Yes, she's inside. Mr. Marston, an old friend of mine, is also with us as are the Parrish's. Do you need to talk to her?"

"Probably better if Tracey stays inside the house," Wayne said, getting out of the car and walking toward Cara. "I don't want to alarm you, Mrs. Summerfield, but we've discovered the identity of the person who... ." His voice trailed off at the frantic gesticulating of Dory. "Just a moment." He walked back to the car.

"What is it?" he hissed at Dory.

"She still thinks Danny died of natural causes," Dory said.

"Right," he said and walked back to Cara. "We have found the person who doped Danny's coffee. We're concerned that the person might attempt to hurt Tracey."

Cara's eyes widened. She covered her mouth with her hand.

"We're going to inform the Sheriff's Office and ask that a Deputy drive by your house several times a day."

PD had gotten out of the car by then and joined them. "We were wondering if Miss Dimond could stay with you for a few days. Just until this threat is neutralized?"

"Of course. I'll ask her if she can stay for the weekend," Cara said.

"Good idea. And, if you're going to be out in the yard or shopping, it would be best for you to go in pairs. Will your husband be home this week-end?" Wayne asked, seeing the tall man who had come out of the house.

Cara looked uncomfortable, but said, "No, my husband is away for a few days. Thank you for your concern. We'll be careful." She waved at Dory and Billie Jo sitting in the car and walked back into the house.

Rafe was holding the door open for Cara. "What did they want?" he asked. He had started to walk back into the sitting room, but Cara reached for his hand to stop him.

"Let's stay here for a minute. I don't know what Tracey has told you about the attempt on Danny's life. Close the door, Rafe, it's getting cold outside."

"Very little, just that he was beaten by a couple of thugs because he couldn't pay some gambling debts," Rafe said. After her husband's rage, Rafe's calm acceptance of the situation gave Cara a sense of relief.

"When he died the police investigated, thinking he'd been murdered. However, the hospital pathologist said he died from natural causes, but added as contributing causes that there was Rohypnol in his system, as well as morphine."

"Go on," Rafe said. He was still holding her hand.

"The Rosedale Investigations group came back just now because they have found the identity of the person who put the Rohypnol in Danny's coffee. They were concerned that an attempt might be made to hurt Tracey. They want her to stay here this week-end."

"I thought I'd stay for a few days as well," Rafe said. "I could get a hotel room, or I could stay here if you have enough space. I'm worried about both of you. I want to protect you, Cara," his eyes warmed and he put his arm around her shoulders. Then he pulled back saying, "Where is your husband, by the way?"

Cara took a deep breath. "He left me, Rafe. When I told him about Danny, he couldn't forgive me and ended our marriage. I begged him to come to the funeral, but he wasn't there. When I saw you in the church, I knew you had forgiven me. Thank you, Rafe," she smiled up at him gratefully.

"I was angry at first, but when you called back, I wanted desperately to see you again. Driving here, to our son's funeral, I had a long time to think. I thought about you and how hard it must have been for you, having a baby at seventeen and giving him up for adoption. If anything, I should ask you to forgive me. I got you pregnant and you must have felt I abandoned you." He put his arm around her waist and pulled her close.

"We're going to be grandparents, Rafe. We never got a chance—either of us—to be parents, but we can be grandparents now. I don't know if you remember, but I was an only child, my parents died years ago, I wasn't able to have a child with Grant and when he left me, I felt totally alone in the world. Now, suddenly I have a daughter-in-law, almost anyway, and next spring you and I will have a little baby to love."

Rafe leaned down to kiss her and Cara lifted her face to his just as the front door burst open. Grant stood silhouetted against the light.

"What the hell is going on here? Get your hands off my wife." His fists were clenched, and he looked like he was about to punch Rafe whose own face was tight with fury.

Cara pulled away from Rafe's arms saying, "Grant, Rafe stop it. Just stop this both of you."

"Who the hell is this guy, Cara?" Grant said between clenched teeth.

"This is Rafe Marston, my high school boyfriend, Danny's father," Cara said.

"It certainly didn't take you long to show up here, Bastard," Grant said. "And you, Cara, you waited all of one day before calling your high school lover to come comfort you!" He shook his head, looking at her with eyes blazing.

"Hold on there, Buddy, Cara said you left her," Rafe said.

"You said you didn't want me in your life anymore, Grant. Now you come storming back through the door acting like a jealous idiot. Keep your voice down. We have company. Danny's adoptive parents and his girl-friend are here. What did you come for this time? More clothes?" Her voice was tinged with sarcasm.

"You're coming with me right now," Grant said, grab-bing Cara by the arm and pulling her into the kitchen. Rafe remained standing in the entryway, looking per-plexed and troubled.

"DROP MY ARM, GRANT," Cara said firmly, as they walked into the kitchen. He did so, backing away and standing against the refrigerator.

"I'm coming back home, Cara," Grant said firmly. "And I want that man out of here."

His words caused a column of rage to rise inside her. Grant's critical response when she had revealed her se-cret, especially when compared with how Rafe had re-acted, had changed her feelings for him. Her husband wasn't quite the man she had believed him to be. She was going to make her own decisions going forward and wouldn't be bullied into an early and possibly in-appropriate decision. "You left me because I kept my pregnancy a secret, and now only days later you want to come back? I wonder if it's because you have for-given me. Have you?"

Grant looked down, unable to meet her eyes.

"Did it ever occur to you that I kept Danny's existence a secret all this time partly to save you feeling less of a man? I went through years of fertility testing all the while knowing it wasn't *my* fault we couldn't get pregnant."

A bleak expression crossed Grant's face. "You shouldn't have kept that from me," he said.

"Looking back, I wish I had told you about Danny when we got serious. I wonder if you would have married me, knowing about the pregnancy. Would you have?"

"Probably," he said, but didn't sound certain.

"I think you wanting to come back home now isn't because you've forgiven me, but because you are jealous. You see another man here, in our house, and you can't stand it. You said you were getting divorce papers drawn. Have you already consulted an attorney?"

He nodded, but reached out a hand to touch her. She moved away.

"Since you have already talked with a divorce attorney, can't say you've forgiven me, or sound at all convinced you would have married me if you had known about Danny, the tables have now turned," Cara said firmly.

"What do you mean?" Grant asked.

"What I mean, Grant, is that I'm not ready to forgive *you* now. I'm going to see an attorney myself and get a separate maintenance agreement drawn up for a period of at least a year. During our separation, I'm going to be thinking hard about how I feel about you. And right now, I'd like you to leave my house."

THIRTY-SIX

Saturday

DEPUTY GEORGE PHELPS pulled into the driveway of the house Detective Wayne Nichols shared with his girlfriend, Lucy, at nine the following morning. He walked up to the front door and rang the bell. Lucy had seen him from her kitchen window and called, "Wayne, George is here."

Wayne opened the front door to let George in. They walked into the kitchen which was warm from the scent of zucchini bread baking.

"Good Morning, George," Lucy greeted him. The timer rang and she took the bread out of the oven.

"Good Morning, Doctor," George said.

"Would you like a slice of zucchini bread?" Lucy asked. "I noticed you were licking your lips."

"Yes ma'am, thank you. I'm really hungry. I didn't get any breakfast this morning. The Sheriff made me show up for roll call at 7 a.m.," his voice sounded hard-done-by.

"George, you are *always* hungry," Wayne said. "It's starting to catch up with you. Your uniform is getting tight. Have you been patrolling the Steeplechase neighborhood and checking the Summerfield house?"

"I already went by the place this morning. Everything is quiet there. Still two cars in the driveway. I checked and they belong to a Tracey Dimond and a Mr. Rafe Marston."

"Good work, George. What's been done to locate Justine Cantwell?"

"We put out an APB on her and her car. It covers all of Rose County. The Sheriff called the Detectives in Nashville and they agreed to look for her too."

"Now *that* must have been an interesting phone call," Wayne said as Lucy invited George to sit down and set a cup of coffee and a plate with a slice of warm bread in front of him.

George, with a mouthful of bread said something that might have been the word "why" but came out as "whmpff."

"The last contact we had with the Nashville Detectives was after the pathologist said Danny Parrish died of natural causes. They knew we were checking the CCTV footage, but we've not talked to them since Billie Jo figured out Justine Cantwell is our perp. What did Sheriff Bradley say about the call?"

"Something about them not being too happy. He said you might want to call them, maybe apologize."

Wayne snorted. Hell would freeze over before he apologized to Stoneman. As he predicted, they had cracked the case with no help from them. "I'll call the Sheriff in a bit. Thanks for coming over with an update, George."

"Would you like a slice for the road?" Lucy asked and George nodded gratefully.

By the time the deputy pulled out of the driveway, Wayne was on the phone to the Sheriff's Office. Having made certain Mrs. Coffin would call him immediately if they located Justine Cantwell, he dialed Detective Pascoe's cell.

"Pascoe," the older Detective answered.

"It's Wayne. No sign of Justine yet and nothing is happening at the Summerfield house. What are you doing today?"

"Thanking God every dentist's office in town is closed on Saturdays. Billie Jo tried to get me an emergency appointment with no luck. So, I'm not doing much until tonight when we see Billie Jo off to the opera. What were you thinking?"

"I'd like to go to the track and meet this James Walters guy. I still believe this case is about more than a jilted woman."

"I agree," PD said in his gravelly voice.

"Let's meet at the Sheriff's Office and go to the track from there."

"I'll be there in twenty minutes," PD said and rang off.

AN HOUR LATER the two men were in PD's old Lincoln headed for the track in Rosedale. The sky was cloudy and the previous night's rain had left the trees standing in skirts of fog. A windstorm and colder temperatures were on the way.

"Did you ever work out the return of the Penrose Insurance company money?" PD asked.

"I did. Met with the woman who embezzled the funds. Beautiful girl with a cloud of long dark hair and a pretty face. I could see why Penrose would have been attracted to her. As we talked, it became clear that she was still in love with him and was very sad about the relationship ending, although I sensed she was on the way to accepting his decision. His wife having breast cancer left her feeling terribly guilty and made it easier for her to understand."

"Where did you two get together?"

"At her apartment. It's a one-bedroom rental in the Cunningham complex south of town."

"I was there once. Those buildings were very cheaply built. The brick fronts were wavy and uneven, some of them looked like they were about to fall off."

"You're right and the condition of the apartments was what gave me an idea. I started off just listening to her. She told me all about their relationship, although I cut her off when she started relating Penrose's prowess in bed."

PD chuckled.

"Penrose had already made her an offer which she declined, but she was willing to return all the embezzled money, provided we could come to terms. She hadn't spent a penny of it. I asked her whether she was willing to relocate and she said she was. Penrose was prepared to give her a glowing letter of recommendation and call some CEO's of insurance companies in Nashville to ask them to give her an interview. I asked her where she would live in the city, saying I knew it was an expensive place. She was unsure. I also asked her if she wanted to be a home owner someday and she said she could never afford to buy a house. She looked so wistful, I thought she would agree to terms if it included a house."

"So, Penrose is going to buy her a house?"

"You have it. He is going to give her the down payment on a house and then make the payments monthly for twenty years until the place is free and clear. Every month when he writes that check I hope he will once again experience shame for his stupidity," Wayne said and his lower lip turned down.

"A very long penance indeed," PD said. "I trust you said we'd send him a bill."

"Billie Jo has already taken care of it," Wayne said. As they continued the drive in companionable silence, Wayne thought about his career in law enforcement. Choosing to join the police force had also been a penance of sorts. Every time he collared a perp, it had been an act of contrition—an apology to his foster mother. Each time he got justice for other victims, he paid for his failure to achieve timely justice for her.

"We're here," PD said turning into the track and following a pot-holed gravel drive that ran behind the stables. A cold rain had started and horses, covered by dark colored saddle blankets sprinkled with water droplets, were being led into the barns.

"How do you want to handle this conversation?" Wayne asked.

"Should we could tell James Walter, we are looking into the death of Daniel Parrish and imply that he is a suspect?"

"That might work," Wayne hesitated. "But, what if we are wrong, PD? What if there is nothing more to this than a broken-hearted woman who decided to kill her lover rather than let another girl have him? Once we have Justine Cantwell in custody we will have certainly fulfilled our charge from Mrs. Summerfield."

PD frowned and gave a deep sigh. "I get your point, Wayne. We could just quit now, but we don't have any new cases on the docket and I remember you saying you thought Austin Cantwell was involved somehow. Plus,

Billie Jo's intuition is normally spot on. I would hate to give up and allow a conspiracy to fix an important race, or injure a thoroughbred."

"And Billie Jo keeps saying it's all about the horse," Wayne said, frowning. "We've both been detectives for too long to give up. Since we're here anyway, let's go talk to James Walters."

AT SEVEN O'CLOCK that evening, Wayne and PD were sitting in the waiting room of Rosedale Investigations. Billie Jo was upstairs with Dory getting ready for the big night out. They could hear the two women arguing over some detail in the girl's outfit. Wayne smiled to himself, betting Billie Jo would prevail.

When the doorbell rang, PD rose and went to the entryway. He flipped the porch light on and opened the door for a young black man who was wearing a tux and carrying a purple orchid corsage in a clear plastic container.

"Come on in. You must be Joel," PD said, holding out his hand to shake.

"I'm here to pick up Billie Jo," the boy said, sounding a bit apprehensive. "Is this the right place?"

"Yes, I understand you're going to the opera tonight," PD said. "The tickets are quite expensive. Hope you enjoy it."

"The tickets were a gift so I only had to rent a tux. The opera is Mozart's *Don Giovanni*. My music professor at the University said it had gotten good reviews." Joel looked very young and handsome in his black tuxedo.

Turning to Wayne, PD said, "I'd like to introduce you

to Detective Nichols who works with me. Investigator Clarkson is upstairs with your date."

Wayne shook hands with the boy. A bit later, they heard the door at the top of the stairs open and all three men went to stand at the bottom. Billie Jo stood at the top step for a moment. She looked absolutely stunning. Her hair was in a complicated up-do, the purple dress with wide shoulder straps and a sweetheart neckline fell all the way to the floor. She wore what looked like a diamond necklace, earrings and a tiara. All three men were silenced by her beauty. Dory was standing behind her, fussing with the back of her dress.

"Hi Joel," Billie Joe said descending the stairs. "Is this for me?" she asked, gesturing to the corsage box.

Joel, still apparently unable to do anything but nod, handed it to her. She took the orchid out of the box and with the help of Dory pinned it to the wide strap of the dress. She handed Joel a white boutonniere.

"Time to go, you two," Wayne said, glancing at his watch.

As the couple walked outside, PD remained standing by the open door. He turned back and asked, "Dory, may I ask who *purchased* those opera tickets?" His voice was silky smooth.

"Why you did, of course, PD." At his shocked expression, she added, "That's what you get for letting Billie Jo have control of the office checkbook."

"Billie Jo, you are paying me back!" he yelled at the girl who was getting into the car.

As her escort walked around the car to get into the driver's seat, Billie Jo flipped PD the bird, her rings glittering in the starlight.

"Was she wearing anything inappropriate with that

outfit?" Wayne asked as the couple drove away. "If she was, I sure didn't see it."

"She was going to dye her hair purple but I put a stop to that nonsense. It's what she *wasn't* wearing that was inappropriate." Facing two clueless men, Dory added, "Not a stitch of underwear beneath that gown, which you also paid for by the way, PD."

At PD's totally exasperated demeanor, both Wayne and Dory laughed.

THIRTY-SEVEN

Monday

IT HAD TAKEN the entire week-end for the forces of law and order in Tennessee to locate Justine Cantwell. Detective Stoneman called Sheriff Bradley Monday morning letting him know the suspect was being held at the Nashville post. Stoneman said they would interview the woman that day, but would have to release her after twenty-four hours because they lacked any solid evidence linking her to Daniel Parrish's demise.

A tense interchange occurred, ending with the Sheriff saying the review of the CCTV done by the staff at Rosedale Investigations had discovered the same individual both doping Parrish's coffee cup and injecting him with a syringe at the hospital. Stoneman was justly pissed that the information had been kept quiet. Ben pushed for the interview to be done in Rosedale. Stoneman reminded the Sheriff that the crime took place in Nashville. Ultimately they agreed on a two-person interrogation, one person from Nashville and one from Rosedale. Detective D'Angelo would partner with whoever the Sheriff named as his representative for the interview.

Wayne was driving to Rosedale Investigations when his cell phone rang. "Morning Sheriff," he said, recognizing the phone number.

"I just got a call from Detective Stoneman. They have Justine Cantwell at their post. It was a knock down drag out fight, but he's finally agreed that someone from here can assist with her interview which is to be done at his post. Do you want to go?"

"I do, but think I should talk it over with PD, Dory and Billie Jo before a final decision is made. I'll call you back," he clicked the phone off and continued his drive into Rosedale. The expected cold snap had come in overnight and a sharp wind wracked the branches of trees. A branch broke off in front of Wayne's truck and skittered to the side of the road. Despite the dark clouds that often produced a low mood in Wayne, he felt his spirits rise. They had the woman in custody. He feared she might have fled the state, but they had her. Walking into the Rosedale Investigations building, he hung his jacket up on a hook in the entryway and went into the kitchen where Billie Jo was making coffee.

"Good Morning, Billie Jo. How was the opera?" he asked.

"Oh, Wayne, it was brilliant, absolutely mind-blowing. I had a blast!"

"I'm not surprised. You looked stunning. However, I see that you have now reverted to your previous style." She was wearing tight jeans with holes in them and a dingy yellow sweatshirt. "Will you be dating the young man in the future?"

Billie Jo shook her head saying he was just an "opera date" as Dory came into the room, followed closely by PD.

"Morning everyone," Wayne said. "I have news. Miss Justine Cantwell was apprehended as she was about to leave the state and is being held for questioning at the Nashville post." He smiled broadly and the room erupted into happy conversation. "Sheriff Bradley has obtained permission for someone from here to participate in her interrogation. It's going to be D'Angelo from their shop since it's a woman and he has a way with women apparently."

"That he does," Dory said. "He could have his way with me, that's for sure."

Wayne frowned, shooting her an irritated look. "So, let's decide who is going to Nashville? What do you think, PD? You worked there for years and are familiar with the post and how they work. Do you want to do the interview?"

PD shook his head. "So far at least, this is a female crime. I think Dory should do it. Plus she and D'Angelo have done one interview together already, although Stoneman was kept in the dark about that."

"Thank you, PD," Dory said, beaming.

"Why not me?" Billie Jo asked, sounding confused and sad. "I was so happy I figured out who mincing woman was. I thought you would be proud of me, PD. I hoped maybe you would even give me a little more responsibility for things around here."

"You, my young friend, aren't nearly ready to question murderers," PD said. "Plus you and I still need to talk about expensive opera tickets and a fancy dress being charged to the office."

Billie Jo looked a bit shame-faced. "I felt like I cracked the case," she said, quietly. "And I did a background on Justine and found out she is a student nurse."

"It was very good work, Billie Jo. Finding out Justine was a student nurse pretty much clinched it, our perp had to be someone with access to the hospital. And we are all proud of you, aren't we, PD," Dory said, looking meaningfully at him. He nodded in reluctant agreement.

"But, even if I do decide to give you a bonus, Billie Jo, it wouldn't be nearly enough to cover the exorbitant cost of opera tickets and fancy dresses," PD said.

"Sounds like Dory is the point person on the interrogation," Wayne said, cutting off any further arguments between Billie Jo and PD. He personally agreed that she had earned a bonus. "I'm going to drive to Nashville with Dory. We can discuss strategy on the way. PD, would you like to join us?"

"No, I think I'll stay here to discuss 'inappropriate office purchases' with Billie Jo," he said and she colored.

DORY AND DETECTIVE D'ANGELO entered the interrogation room confidently, having agreed on their interview strategy. Dory would be the "bad cop", given what she called D'Angelo's "virtually instant rapport with women." Wayne Nichols and Detective Stoneman would observe from the one-way view window. The CCTV tape had already been cued to the three appropriate segments—the first segment showing Danny's coffee mug being doped with Rohypnol in the stable, the second showing him rescued by the ER nurse and the third segment with Justine entering and exiting Danny's hospital room. As Dory and D'Angelo opened the door to the interrogation room they saw Justine for the first time. She had a narrow face, bright blue eyes, lank blonde hair and was wearing the usual orange jumpsuit issued to prisoners. She looked like a furious cornered cat.

"Hello, Justine," D'Angelo said pleasantly as they entered the room. "I'm Detective D'Angelo and this is Investigator Dory Clarkson. We're going to be talking with you today. This interview is being recorded and I'm turning on the video recorder now." He turned toward the camera saying, "Detective D'Angelo and Investigator Clarkson interviewing Justine Cantwell Monday, October 21st regarding the murder of Daniel Parrish." He turned back to Justine asking her how she was feeling and if she would like a glass of water.

"There's no time for that," Dory said crisply, narrowing her eyes at D'Angelo. "Justine, you have been informed of your rights. If you asked for an attorney, he or she isn't here. Until an attorney arrives we are going to establish certain facts. I'm going to start by showing you some CCTV footage from the Cantwell stables in Nashville. Dory pushed a button on her remote and the office in the stable came up on the television. A small person clad in a hooded sweatshirt entered the room, took a little bottle out of a sweatshirt pouch and poured some liquid into Daniel Parrish's coffee cup on the desk. Then the individual picked up the cup and carried it into the stables.

"Where were you the afternoon of Thursday, October 10th from 4–6 p.m. when this happened?" Dory asked. *The girl looked absolutely petrified and they had hardly started.* This was no career criminal. When she checked Justine's juvenile record there was nothing except a single charge for minor theft. She'd stolen some cosmetics from a local drug store when she was fourteen. It has been tossed out of court.

"I was at home, in my apartment," Justine said.

"Can anyone confirm that," Dory said. "Do you have a roommate? A boyfriend?"

"We're just trying to eliminate you from our inquiries, Justine," D'Angelo said, kindly. "If you can prove you were at home during that time, you could be released." He smiled.

"Unfortunately, I was alone," she said, taking a deep shaky breath.

"What was your relationship with Daniel Parrish?" D'Angelo asked her. "Was he your boyfriend?"

Sadness washed Justine's pale face. "Yes, he was. We were together for a year and he was about to move in with me before he met…"

"But you weren't together at the time in question, were you," Dory said, unfeelingly. "We already have your fingerprints on Danny's coffee cup, Justine. You roofied him. The Rohypnol you put in his coffee cup made him virtually unconscious."

Justine looked pleadingly at Detective D'Angelo, but didn't speak.

"This next segment shows Danny being brought from the parking lot behind the hospital to the place he was left behind the ER," Dory said.

Watching Justine's face as she saw her former lover brought to the hospital by the stable boy, it was obvious she was devastated. Clearly, the girl felt terrible about what she had done.

At that moment an all-too-familiar figure opened the door and entered the room. It was local defense attorney Ramsey Tremaine. All the members of the staff at the Sheriff's Office in Rosedale knew and detested the sleazy character. After all their hard work investigating crimes, gathering evidence and arresting criminals, Tremaine often got them off.

"Damn it," Dory whispered under her breath. *Of course it would be Tremaine who was the girl's attor-*

ney. The Cantwell family had obviously engaged the
expensive rat to represent their niece.

"I'm Ramsey Tremaine, Miss Cantwell's attorney,"
he told the startled girl. "Just a moment officers while
I confer with my client." He took a seat next to the
girl and a whispered consultation took place. When he
looked back at D'Angelo and Dory, Tremaine had his
hand on Justine's shoulder. "What has my client told
you so far?"

"Nothing. We were just getting started," Dory said.
Over the years she had learned not to give any information at all to defense attorneys. "Mr. Tremaine, if
you haven't met, this is Detective D'Angelo from the
Nashville police post." The two men shook hands. "We
were about to show Justine some CCTV from Vanderbilt hospital. If you have no objection, we will continue
viewing the tape."

Tremaine nodded and whispered to his client that he
didn't want her to say anything.

Dory pushed the "start" button on the remote and the
hall outside the ICU at Vanderbilt came into view. She
fast forwarded a bit, until the time stamp in the upper
corner said 1:45 a.m. "Justine, I'd like you to pay close
attention now," Dory said as a small figure in scrubs
walked quickly down the hall and entered Daniel Parrish's room.

"I'd like you to confirm that you were the person who
entered Daniel Parrish's room at that time," Dory said.

"My client has nothing to say," Tremaine said. "I am
personally unable to tell whether that individual was
male or female. You have no evidence that Justine was
the person on the tape. However, as I'm sure you know,
my client is a student nurse on rotation at Vanderbilt

hospital. As such, she had a perfect right to walk in and out of patient rooms. I will also remind you that the pathologist listed natural causes on Daniel Parrish's death certificate."

"Being in the hospital and on the intensive care ward at the exact time the crime occurred is *opportunity*," Dory said coldly. "We also know that Justine has *motive*. She was dating Danny Parrish until he fell in love with Tracey Dimond. Although it was not reported to the police, Justine stalked Danny for months and even appeared at his funeral. As you know it's a common thing for murderers to do." *It actually wasn't, but it was a belief held by most of the populace.*

"Lot of couples break up. It's not a motive for *murder*. Justine hasn't been convicted of a single crime and we all know that most killers start with a long line of arrests for Grievous Bodily Harm, affray and criminal assault before they get to murder. My client doesn't fit the profile and most damning of all," Tremaine paused, giving Dory a victorious look, "You don't have the means. You have no murder weapon."

He was right about that one, Dory knew and her heart sank. Nashville's CSI unit had meticulously searched all the disposal bins in or near the ICU unit of the hospital for syringes. Unfortunately, there were hundreds of them and Captain Paula Crawley had drawn the line. She wouldn't approve doing fingerprint and DNA tests on so many. It was cost prohibitive. They had to show Justine entering and then exiting Danny's room with a syringe in her hand. And they had to get a solid confession.

Dory cast a quick meaningful glance at D'Angelo, pushed the play button again and said, "Here you are again, Justine, looking guiltily from right to left as you exit Danny's room. The video experts from Nashville are enhancing this part of the tape and making close-up photos of the syringe. We will be able to get your fingerprints off it."

"No, no, no," Justine said, shaking her head from side to side. She was starting to cry.

"The only thing we don't understand, Justine, is how you got the morphine, since it's kept in a locked cabinet, and we are aware student nurses don't have independent access to morphine. We also want to know why you spent almost ten minutes in Danny's room before you injected the morphine into his IV," Dory said.

"Were you talking to Danny during that time?" D'Angelo asked quietly. "Did he say something that tipped you over the edge? It could help prove you didn't plan this, but acted on the spur of the moment."

There was always a point in any interrogation when the suspect begins to crumble. It is visible in their body language. When that moment appears, it's as if the person has reached the edge of a cliff a thousand feet above a curving silver river. Justine had come to the point of no return. She was breathing raggedly, tears falling from her eyes.

"My client is obviously under extreme duress," Tremaine said. "She's can't answer any more questions. You need to stop this right now."

"You don't understand," Justine said softly, turning toward D'Angelo.

"If we don't have it right, Justine, I'm ready to listen to your side of things. My partner, Investigator Clarkson, won't understand, but I will," D'Angelo said. Dory gave him a scorching look.

"Don't say anything, Justine," Tremaine said firmly. "Just stop talking."

"No, Mr. Tremaine. *You* stop talking," Justine said. "I have something I want to tell Detective D'Angelo. I want you to know I never wanted Danny to die. I only roofied him because we are studying hypnotic drugs in class and my instructor said that Rohypnol gave patients amnesia. All I wanted to do was to have Danny forget Tracey," she wailed.

We're almost there, Dory thought. She crossed her fingers that Justine would continue talking and Tremaine couldn't stop her.

"Then why did you add the morphine to his IV?" D'Angelo asked gently. "Didn't the Rohypnol make him forget Tracey? Was that the reason?"

"Justine, stop. Stop right now," Tremaine said, urgently. "I can get you off with just the doping."

Dory felt an almost undeniable urge to strangle his scrawny neck.

"When I went into Danny's room that night, I brought the syringe," Justine admitted. Dory glanced quickly at the one-way window, knowing Wayne was watching. Knowing they almost had her.

"Tell me happened in that room, Justine," D'Angelo said softly, and the silence intensified.

"Danny was conscious when I walked in. I asked him if he knew who I was and he said he did. Then I asked him if he remembered who Tracey Dimond was and he said, 'I will always remember Tracey. I love her and I'm going to marry her, Justine. There's nothing you can do about it.' That's when I did it."

Dory felt an upwelling of pride. The young man she had felt so sorry for in the hospital was going to get justice. Justine Cantwell was going down. "Interview suspended at 2:45 p.m." she said and clicked off the recording.

The door opened and a uniformed officer came in, took Justine by the arm and escorted her from the room. Tremaine followed them, still telling her to be quiet. Detective Stoneman entered into the room and shook D'Angelo's hand, congratulated him and slapped him on the back. Wayne gave Dory a huge bear hug.

"You did it, Dory. First time interrogating a murder suspect and you got a confession," Wayne said. "I'm proud as punch of my partner."

"I did, didn't I?" Dory said, but her voice trailed off.

"What's wrong?" Wayne asked.

"I just hate to think of Justine spending her whole life in jail. Maybe because she's young, has no record and the crime wasn't premeditated, the Judge will give her a short sentence."

Wayne looked at his partner and frowned. "I don't think you need to feel too badly for that girl, Dory. Remember, she brought a morphine-loaded syringe into Danny's room. She might not have decided to kill him when she entered his room, but she was definitely prepared to do so if he said he was going to marry Tracey."

THIRTY-EIGHT

PD AND BILLIE JO were both waiting on the front porch of Rosedale Investigations when Wayne pulled into the parking lot. Dory jumped out of the truck and raised both her arms in the air. She did a little twirl and PD and Billie Jo launched into congratulations. Once seated in the conference room, Dory told them the whole story, receiving her well-deserved accolades for eliciting Justine's confession.

"Did you or D'Angelo learn how Justine got the morphine?" Billie Jo asked.

"As a student nurse, she was shadowing a senior nurse who was getting some morphine a few days earlier. There's a code that has to be entered into the locked system which opens the cabinet. Justine watched the supervisor, memorized her code and was able to get a full syringe of morphine that night. All she had to do then was add it to Danny's IV."

"Definitely premeditated," PD said. "They will get her on murder one."

"If Danny hadn't said he was in love with Tracey and planned to marry her, I doubt it would have happened. That was what tipped the balance," Dory said.

"Dory had a moment when she felt sorry for Justine before the uniforms took her away." Wayne added.

"Justice is blindfolded as she weighs the scales," Dory said. "I just hope the judge's eyes are wide open and he takes Justine's age and lack of a record into account when he pronounces the sentence."

"So, what's next on the docket for us, PD?" Billie Jo asked.

"We have a client coming in this afternoon with a request for someone to follow a philandering wife," PD said. "We are going to do the stake-out this evening. Anyone willing to volunteer?"

"I will," Billie Jo said. "I've never done a stake-out before. Sounds fun."

PD snorted. "Ah, the enthusiasm of youth," he said.

"I'll join you," Dory said. "I've done tons of stake-outs and know exactly what we need to bring. Let's go upstairs and I'll help you pick out an outfit."

"Let's not forget we need to contact Mrs. Summerfield and tell her the person who killed her son is in custody and likely to receive the maximum sentence," Wayne said to PD as the two women left the conference room.

"I'll take care of that," PD said. "Do you want the afternoon off, Wayne? We've all been working long hours. I'm beat and I'm sure you are too."

"Good idea, although I did think about returning to the track. We didn't get much from James Walters, but we both came away from that conversation thinking that there's something bad going on down there."

"I would go with you, but I'd like to tell Mrs. Summerfield about Justine's arrest and confession personally, plus our new client is coming in. We haven't made much money on the Danny Parrish case, so I need to hang around here. This new client is loaded."

HAVING SPENT THE afternoon catching a nap followed by washing and waxing his motorcycle, Wayne suggested taking Lucy out for an early dinner. She had a shift starting at seven o'clock.

"Where do you want to eat?" he asked her.

"I thought we'd try that new Indian place. Supposed to have great curry and Vindaloo," Lucy said. She was wearing a long black skirt and turtleneck. Standing in the entryway, she took her newly dry-cleaned white lab coat out of the closet. Tucking the garment into her oversized shoulder bag, she said, "I'll drive separately so I can go directly to the hospital after dinner."

"Okay," Wayne said, trying to keep the grumpiness out of his voice. He had been hoping for steak and mashed potatoes. To his surprise, however, the food was excellent and not as expensive as he'd expected.

"I'm relieved this case is over, to tell you the truth," Lucy said as she sipped her coffee after the meal. "I had a funny feeling about this one. Like you might get hurt or something."

"Closest I came to an injury was moving out of the way so a racehorse didn't step on my toes," he said. "And I'm smart enough to be careful of those big guys."

"Nonetheless, I'm glad you got your perp and that you're fine," she said, but a shadow seemed to cover her face for a moment and Wayne patted her hand as it lay on the table.

"Lucy," he said, shaking his head, "you're turning into an old gypsy carnival woman with these premonitions."

"Just be careful. Promise me, Wayne," she said. He nodded.

THEY KISSED GOOD-BYE in the parking lot. It was already getting dark and the wind was rising when Wayne got into his pick-up truck. He hadn't told Lucy he was going back to the track. Her uneasiness didn't need to be fanned up.

An hour later, Wayne drove down the lane behind the loose boxes for the racehorses and parked. He knew which stalls belonged to Austin Cantwell by then. When he turned off the pick-up, he heard a loud neighing. It sounded like it was coming from Boyd's Boy. Then everything was silent. He got out of the truck and stood listening to the sounds of the night for a few minutes. The moon was full. He caught sight of a barn owl, gliding silently over the stables. He was hunting and Wayne wished him luck. A yellow tomcat skirted the end of the building. The animal looked fat and sleek; his hunting had obviously been going well. The cat stopped and regarded Wayne with acute feline displeasure.

"Recognize a fellow hunter do you?" Wayne said in a whisper. "Don't worry, I'm after bigger game." Then he heard voices. It was two men talking. He walked silently to the area behind the stalls where the voices were coming from.

"What are you giving him?" a man asked.

"It's a special cocktail I've developed. Sort of a milk-shake that will slow him down."

"What if they test him after the race?"

"Nothing will show. That's the beauty of it. By the time they get around to testing, it will all be out of his system."

"And if this doesn't work, our plan is to use the blind switch, right? Is that all arranged?"

"Yes, we've got the jockeys on board. They all want to qualify for the Derby too, so there was no resistance to my request. Boyd's Boy will be caught in a pocket between horses so that he can't possibly win. Easy Money will have a clear shot."

Wayne was close enough to hear the stallion's nervous movements. Whatever the men were doing to Boyd's Boy, he didn't like it. Then he heard harsh breathing coming from behind him. He whirled around, saw a bright flashlight and heard a sharp exclamation. Then an almost overwhelming pain exploded on his right side and he fell, feeling the gravel scrape against his face. His last thought was, *Lucy is never going to forgive me.*

WAYNE WOKE TO the scent of freshly starched sheets. He tried to open his eyes but the light was too bright and his head ached. He managed to turn his head and peer at a window. It was still dark. He felt his right side gently, wincing when he encountered a bandaged wound, a drainage tube and a padded dressing.

Much later the door to his room swished open and he saw the slender outline of a person entering the room. The morning light was coming in through the window. The person sat down in a chair by the foot of his bed.

"Who's here?" Wayne asked, feeling the pain of saying even two words.

"It's me, Frank Stephenson. How are you feeling?"

"What happened?" Wayne asked.

"Somebody stabbed you. Whoever did it, dragged you from behind the stables and left you bleeding out in the parking lot. We think someone must have scared the perp off because when Detective Pascoe got no answer to his phone call, he raced to the track and found you. Lucky he got there when he did. You were almost a goner. When your partner, Miss Dory, left this morning, she asked me to come stay with you. There's this pretty lady doctor who keeps coming in and out of your room. She seems kinda…pissed. I didn't think doctors were supposed to get mad at their patients."

I must be at Rosedale General, he thought. "I'm going to sleep now," he told Frank. As he closed his eyes he was glad for the heavy pain-killers Lucy had probably requested, pleased he wouldn't have to face an enraged girlfriend for a while.

When he opened his eyes again, Lucy was standing over him with clenched teeth and a furious expression on her face.

"So, I'm an old gypsy woman with silly premonitions, am I? You promised me, Wayne! What are your promises worth, I ask you? No sooner do you say you will be careful than you leave for the track, get stabbed and practically killed," her face crumpled and she started to cry furiously. "I could murder you myself I'm so mad. What the *hell* were you doing out there? And alone? Could you not have taken PD with you? Jesus, Wayne."

Wayne swallowed but couldn't manage to say a thing.

Dr. Lucy turned on her heel. Looking back over her shoulder she said, "You and I have a lot more talking to do, Wayne Nichols, but in view of your injury, I'm cutting you some slack. Whoever stabbed you put the knife in between your ribs, if they just had pushed it in just a little further, it would have penetrated your heart. Don't think for a moment this has been forgotten."

THIRTY-NINE

Tuesday

WITH THAT OMINOUS PRONOUNCEMENT, his girlfriend left the room. Wayne heaved a sigh of relief but then winced from the pain. He could hear her voice speaking to someone out in the hall. When the door opened, it was the entire Rosedale PI team: PD, Billie Jo and Dory. They were all talking at once.

Wayne raised one finger to his pursed lips and PD was able to silence Dory and Billie Jo. "We have lots of news for you, Wayne, but first how are you feeling?" he asked.

Wayne patted his side and made the "go on" gesture with his hand.

"We've been assured you will make a full recovery and will be home in a few days. Detective Stoneman called this morning and actually apologized. He said they had been wrong not trusting your instincts about Parrish being murdered. Furthermore, he and D'Angelo are working your stabbing hard. They didn't originally catch the case, but insisted on their right to investigate it. Said they didn't trust anyone else," PD smiled.

"It's so funny, Wayne. They keep talking about how they are going to nail the guy who stabbed you. They are calling you 'one of their own' and a 'brother'," Billie Jo grinned.

"What happened that night?" Dory asked. "You must

have pissed somebody off pretty badly to end up bleeding out in the parking lot."

"Doping Boyd's Boy." He could only manage those three words before he was caught by a stabbing pain.

A nurse opened the door saying it was time for Mr. Nichols' pain meds and gave him two pills.

"Don't make your visit too long," she said. "He's in a lot of pain and is having a hard time talking."

When the nurse left, PD said, "I'll call Stoneman and have them hold off until tomorrow before getting your statement. They are hell-bent on catching the bastard that damn near killed you," he smiled and patted Wayne's shoulder.

"We'll talk and you can listen," Dory said. "When Dr. Llewellyn-Jones heard you were in the hospital, she went over her findings on Danny again. Turns out morphine is only discoverable in the human bloodstream for about eight hours. The Narcan would have been gone by then as well. So, when Danny's body was brought down to the morgue, she checked his patient record and saw that morphine had been ordered by the Hospitalist. Because it was prescribed, she didn't request testing for the *level* of morphine in his body. Later, when Dr. Harding called to let her know your suspicions that a hospital employee had injected Danny with an extra dose of morphine, the drug was already gone. Now that Justine has confessed, Dr. Jones has amended the death certificate to say that Danny's death was *likely due to a substance added to the patient's IV that stopped the heart.* That is going to help with the court case."

"The Nashville Detectives already have James Walters in custody. He apparently had another trainer with him the night you heard them talking. The other guy's name is Dudley Pierce. They have picked him up as well," PD said.

Wayne held up three fingers.

"You're right there had to have been a third guy who stabbed you. They intend to pound his name out of the two trainers," Dory said.

"Boyd's Boy?" Wayne whispered but so quietly that nobody caught it.

"There was some good that came out of that night, Wayne. Both trainers have been scheduled for investigation by the Stewards at the racetrack. It's likely they will be banned from all the tracks in the state," Billie Jo beamed. "Walters, it turns out, had already been in trouble for doping in California. That's why he changed his name."

"Boyd's Boy?" Wayne said again.

"The Syndicate brought in the best horse vet in the State for him. They don't know if Boyd's Boy will race again, but he's already in demand for stud. And being in lush pastures with a bunch of willing mares in season is a lot nicer life than pounding the track," Dory said.

Wayne felt his eyes closing. He heard PD say, "We need to let the man sleep," and the sounds of them leaving.

IN THE LATE AFTERNOON, Wayne woke up to see Lucy sitting in the chair in his room. She was dozing. The last thing he wanted was a fight, but knew he had it coming. He watched her, thinking how much he loved her and fearing his stupidity in going to the track might have caused an irreparable rift between them. When she opened her eyes and met his gaze, she didn't look mad any more. She looked sad. He didn't know which was worse. He patted the side of the bed and Lucy rose, walked over and sat down beside him.

"I'm sorry," he whispered. "So sorry." He grimaced with the pain. It had taken all he had to say that many words.

"It's not just that you took such a risk, Wayne. It's that you were only thinking of yourself and the case—the stupid case! You never gave a thought to me and what I would suffer if you got hurt or died."

"So sorry," he forced himself to say again.

"Don't you think I know every case is a penance for you? Your whole career has been one long dreadful atonement, and I have had it! You did get your mom out of jail, she died peacefully with her family. And you will pledge *here and now that you will never investigate a violent crime again*, or I am simply not willing to continue this relationship." Her breathing was shaky, but he could see she was unwavering.

Wayne felt his breath come faster and started coughing. The agony was almost overwhelming, but the possibility of losing Lucy was worse than the pain of the knife wound. When he was able to stop coughing, he raised his right hand and put it on his heart.

"Never...again," he said.

"I mean it, Wayne," Lucy's voice and face were serious. "I won't take you back if you *ever* put yourself in harm's way again." She took a deep breath. "I know you feel like you are alone in the world, but you're not. In case you have forgotten, I found my mother dying when I was a kid. I knew my father had killed her. He never paid the price for it and my only sister is a lost druggie."

Wayne nodded. He knew her tragic history well. While her father was dead now, someday he hoped to track down her sister.

"If I had even known first aid, I might have saved my mother. Her untimely death was the reason I became a doctor, but I've stayed in medicine for other reasons. Unlike you, I got *past* my guilt for not being able to rescue her. When I lose a patient now, I just try to learn from the case and become a better doctor," She had tears in her eyes when she said, "You'd think a man would owe some loyalty to his *fiancé* and not take…"

Fiancé. The word exploded in his mind like a firework. He didn't even hear the rest of her sentence. Stunned, he reached for Lucy's hand, still hearing the word fiancé reverberate around the room.

He looked at her questioningly, touching her ring finger.

"Well, you would have to *ask* me, Wayne," she said with an oblique glance. "And it's no small matter because I want something else, too." She stopped and took a breath. "I want a child. I'm probably too old to conceive, but we could adopt." Her face looked so pensive, it touched him deep inside. "I've come to the decision that I want to be a mother, but fathers are so important to children that…" her voice trailed off as she looked at him.

Becoming a father was something Wayne hadn't thought about since he was a young man. Lucy was in her mid-forties now and he would be turning sixty soon, but when he saw the expression on Lucy's beautiful face, it was clear she was absolutely committed to the idea.

"Well?" she said, frowning at him questioningly.

He swallowed as he thought of the words he wanted to say and Lucy waited. He took several deep breaths before he managed, "Always wanted…to be a dad."

Then, at long last Lucy's determined expression softened and she smiled.

FORTY

Six Months Later

IT HAD BEEN a lovely spring in Rosedale. It was May and the roses were already blooming: old roses, damask roses, tiny tea roses, climbing roses. The luscious scent was carried by the breezes in through the windows of the building which housed Rosedale Investigations. Billie Jo had finally convinced PD that air conditioning was critical to her work performance. Wayne was talking with the A.C. installation guy who was connecting the unit behind the house. Dory was sitting at Billie Jo's desk finishing a report on a previous case. PD was in the kitchen making coffee. Billie Jo was upstairs in her apartment looking regretfully at the red shorts and halter top lying on her bed, before donning a blameless little black skirt and a white blouse with black edging on the collar. She thought it made her look like a pre-school teacher and not the maverick she wanted to be—when she spotted two people walking up the sidewalk to the front door. Quickly grabbing two small gifts she had purchased for Wayne and Dory and a large file folder, she thundered down the stairs.

"Guys," she shrieked, "They are here!" She clattered down the stairs, ran into the kitchen and grabbed PD by the sleeve, tugging him with her. "Get Wayne," she told Dory and dashed to the front door to welcome the couple. Cara Summerfield was walking up the path accompanied by a good-looking man about her age. She wore a light blue sarong dress, heels and silver earrings. She was carrying a bouquet of white roses tied with a blue ribbon. When Billie Jo opened the door, Cara hugged her tightly, gave her the flowers and said, "These are for you and Dory as a special thank you for all you did for me."

"Come in, come in," Billie Jo said excitedly and led the couple into the conference room.

Everyone got seated and PD began by saying, "Mrs. Summerfield, we are delighted you have stopped by. We have wondered many times about you, Tracey and the baby. Would you like to make the introductions?"

"Thank you. I'd like to introduce you to my dear friend and Danny's father, Rafe Marston. Rafe, this is Detective Pascoe, Detective Nichols, Investigator Clarkson and Billie Jo Bradley. I came by because I knew you would want to know how our story turned out. As you learned at Danny's funeral, his girlfriend Tracey was pregnant when he died. She was struggling to make ends meet in Nashville. At the time, since Grant and I were separated, I invited her to move in with me." She sounded pleased with her decision.

"What did your husband think about that?" Wayne asked, raising his eyebrows. "We are still separated so his opinion isn't relevant at this time," she said calmly. "You will remember that Grant's running for State Representative for our District. He's very busy with the campaign. He was worried that his bid for the seat would be derailed when people learned about my pregnancy at seventeen and that he didn't know about Danny for many years. To my surprise, his supporters have been overwhelmingly understanding. So many of them have had such big issues to deal with in their own families that a teen-age pregnancy seemed tame by comparison. However, he's having a hard time agreeing to some conditions I am insisting on before I can agree to his return," Cara said.

"What would those be?" Dory asked.

"That Tracey and the baby will continue to live with us for the foreseeable future, and as Rafe is now a member of the family, Grant must be cordial and welcoming to him. He seems to be having a particularly difficult time with that one."

"Way to stick up for yourself, Cara," Billie Jo said.

"Always knew you had it in you to be a bad ass," Dory added.

Cara reached into her purse and pulled out some little folded notes. She passed them around the table. "The baby was born two days ago. Our grandson, Daniel Kidd Dimond weighed 7lbs and 9 ounces and was twenty inches long. Both mother and baby are doing well. Tracey and baby Danny come home tomorrow. Rafe was present at the birth and Grant has been up to the nursery several times. I was concerned that he might not be very interested in the baby, but he seems pleased with the little guy," she said.

The room rang with congratulations and Cara turned pink with pleasure.

"How do you feel about this complex situation, Rafe?" Wayne asked him quietly. The man hadn't said a word since they sat down at the table, but his eyes never left Cara's face. It was clear he was deeply in love with her.

"Whatever Cara decides about Grant, I'm staying in

Rosedale. In fact, I've bought a small house in town. I want to be here for Cara, for Tracey, who I consider a daughter, and for my grandson," Rafe said and reached for Cara's hand. She didn't take her hand away, Wayne noticed.

"Now that the case is over and done with, I have some questions," Cara said. "I know it was Justine Cantwell who put the morphine in Danny's IV in the hospital. And I know she did it because she was still in love with my son and couldn't move past his decision to choose Tracey."

"That's right," Dory said. "Her obsession totally consumed her."

"The murder case is coming before a Judge and jury soon. The Prosecutor will be alleging premeditated murder," Wayne said.

"And it's likely a jury will agree because Justine had to follow a senior nurse to the locked morphine cabinet, watch while she punched in her code, and memorized the number ahead of time. Then the night of the attack, she went to the cabinet, opened it and pulled out a syringe pre-filled with morphine. All of that indicates clear intent and planning," PD said.

"It does, but I still believe if Danny had told Justine he would return to her, she would never have injected him," Dory said. "It's been hard for me to think about her locked up for life. She's so young."

"People always think women are unlikely to kill, but as we know 'Hell hath no fury like a woman scorned,'" Wayne said philosophically and PD nodded.

"When you came to us originally, Mrs. Summerfield, we thought the only crime we had to look into was your son's disappearance and later his murder—

which Billie Jo suspected had something to do with his horse, Boyd's Boy. As it turned out, it was a lot more complicated," PD said.

"Yes, I heard there was another crime, one involving Danny's horse. You discovered the plot, right Detective Nichols?" Cara said.

"I did, but I was stabbed before I was able to stop them giving the horse a concoction of drugs to make him run slower."

"How are you feeling by now?" Cara asked.

"I'm all healed up. The Nashville detectives nabbed the two trainers involved and a guy named Carl Sabaris is under arrest for stabbing me. The Stewards have banned both trainers from the track. Neither one will be training horses in Tennessee again."

"What is Boyd's Boy's situation?" Cara asked.

"The stallion is now in peak condition and may even race again," Billie Jo said smiling.

"Wonderful news," Cara said. "I did have one other question. What was Austin Cantwell's role in all this?"

"It took us a long time to figure him out," PD said. "It's important to remember that all the money in the Cantwell family came from the wife's father. Mr. Cantwell's ego demanded being seen as a big wig in the horse racing game, but Mrs. Cantwell was starting to put the brakes on his spending. Cantwell was losing money big time, buying horses with little potential and paying for trainers, stable lads, vet care and renting stables they couldn't really afford. That's where Carl Sabaris came into the picture. Tell them about him, Wayne."

"Carl Sabaris and Austin Cantwell had known each other since they were kids, but whereas Cantwell went to college and married into money, Carl Sabaris got in trouble with drugs and the law. His record shows he was convicted for armed burglaries and home invasions. In both cases, he used a knife. When he was released from jail for those crimes, he wormed his way in with the Syndicate and learned they wanted Easy Money to qualify for the Derby. He rekindled his childhood friendship with Cantwell, saying he knew how they could make a killing on the horses. The first thing they needed to do was to get Danny out of the picture because he was doing too good a job. He really was a fine trainer, Mrs. Summerfield," Wayne said.

Cara smiled. "Thank you for saying that, Detective. Please go on."

"At the Syndicate's request, James Walters left his original stable to work for Cantwell—lured by promises of big money if he could get Boyd's Boy to lose a qualifying race."

"I don't understand. Cantwell owned that horse, why would he want him to *lose* a race?" Cara asked, frowning.

"Because he was going to bet on Easy Money making it to the Derby and that Boyd's Boy would be out of the picture. In effect he was betting against his own horse," PD said.

"So Cantwell was going to bet Easy Money would be a Derby starter and Boyd's Boy wouldn't?" Cara asked. "Why would he do that?"

"Since Boyd's Boy was the odds-on favorite, betting on Easy Money making it to the Derby would result in a big pay out for Cantwell. On the night I went to the track and was stabbed, James Walters was giving Boyd's Boy a benzodiazepine cocktail that would tranquilize him before the final race he needed to become a Derby starter. If that wasn't enough, they were prepared to use a trick called a *Blind Switch*. It's basically using other horses to trap the favorite horse in a pocket which prevents a free course from being pursued," Wayne said.

"Thank you for explaining all this. One last thing. Austin Cantwell is a big supporter of my husband's candidacy. I don't want Grant connected to him if he had any part in this."

"Austin Cantwell is a weakling. He was willing to do practically anything including firing Danny, replacing him with James Walters and turning a blind eye to whatever the Syndicate planned to do to Boyd's Boy—all to be considered one of the racing big wigs. In fact, if Boyd's Boy was damaged by the drugs or other horses, Cantwell was prepared to have him shot and killed, just to collect the insurance money," PD said in disgust, shaking his head. "Later on, the Prosecutor learned Cantwell suspected his friend, Carl, of Wayne's stabbing, but he didn't tell the cops. What he did was obstruction of justice, but since they had Sabaris' confession by then, the Prosecutor decided not to pursue the matter. Austin Cantwell is morally corrupt," PD said. "It's your call, Mrs. Summerfield, but I think Grant should keep his distance."

"I agree. The situation certainly was more complex than I ever guessed the day I asked you to find Danny. Thank you all so much. Rafe and I need to get going. We're picking Tracey and the baby up from the hospital tomorrow and I still have some things I want to do for the nursery. I have two checks for you, Billie Jo. One is the cashier's check for $15,000 I originally planned to send Danny but sadly he died before that could happen. I've made the recipient Rosedale Investigations. There's also a check from Mr. Marston for twice that amount. Please let me know if I owe you anything more."

Billie Jo looked at the check and her eyes widened. "Not another thing, Mrs. Summerfield. You are all paid up."

Cara and Rafe bid everyone good-bye and walked out the front door. Rafe held out his bent arm for Cara and she took it, smiling up at him as they walked.

"IT WAS GOOD to hear about the outcome for Mrs. Summerfield," PD said. "The case turned out well, especially with your complete recovery, Wayne. So, let's take a short break. When we're all back, I have some housekeeping issues to discuss before we talk about our next case.

Before we break, I've got a question for you, Billie Jo," Wayne said. "When Dory and I started here, you talked about us mending spider webs. It was a new concept for me, but I've gotten used to the team approach and have to say it works. What I'm wondering is whether you still see our jobs as mending spider webs?"

"No. Now that I've seen a murder and conspiracy case all sewed up, I'd have to say my metaphor was a bit off. What we do is closer to each of us holding the corner of a safety net for our clients. If anyone drops their corner, our clients won't land safely on their feet," Billie Jo said.

"How are you feeling about being on a team as a PI, Dory?" PD asked.

"I love it, PD. I'm happier than ever," she said.

"What about you Wayne?"

"I've really enjoyed working this case with you," Wayne said, but knew he couldn't echo Dory's unreservedly positive statement. Since the Daniel Parrish case had overlapped his former role, it was going to take some time before he could be certain he had made the right decision in leaving the Sheriff's Office.

FORTY-ONE

Ten minutes later, with everyone once again around the table, PD said, "I've talked to Dory and Billie Jo about this, Wayne. Hope you will be okay with it. Dory is going to become the Chief Financial Officer, the CFO, for Rosedale Investigations. I've raised her salary commensurate with her new responsibilities. Billie Jo has handed over the office checkbook and credit card. Right?" PD said pointedly, looking at the girl who nodded.

"She sure did. I have them right here," Dory said.

"Dory being CFO for the business is a good decision. She's always been good with money, prepared budgets for the Sheriff's Office and approved overtime. I did want to ask what happened about the opera tickets and the purple dress," Wayne said.

"Once I got over being about to *murder* our youngest colleague, I looked into whether we could give Billie Jo the opera tickets as a bonus. We can, but it's iffy as to whether she is required to pay taxes on the amount. Our new CFO is looking into that," PD said smiling at Dory.

"Looks like the amount has to be added to her salary and she will be paying taxes on it. Sorry, Billie Jo. I also looked into whether the business could deduct the event as an entertainment expense. It's apparently okay if the expense was for entertaining guests of the business. It's a bit iffy though, since Billie Jo's date wasn't seeking our services. Still researching that one. The dress, however, is quite another matter. Billie Jo had agreed to pay the office back for the cost of her fancy outfit."

"I have. It might take me several months to pay for my purple gown, but I'm determined to do it. And, I'm grateful for the bonus to cover the opera tickets. I wanted to show my appreciation for you all for putting up with me, so I have gifts for each of you." Billie Jo grinned as she pulled two small wrapped packages from under her chair and pushed a file folder toward PD. Handing Wayne and Dory each a gift, she said, "I've tried to celebrate the essence of each of you. Hope I did it. Go ahead and open yours, Dory."

Dory unwrapped her gift and pulled out a coffee mug. "You're going to have to explain this one Billie Jo," she said showing the cup to PD and Wayne. "It says, *'How wonderful it is that nobody need wait a single moment before starting to improve the world.'*"

"It's a quote from Anne Frank, the young holocaust victim. That's what you do, Dory, you improve things everywhere you go and for everyone you encounter," Billie Jo said.

"Lord knows you needed my help, Girl," Dory said. "It's funny. Here I am, a well-nourished African American woman who is close to retirement age, (Wayne snorted) and Billie Jo here is a skinny white chick who looks barely legal, but the kid is actually a younger version of me," Dory grinned.

Billie Jo stood up, walked over to Dory and hugged her. "It's your turn now, Wayne," she said.

Wayne pulled the paper off his gift. "My mug reads, *'In the confrontation between the stream and the rock, the stream always wins. Not through strength, but through persistence.'"*

"It's a quote from Buddha and it embodies what I see as your approach to your job. You never give up. It was because of your persistence that the racehorse's life was saved," Billie Jo said. She rose and planted a kiss on Wayne's grizzled cheek.

"Thank you Billie Jo, it's been a pleasure working with you," Wayne said, looking moved. "What is PD's gift?"

"His is a bit different. As you know, I have no family and neither does PD, who is my honorary grandfather. I had to consult with Dory on this one. She took me to meet her friend Evangeline Bon Temps, the lawyer. I wanted to learn about adult adoption," Billie Jo said passing the file to PD.

PD opened the folder and briefly read the document. "I think Miss Bon Temps has made an error, Billie Jo. This document isn't for me to adopt you."

"I know. This document is for me to adopt you! It turns out that an adult adoption may occur once the potential adoptee reaches the age of 18 or older. Pretty sure you're over 18, PD," she said grinning. "The only consent required is that of the adult wishing to be adopted, and of course, the person willing to adopt. So, if agree to this adoption, PD, all you have to do is sign the form," she giggled.

"I would be honored to be adopted by you, Billie Jo," PD said with a quirky grin, signing the form with a flourish. "Thanks for being a good sport about paying the business back for the dress."

"It was the right thing to do," the girl said, looking at Dory who nodded.

"All right then, people, enough of this touchy-feely stuff. Let's talk about our next case. This afternoon we will be meeting our new client who is bringing us a missing person's case. Lexie, as she prefers to be called, recently lost her father. She was saddened by his passing, but he had been ill for some time. A few weeks after her father died, his lawyer called to say she needed to come by the office to learn of a special condition in her father's will. It seems the father had a son from another relationship and left half his estate to the boy. Lexie never knew of her brother's existence. She is required by the terms of the will to find him."

"Interesting," Wayne said, looking outside at the bright sunshine. He wasn't paying attention. Ever since Mrs. Summerfield left with Mr. Marston, he'd been thinking about the word *fiancé*. In fact, he'd been thinking about the word for months.

"Does Lexie want to get to know this brother? Perhaps welcome him into the family?" Dory asked.

"Apparently not. I asked her about it and she said didn't want to have anything to do with him after he got his inheritance. It's all because of a second teddy bear," PD said, frowning and looking perplexed.

"So our next big case is going to be the Teddy Bear caper?" Dory said, grinning. "That ought to please your girlfriend, Wayne."

Wayne nodded, although his mind was elsewhere.

"If you give me Lexie's surname, I'll see what I can find out about her before she gets here," Billie Jo said.

"Good idea. I've got it written down in my office," PD said and the twosome left the conference room.

"What's up?" Dory asked turning to her partner. "You've been awfully quiet. What's on your mind?"

"Just thinking about Cara and Rafe. Did you notice every time she mentioned Grant, it was to discuss his candidacy? The man's an idiot to delay agreeing to her conditions. By the time he gets elected and has time to attend to his marriage, I have the feeling Cara and Rafe will once again be a couple."

"I wouldn't be at all surprised. Did you know Cara insisted on a legal separate maintenance agreement with Grant? I told her about our favorite attorney, Evangeline Bon Temps, who took care of it right away. Why is this hitting you so hard?" Dory asked.

"I just don't want to make the same mistake," Wayne said. He paused before saying, "Dory, do you know the name of a good jewelry store?"

"Why yes, Detective," she said, grinning a little. "I do. May I ask what you are planning to purchase? And whether you could use a little consultation?"

Wayne looked down, slightly embarrassed, before raising his eyes to Dory. "Could we go now? I'm afraid if I hesitate, I might lose my courage."

"PD, Billie Jo," Dory called, "Wayne and I have an errand to run. We'll be back in time to meet the new client."

They heard PD's slightly distracted voice say, "Fine, see you later."

Walking out to Wayne's truck, Dory said, "I didn't think Lucy's birthday was until the end of the summer. I presume you are buying something for her?"

Deep in thought, Wayne didn't answer. He started the vehicle and backed out of the driveway before he said, "Don't tease me, Dory. I'm having a hard time with this bended knee business."

"Bended knee?" Dory asked and then chuckled.

"Well, well, well. It's about time, Partner. You have certainly waited long enough. Could you use some help in choosing a ring, perhaps?"

"Indeed I could. I just hope Lucy says 'yes' because, like Cara Summerfield, my girlfriend also has a condition. And it's a big one."

"You can tell me all about it on the drive, Partner, but she won't be your *girlfriend* in the future. If she accepts your proposal, Dr. Lucy Ingram will be your *fiancé*. And eventually your *wife*."

As the two partners drove to the jewelry store, Wayne swallowed, realizing he now had two very big words in his head.

* * * * *

ABOUT THE AUTHOR

Lyn Farrell is the penname of Lynda Farquhar, Ph.D., the co-author of the Mae December mystery series. She also writes YA fantasy, is a master gardener, a talented amateur interior designer and "dog mom" for Dezi, a Cavalier King Charles Spaniel who is jealous of her cell phone and tries everything he can think of to distract her from writing. She has two biological daughters, Lisa is her co-author for the Mae December series, six step-kids and twelve grandkids.